CW00863070

Dying

for

Justice

Iain Cameron

Copyright © 2022 Iain Cameron
ISBN: 9798786267939

The right of Iain Cameron to be identified as the author
of this work has been asserted by him in accordance with
the Copyright, Designs and Patents Act 1988.
All rights reserved. No part of this publication may be
reproduced, stored in a retrieval system, or transmitted,
in any form or by any means, electronic, mechanical,
photocopying, recording or otherwise, without the prior
permission in writing of the copyright owner.
All characters and events in this publication, other than
those clearly in the public domain, are fictitious and any
resemblance to real persons, living or dead is purely
coincidental.
All rights reserved.
To find out more about the author, visit the website:
www.iain-cameron.com

DEDICATION

For my sister Linda, I miss you so much

ONE

It was a freezing cold night. Martin Turner wasn't sure if his shoes were slipping on patches of ice, or if he had lost control of his legs, but walking along Queens Road towards Brighton Station was proving tricky. He knew the station was there; it was the great big bloody thing at the end of the road, but he couldn't see much else.

Nights like this, sitting in a bar until closing time before going on to a restaurant or a nightclub and drinking non-stop for five or six hours, were becoming more frequent. He did it because he enjoyed it, he thought, bringing a smile to his face. Of course, it also helped him forget about the shitty things in his life: the scumbags he defended, his failure of a marriage, and the poor excuse for a human being he worked alongside.

Turner walked into the station and stopped to look at the departures board. He tried to keep his body still for a few moments to focus on the information being presented, but it continued to sway, as if he was standing on the deck of a boat. There was an app on his phone which could tell him the times of the trains, but even if he used it in the pub, while still sober enough to select a train, the evening's events had a habit of taking over.

An 'important notice' was displayed at the bottom of the screen. He screwed up his eyes to try and decipher it. He could make out 'tree fall' and 'cancellation'. A few seconds later, the words sorted themselves into some sort of order, and he let out an exaggerated sigh in response. It sounded more like the yelp of a terrier, but it didn't faze the half-dozen people in the station, many of whom looked as though they were in there to shelter from the cold weather.

Plan B, he said to himself, but he must have said it out loud, as a girl looked round. He giggled to himself as he walked outside. He understood enough about popular culture, courtesy of a teenage son and daughter, to know that Plan B was a rap star. Perhaps the lass had turned, thinking he'd been spotted.

He was still smiling to himself as he turned into Trafalgar Street, a tricky undertaking as it was a downward slope and the pavement was glistening with frost. Once a scruffy part of Brighton where no sensible person would venture out at this time of the morning, it had been gentrified with offices and apartments. How he wished he'd bought an apartment in this area and not Haywards Heath, but at least it contained the next best thing: the offices where he worked.

He turned left and walked past a large office complex, looking like a ghost town at this hour. He approached the main door of Linden House and used his pass key to open the door. The reception area was unmanned at this hour, but the glassy eye of the CCTV camera was unblinking. His saving grace was that the security guard rarely looked at it unless something had gone wrong in the night.

The offices of Jonas Baines, on the second and third floors, were deserted. While lawyers and paralegals were not 9-5 workers, and would continue beavering away on a case if they were required to meet a deadline, he couldn't recall the last time anyone had burned the midnight oil. Just as well; it wouldn't do for someone to be engaged in an important client meeting, only to be interrupted by his snoring.

He entered his office and closed the door. He shared it with slime-ball Trevor Robinson, who never arrived for work before 9am. This gave Turner plenty of time to freshen up in the well-appointed toilets, complete with shower and fresh towels, before Robinson would put in an appearance.

He pulled out a self-inflating mattress and blanket from the cupboard and lay them down on the floor. He removed his jacket, shirt, trousers and shoes, and was fast asleep seconds after pulling the blanket over his shoulders.

He was dreaming. A man looking like Mad Max, but with the face of one of his former clients, Bruce Nolan, was hammering a huge nail into his skull. The bastard! After all the help he had given him! The dream felt so vivid it woke him up.

He lay still, his head spinning, mouth tasting like the inside of a tramp's underpants, and his painful bladder informing him he needed to pee or his mattress would turn into a lilo. He was trying to summon the energy to get up and walk to the bathroom when he heard something. It was a distinct *thump-thump*, but coming from where? He stopped and listened. Someone was in the office next door. The office belonged to Alex Vincent, a divorce lawyer and a man who would get a nose bleed if he worked beyond 6pm.

He levered himself up. Then, when his head had stopped spinning and he knew he wouldn't puke, he tried the next stage. He stood for a moment, waiting until the room stopped moving from side to side, before walking to his office door and opening it quietly. He was tempted to first make a detour to the bathroom, as his bladder was starting to feel like an inflated beach ball, but curiosity triumphed.

The offices on this floor were glass-panelled, and he saw the flickering light before he got there. He peered through a gap in Vincent's vertical blinds, trying to focus. If he'd had trouble reading the Brighton Station noticeboard under the full glare of station lights, he had little chance with this. He could see shadows and movement, but couldn't be sure if someone was in the office, or if it was the reflection of something going on outside. Surely their window cleaners didn't work at this time of the night?

Moving as quietly as possible, he eased the door open and peered inside. This was a better view than through the glass, as he now could see the figure of a man covered in black clothing. He was removing box files from the bookshelves behind the desk, opening them on the desk, and pulling out the papers inside. He then shoved the boxes back on the shelf, two at a time, making the *thump-thump* noise Turner had noticed earlier.

'What the hell is going on here?' Turner said, trying to sound forceful and authoritative, but it came out fretful and more high-pitched than he intended.

'What the fuck!' the man said. He threw the boxes he was holding on the desk and came striding towards Turner.

Martin Turner used to be a keen boxer in the days before pubs and young women took precedence over boxing gyms. The guy's intention was clear, and before he came any closer and did some damage, Turner landed a haymaker on his jaw.

He took pride in the amount of power he could deliver in a punch, one was often enough to drop a normal opponent, but either the booze had made him weak, or this guy didn't feel pain. He rubbed his jaw with his hand and continued his advance. The guy was bigger than Turner and the lawyer had no defence against the heavy blows that were soon pummelling him against the wall.

The attack stopped for a second and Turner used the temporary hiatus to land another blow on his opponent. Far from stopping him, it only seemed to enrage the guy, and he saw, only too late, the unmistakable glint of a blade in the man's hand.

Turner was punched once, twice, three times in the stomach before he slumped down the wall, the life leaking out of him with every drop of blood that landed on the office carpet.

TWO

'It's not often we get called out to a crime scene during office hours,' Detective Sergeant Carol Walters said.

'Makes a change,' Detective Inspector Angus Henderson replied, as he turned the car onto Trafalgar Street. 'It's more likely at two in the morning, when I'm recovering from a late night or I've been out for a long run.'

'Talking of late nights, are you still seeing the woman living above you?'

'What? Sharon Conner?'

'Yeah.'

'I can hardly avoid her, as she lives in the same building. We go out now and again, but it's not what I would call serious.'

'How very modern.'

'What do you mean?'

'Youngsters nowadays, I'm told, don't think they're in a relationship until both parties agree that they are.'

'It sounds so very formal.'

Henderson drove into a private road called Trafalgar Arches; on one side, the station, and on the other, a large office development. He slotted the car into a space beside Linden House, the building housing the offices of Jonas Baines, Solicitors and

Notaries. The two detectives got out of the car and walked towards it. They showed their ID to the security guard. Heading towards the stairs, Henderson noticed the CCTV camera. On the second floor, the hive of activity and visible crime tape told them where to go.

Before approaching the pathologist, Grafton Rawlings, who was on his knees, examining a blood-stained body with gloved hands, Henderson and Walters donned an oversuit and covers for their shoes.

The DI knelt down beside the pathologist and the victim.

'Morning, Grafton.'

'Morning, Angus. For a change, we're both not looking bedraggled and counting the minutes until we're back in our beds.'

'There's always a first. Multiple stab wounds, is it?'

The injuries to the victim's stomach were obvious, but the clothes he was wearing, or in fact, not wearing, were incongruous with the sombre surroundings. Despite the grief evident in many of the neighbouring offices, he could see a high standard of dress: smart suits for men and women, shirts and ties for the men. The victim, by way of contrast, was wearing a t-shirt and shorts; no trousers, jacket, or shoes.

'He's been beaten, which you can see on his face and arms. I'll be in a better position to see the extent of it when I get him back to the mortuary. But that aside, yes, I can say at this stage he died from multiple stab wounds.'

'Any idea of the time of death?'

'Not too difficult in this case as rigor mortis hasn't set in. I would say within the last four to six hours.'

Henderson looked at his watch: 8.30am. 'Sometime between two and four this morning?'

'Sounds about right.'

'Would this be Alex Vincent, given the nameplate on the door?'

'No it isn't. I'm told the victim's name is Martin Turner. His office is the one next door.'

'Thanks Grafton,' Henderson said, standing. 'I'll see you at the PM.'

'Not if I see you first. Are we still on for the pub at seven on Thursday?'

'We certainly are. See you later.'

Henderson joined Walters as they looked around the room. It contained a large desk with a computer, and behind the chair, bookshelves full of legal books and box folders, which he presumed were case files.

'Not much to see, is there?' she said.

'No, you're right. Let's go talk to the senior partner, or whoever is in charge.'

They walked out of Vincent's office and Henderson took a quick look inside the one next door, which confirmed what he had suspected.

Ten minutes later, the detectives were seated in the well-appointed office of the managing partner at Jonas Baines, Robert Haldane. The door was closed and all three had a cup of hot coffee to drink. Not a bad start.

'First of all, Mr Haldane, please accept my condolences for the loss of one of your own,'

Henderson said, 'and my apologies in advance for any disruption my officers may cause.'

'The victim of this horrendous crime was my beloved friend and colleague, Martin Turner. He ran the criminal side of this practice, and it's no exaggeration to say it was through his efforts that it has become the powerhouse it is today.'

Haldane was mid-fifties and looked every inch the successful partner in a large legal practice. His salt-and-pepper hair was slicked back, no doubt to look good in the convertible Jaguar sports car Henderson had spotted in the reserved space in the car park. He wore an expensive looking shirt and suit, a fat gold watch, and his skin exuded a healthy tone not gained from lying out in wintry Brighton, more likely a recent holiday in the Middle East or the Caribbean.

'I've come across Mr Turner several times in the past,' Henderson said, 'and I've always found him to be tenacious but fair.'

'It's a good assessment, Detective Inspector.'

'Tell me, Mr Haldane, did Mr Turner often sleep in his office?'

The well-coiffured and unflappable expression of Robert Haldane's face faltered, changing to something that Henderson thought looked like disappointment. The expression of a father who found out his favourite son wasn't capable of taking over the family firm, or had been dating a girl he regarded as unsuitable.

'Martin started to fray around the edges about three years back, not long after his wife initiated divorce proceedings. In this legal practice, that side of things is run by Alex Vincent, whose office all your people are occupying. Alex and Martin were good friends, and I imagine when talking about cases over a drink, Martin always thought it was something that happened to other people. He wasn't a man who took failure easily.'

'Was his marriage breakdown due to the pressure of work?' Walters asked.

'No. I wish it was, as then I could have done something about it. No, it was his wife's infidelity with her son's piano teacher.'

'All the same,' Henderson said, 'many people go through divorce and don't end up sleeping on the floor of their office. I imagine a successful lawyer could afford something better.'

Haldane bristled; clearly this was a touchy topic. 'Oh, he could, and did. He owned a smart apartment in Haywards Heath. However, now and again a thick black cloud would descend, and those working close to him would know that night he would go on a bender. More often than not it was easier, and safer, for him to sleep here than catch a train home. As long as it didn't become known among the younger and more impressionable members of staff, I decided I would let it go.'

'Early indications are,' Henderson said, 'Mr Turner was killed by an intruder.'

It was the only logical conclusion Henderson could draw at the moment, until he knew more about the Jonas Baines business. This was based on the victim's injuries and the time of death, which excluded an argument with a colleague or client. Haldane's lack of reaction told him the lawyer was thinking the same.

'Have you any idea who that might be, Mr Haldane? It looks like either a person was lying in wait to attack Mr Turner, or there was someone here for some other purpose, and Mr Turner disturbed them.'

Haldane steepled his fingers, considering the question. 'As a consequence of Martin spending his days defending serious criminals, it would be logical to point the finger at one of them. However, his job was helping those people, not trying to send them to prison. The only time I think resentment would fester would be if Martin had done a sloppy job, but that option wasn't in his toolbox.'

'Nevertheless, you can understand why his working with criminals does interest us.'

Haldane sighed. 'Yes, I can.'

'If we consider the second scenario, of him being in the wrong place at the wrong time,' Henderson said, 'do you keep, beyond the obvious electronic equipment, any valuables in your offices? I'm thinking here about cash, cheque books, jewellery, bearer bonds, anything that a thief might want to steal.'

He shook his head. 'I know some legal offices hold assets on behalf of clients, but we do not. If, as you say, Martin was killed by an intruder, I don't have the faintest idea what he or she thought they might steal. On the other hand, if their metabolism was full of drugs, which Brighton seems to be awash with at the moment, who knows what twisted logic was going on inside their heads?'

The two detectives left the offices of Jonas Baines ten minutes later. They now had the address of Martin

Turner's ex-wife, and that of the apartment he owned in Haywards Heath. Robert Haldane also promised to supply them with a copy of any CCTV feeds from the previous night, and a list of all Turner's clients by the close of business.

'What are you thinking, gov?' Walters asked as they walked back to the car.

'Given there's no sign of an intrusion in their offices, or even in the building, the CCTV is going to show the intruder, but the camera is so obvious, any idiot would know to shield their face. If we don't get a good image, we'll need to trawl through Martin Turner's life, with the added spice of a big list of criminal clients. I think with this one, we're in for the long haul.'

THREE

The village of Woodmancote was located in Mid-Sussex, ten miles north of Brighton. Henderson and Walters found Blackhouse Lane without too much trouble, but locating the house occupied by Joanna Turner was proving a little more difficult. None of the houses displayed numbers, only names, and some of those were obscured by overhanging branches, or accumulated dirt.

At last, Forest House appeared. They stopped the car and the DI leaned out of the window and pressed the buzzer beside the gate. Henderson had decided that if Mrs Turner wouldn't open the gate until she knew why they were there, he would try to be circumspect with the details. He would give her enough information to believe it was important business, but nothing more. No one wanted to hear bad news over an electronic loudspeaker, no matter how sophisticated the system might be.

His concerns became academic when the gate slid open. Henderson drove in. He had driven into boutique country hotels smaller than this. The house was arranged in an L-shape. On the long arm, he saw what looked like the main reception rooms with bedrooms on top, and on the small arm, a triple garage with accommodation above, perhaps a granny flat or studio.

The door opened and a woman appeared, drying her hands on a towel.

'Good morning, Joanna Turner?'

'Yes,' she said. 'What can I do for you?'

She was tall, of slim build with short, dark hair, and an outdoor, ruddy complexion. Her accent wasn't Sussex, somewhere further north.

'I'm Detective Inspector Henderson, and this is Detective Sergeant Walters, from Sussex Police.'

'Can I see some identification?'

Henderson walked towards her holding out his ID. Walters did the same. She took them from the detectives and gave them a studied look. This was unusual, as most people, once they'd spotted the Sussex Police logo, would hand them back.

'A Detective Inspector, eh? I'm honoured. My father only made it to sergeant.'

'We'd like to talk to you about Martin, Mrs Turner. Can we come in?'

'Yes, of course.' She handed back the warrant cards and stood to one side to allow them to enter. She closed the door behind them. 'I'm no longer a Turner or a Mrs, Inspector. I call myself Woodford now, my maiden name, even though I do think it does sound ghastly. For the purposes of your visit, please call me Joanna.'

'Thank you.'

'Don't think I'm blasé about letting strangers into the house, despite the official-looking ID. There are two big dogs in the kitchen and, if I tell them, they would do anything to protect me.'

'I'll need to remember that.'

Part way down the hall Henderson reached what looked like the sitting room.

'Just go in,' he was told.

Henderson ducked under a low beam and walked into a traditional living room. It was large, taking up the whole width of the house, and full of dark, solid wood furniture with chintz patterns on the chairs, settee, and curtains, and at the centre, a large open fireplace with an ornate mantlepiece.

'Before we start,' Joanna said, 'let me make you both some tea. In my experience, police officers always like something to drink before discussing anything of importance.'

In a situation like this, Henderson would normally ask the officer accompanying him to make tea while he imparted the bad news. However, Joanna was gone before he could do, or say, anything.

'It looks a traditional sort of room, this,' Walters said. 'It's a bit old-fashioned for my taste, but this settee is comfy. You just sink into it.'

'It is, but watch you don't get too comfortable. So many of those modern, stylish ones are either as hard as a brick, or you find yourself sliding down the cushions.'

Several pictures were dotted around the room, but Henderson didn't need to leave his seat to look at them. Most were large, including two framed portraits of a girl aged about sixteen, and a boy about twelve, blown up beyond life-size. Haldane had told them that the boy, Seb, was now sixteen and a pupil at Hurstpierpoint College, a fee-paying boarding school in the locality, while his sister, Lidia, was twenty, and a psychology student at Nottingham University.

Joanna entered the room bearing a tray. Henderson stood, took the tray from her and placed it on the table.

'Thanks, it was killing my arms. Note to self, must do more exercise.'

Henderson waited until the drinks were poured and Joanna was seated.

'You said when you arrived, this was something to do with Martin. We've been divorced for over two years now, and I have to tell you, I'm over him. In fact, I was over him about five years after we married. He married me, but I didn't realise he was already married to his work. In my mind that makes him a bigamist.'

'Joanna, I'm afraid I am the bearer of bad news.'

'How bad?'

'In the early hours of this morning, Martin was found dead at the offices of Jonas Baines. He'd been murdered, stabbed by an intruder, we think.'

'Oh, my Lord,' she said, a hand shooting to cover her mouth.

Walters rose from the settee, intending to comfort her, but a raised hand waved her away.

'Don't waste your empathy training on me, Sergeant, I'm made of stronger stuff. I was just shocked to hear the word murder, that's all. I mean, I'd heard it often enough at home when Daddy was in the force, but I didn't expect to hear it in this house about someone I know.'

'You and Martin weren't close?' Walters asked.

'Let's just say the news has saddened me just as much as it would if we were talking about our former next-door neighbour in Hove, although I admit, the children are less stoic and it will be hard breaking it to them. I suppose the great Robert Haldane has filled your heads with stories about my infidelity with Seb's piano teacher?'

Henderson nodded.

'He's such a misogynistic prig, that man. My so-called affair happened after we were separated and lasted less than a month. No, what caused our eighteen-year marriage to break down was his continual drinking, and afterwards going to clubs where he would sleep with any girl who was stupid enough to have him. The final straw came when he picked up an STD, a Sexually Transmitted Disease if you will, and gave it to me. Syphilis, to be precise.'

Henderson wasn't expecting to hear this and was momentarily taken aback. Regaining his composure, he said, 'I see.'

'So, you can no doubt tell, my ex is not high up on my Christmas card list. In fact, he isn't even on my Christmas card list.'

'Did he have any enemies?'

'Beyond me, you mean?'

'I wasn't suggesting...'

'I know. I didn't much like the man he had become, but that doesn't mean I'd wish him any harm. As long as he didn't come near me, I was fine.'

'What about other enemies?'

'Hmm, I wouldn't call him an enemy, but he thoroughly disliked the guy he worked beside and shared an office with, Trevor Robinson. They were buddies for a time, and happy drinking companions, but something happened. I know no more and only heard it second-hand from Lidia, after she had been to visit her father.'

'Is there anyone else you can think of?'

'No, not among his friends, the likes of Will Slater and Stephen Bradshaw, or any of his acquaintances.'

'Slater and Bradshaw, they are close friends of his?'

'Oh, yes, and have been since school. You see, Inspector, men like Martin have attended good private schools, and are fans of the same things: cricket, sailing, drinking, and eyeing up young women, all the things they did when they were young men. When the likes of houses and children come along, wives change and become carers and act accordingly, but those men stay the same. As a result, it's all laughter and bonhomie. People like that don't make enemies, Inspector, they form alliances. They have friends, associates, and a wide network of contacts, but never enemies.'

'What about his client work?'

'The rogues and scoundrels, as he called them. Yes, there are some serious criminals on that list. Let me think.' She paused. 'He defended John Pope, who I think is dead now, Bruce Nolan, Dominic Green, Raymond Schofield. There's more I'm sure, but someone at Jonas Baines can tell you better than me.'

Henderson knew the name Bruce Nolan, but couldn't remember the crimes he had committed. Dominic Green was a well-known drug big shot Henderson had been responsible for sending to prison. Raymond Schofield was a mega-rich businessman who was acquitted of murdering a business rival, Allan Blake. Blake died in the middle of negotiations to sell his chain of health clubs, after falling from Schofield's yacht and drowning. He was sure the list that Jonas Baines supplied would have others on it. However, the fact that Joanna could still recall those four without much trouble suggested they were in the Premier League and the rest were playing in the lower divisions.

'One final question. Robert Haldane mentioned an apartment Martin owned in Haywards Heath.'

'Yes, it's in a modern block near the station. I was surprised he bought it, as you can see from this house he prefers the more traditional. I suppose it doesn't really matter, as he didn't stay there often. He had a serious drink problem, you see, and when things started to become a bit sticky, he would often be found surfing on friends' couches or sleeping in the office.'

'That was a weird one,' Walters said a few minutes later when they had returned to the car and were driving away.

'You don't think maybe she's a private person and is saving her tears for a time when she's alone?'

'I'd like to think so, but the rift between her and her ex seems to have cut too deep. They were married for eighteen years, according to Joanna, but she said herself the spark had been lost after five.'

'He must have had some constitution to drink all night and then perform like a professional lawyer the next day. I know I couldn't do it.'

'I'm sure you could manage it gov, you just need to put in a bit more practice.'

FOUR

'Here boy. Here boy! What the hell are you doing?'

Raymond Schofield ducked under the branches of an alder tree to see what the damn dog was up to. He was digging as if his life depended on it, and a few moments later found what he was looking for: a bone. At first glance it looked like the leg of a fox, but before he could take a closer look, Viper scampered off with his booty.

He sighed. When the dog was younger, Schofield was assiduous about not letting him eat strange things he came across in the garden. He knew enough about plants to understand that pretty plants such as foxglove, hemlock, and wolfsbane, could kill. He had instructed his team of gardeners, who maintained the seventy acres around Mayfield House in Warninglid, to pull out any poisonous plants they found, and to bury any bones and dead animals.

However, now that he had reached the ripe old age of fifty-five, and his Cocker Spaniel, seven, his concern for the dog's wellbeing had waned with the passing of the years. It was Schofield's birthday today, and perhaps the reason why he was feeling more reflective than usual. When he had set out in business all those years ago after leaving school, he had big dreams. He wanted, by the time he reached fifty, to be the boss of a large multinational company, have a big office overlooking the rooftops of central London, and be jetting off several times a month to far-flung destinations to review his business interests.

His younger self would be delighted to see that he had fulfilled all his ambitions, but perhaps not so thrilled to know the ink was now dry on the contract to sell the last remaining part of his former burgeoning business empire. It was Marilyn Monroe who once sang 'After you get what you want you don't want it.' No truer words were spoken.

He picked up the ball launcher that Viper had been so interested in before finding his snack, and walked through the woods towards the house. With the sale of a hotel chain in Spain, the last of his brick-and-mortar businesses, he wasn't the Chief Executive of anything anymore. Now, perhaps the big fuck-off twelve-bedroom house set in seventy acres of picturesque Sussex countryside wasn't a statement he needed to make any longer.

If he was being honest, it wasn't his age, or the closure of a major chapter in his life that was encouraging his reflection; it was his impending divorce. It wasn't the fear of losing the love of his life that so vexed him, as Rebecca had been living her own independent life for many years, but handing her a substantial slice of his recently liquidated fortune.

She was demanding fifty percent of the whole caboodle, claiming that she had been integral to the success of the business. It was her idea in the first place, she maintained, to start an Italian coffee business in the UK, and then to open a chain of boutique hotels in quirky locations: beside windmills, water towers, and inside former railway stations.

In an effort to leave his old life behind and start anew, he had, by accident, done her and her rapacious lawyers a very big favour. No way could he have stumped up the one-hundred-and-seventy-five million plus she was claiming, or the lower amount being proposed by his legal team if his money was still tied up in hotels, coffee bars, marinas, and health clubs.

He had worked hard to build up that fortune, and no matter who had the idea in the first place it was his drive, ambition, and ruthlessness that made sure it became a success. No way was Rebecca going to take the lion's share just to piss it away on an over-priced condo in Florida, and on the young guys she met on Palm Beach, entranced by her remodelled wares, courtesy of the surgeon's knife.

He walked into the house and headed over to the worktop in the kitchen, where he poured himself a cup of coffee. He took a seat at the table overlooking the garden. The garden was still in winter mode, the trees bare, the bushes hunkered down against the cold, and the grass glistening with overnight frost. Viper was lying out there gnawing at the bone as if he hadn't been fed for weeks, his damp brown coat looking like a pile of dead leaves the gardeners had forgotten to take away.

Suddenly, the dog looked up, his ears cocked. He leapt up and raced towards the driveway, barking. Minutes later, Schofield's former financial director and now business partner, Clare Mitchell, walked into the room. Raymond got up and greeted her, giving her a warm hug and kissing her with unrestrained passion.

'Happy birthday, darling.'

'Thank you.'

A few moments later, they stepped apart. 'What's that you're carrying?'

'Something special for the birthday boy, but we'll open it later, we've got work to do this morning.'

'I know,' he sighed. 'What do you fancy for breakfast?'

'Whatever you're having.'

'I fancy scrambled eggs with a generous chunk of salmon. Okay for you?'

'Ideal.'

As if on cue, his housekeeper, Lyn Malone walked into the kitchen. 'Did I hear scrambled eggs for two?'

'You did indeed, Lyn.'

'Coming up.'

Raymond and Clare moved to the kitchen table and took a seat. 'Did the deal go through?' Clare asked.

He nodded. 'I received a confirmation email this morning.'

'Fantastic! Congratulations, Ray. It's a champagne breakfast we should be having.'

'We'll sit down to one of those just as soon as the money hits my bank account. You know what they say, *It ain't over 'till the fat lady sings*.'

'I'll look forward to that.'

Lyn put a pot of tea on the table for Clare, and topped up his coffee.

'How does it feel,' Clare asked, when Lyn had departed, 'to no longer be the captain of your own ship?'

'It's taking time to sink in. I think I'll notice it,' he said, smiling, 'when I have a problem with my laptop, and I shout for Alex or Mel and no one comes.'

'They say it's the hardest part to get used to, not having staff.'

'It's so easy to forget all the things people did for you, until you have to do them yourself.'

A few minutes later they were both tucking into breakfast. 'Tucking' was perhaps a relative term in Clare's case, as she was slim and never ate much. That didn't mean she didn't enjoy food, she knew more about food preparation than most, but she didn't eat large quantities of anything. Lyn was aware of this, and while she gave Ray a good helping with two bits of toast and plenty of salmon, Clare received about half that amount.

Clare's thirty-ninth birthday was two weeks before his. She had been his financial director when he ran Raybeck Leisure, the holding company for all his business interests. In that time she had not only been his aide-memoire, reminding him of meetings, giving him a précis of reports he had failed to read, or offering him a quick bio of people he was about to meet, but also his lover.

To those that didn't know and were prone to making snap judgements, they would say he had traded Rebecca for a younger model. On the face of it, they were both blonde, slim, good-looking, smarter than average, and took care of themselves. This was where the comparison ended. Clare was intellectually as sharp as a knife, and business savvy in a way that Rebecca never was. She would challenge Ray's decisions and advise him on the best course of action, while his former wife was good at coming up with suggestions, but not at developing them or persuading him to implement.

'This is good, Lyn,' Schofield said to his housekeeper. 'Don't you think, Clare? It's even better than what they serve at the Savoy.'

'If you remember, I had a bad meal at the Savoy the last time we went there, so my judgement's somewhat coloured. Ray's right though, Lyn, you do make a very fine plate of scrambled eggs.'

After breakfast, they walked down the hall to his study. It was a large room, in keeping with the grandiose dimensions of the house, and around the same size as the one he'd once occupied on the top floor of a tower block in Leadenhall. By anyone's standards it was an impressive room, with bookcases lining the walls, and a large open area between the door and his desk at the far end of the room. It was floored with wood, while his chrome and glass desk sat on a twenty-five-thousand-pound rug imported from Turkey.

The study in other people's houses was often the place where they kept up with football and celebrity stories, or placed Amazon orders. In his case, and for the last ten years he had been in business, it had been an extension of his main office in London. He would conduct key meetings at home, meet foreign dignitaries, and sign important documents. Even now, it was to become the nerve centre for his latest business venture. It was also the place where he and Clare had first made love, the cleared desk used for a purpose unintended by the Italian manufacturers.

Clare sat at his shoulder while she looked at the email from the corporate financiers who had brokered the deal to sell all the businesses in the Raybeck group. After reading, she gave him a passionate kiss.

'Well done you. You've at last realised your dream, four years in the making.' She pulled away just as his hand reached her breast and started to massage. She took a seat at the other side of the desk. It not only stopped him going further, it created a formal barrier, a cue to him that she wanted to talk business.

For the next hour they discussed the next steps they would take in trying to become investors in technology start-ups. As usual, he was gung-ho and keen to make an immediate start, but Clare hauled his reins back. She said they first needed to develop a corporate statement, spelling out the type of companies they wanted to invest in, the relationship they wanted to have with them, and any ethical barriers that would stop them investing. The statement wasn't only for them, it was also for the target companies, to give them an idea of their financiers' long-term objectives.

All investments would be made from a vehicle owned by Clare and himself. She had money to invest, as she had taken his advice on several occasions in the past, and had bought shares in companies that he was convinced were expected to rise in value. He had also gifted her ten million when he'd sold his 'baby', a chain of two hundred and fifty coffee bars with branches in all major towns and cities in the UK, and the same coverage in many other European countries.

She was the love of his life. The reason why he had initiated an expensive divorce, why he had liquidated all his assets, why he had started a new business with her as an equal partner.

His phone rang. When he saw who it was, he signalled to Clare, who got up and left the room. She would think it was a terse call from his soon-to-be ex-wife, complaining about the behaviour of his lawyers, but it wasn't. It was Pete Hammond, the man who sorted all the problems he couldn't.

'Hi Pete, tell me some good news.'

'I got what you wanted.'

'Excellent news. Did it give you any problems, anything I should know about?'

'Nah, nothing I couldn't handle.'

'Great. I'll meet you at the usual place; you bring the coffee, I'll bring the doughnuts.'

'Ha. See you then.'

FIVE

Following the Thursday evening briefing of the murder team, Henderson called his three sergeants: Carol Walters, Harry Wallop, and Vicky Neal, into his office. They sat around a laptop, looking at the CCTV pictures taken by the camera in the reception area of the Jonas Baines building.

They first viewed a drunken Martin Turner arriving. He entered the building and staggered towards the stairs, and if not for the hand reaching out and grasping the banister, would have fallen flat on his face. When he disappeared upstairs they spun the pictures forward, and using a printout from the security system, stopped it seconds before the intruder arrived.

They ran the sequence but spotted nothing of value, as for most of the time, he had his back to the camera. They spun it forward once again and started the playback moments before the intruder came down the stairs.

After a minute or so Henderson said, 'Stop right there.'

Walters halted the picture and bumped it back a few frames to try to sharpen the image.

'It's the best I can do, gov.'

'This person,' he said, pointing at the screen, 'is clad from head to toe in black. For good measure, he's also wearing a woolly hat and a scarf around his mouth. A protection from the cold outside, for sure, but I also suspect to hide his face. What else can we discern?'

'Comparing him to the height of the reception desk, he looks taller than average, and well-built; not fat, but muscled,' Carol Walters said.

'Do we all think it's a man?' Vicky Neal asked.

'Based on his shape and size, I do,' Henderson said.

'What about you, Harry? You're very quiet?'

'I suppose so,' Harry Wallop said. 'He doesn't have the build of any woman I know, except maybe a Russian athlete.'

'You need to get out more,' Neal said.

'Anything else visible?' Henderson asked.

'What's that on his hat?'

'I'll zoom in.'

'I'm not sure what that is. Three C's?' Neal said.

'Ah, I recognise it,' Henderson said. 'It's the Canterbury Clothing Company. They're big in Rugby circles.'

'The letters are in the shape of an animal.'

'It's a kiwi. Canterbury are from New Zealand.'

They stared at the screen for another half-minute.

'I don't think there's much more we can extract from this,' Henderson said. He looked around at the faces of his colleagues, and they nodded. The laptop was pushed to one side.

'What do we know about the entry card used by the perpetrator?' he asked.

'It belonged to a lawyer at Jonas Baines called Trevor Robinson,' Neal said. 'He reported it missing yesterday.'

'The name Trevor Robinson rings a bell. Ah yes, isn't he the guy who shared an office with our victim, Martin Turner?'

Walters flicked through her notebook and scanned several entries. 'Yeah. They shared an office and both are involved in criminal defence. Martin being the senior man.'

'What's the age difference?'

Walters consulted her notebook again. 'The victim's forty-five, Robinson, thirty-three.'

'Okay,' he said, 'let's assume this: Trevor is a lad about town, and while in a bar or a club, he leaves his jacket on a stool. When he's not looking, someone dips his pocket and takes his key card.'

'Sounds plausible.'

'Is it though?' Henderson said. 'How would the thief know which building the card was for? Most of these things don't bear a company name. Do the ones at Jonas Baines?'

'I don't know,' Neal said, 'but I'll find out. What if the killer saw him coming out of Jonas Baines and pickpocketed him, or removed it from his abandoned jacket after following him to a pub?'

'Possible. On the other hand, wouldn't it be easier if someone was visiting their office, and either took it from Robinson's jacket if it was perhaps hanging on a peg, or picked it up from his desk?'

Neal's face lit up. 'If so, all we need to do is find out the names of everyone who was in their office the day Trevor thought his card went missing. One of them will be our killer.'

'Maybe not our killer, Vicky, but perhaps the person who stole Robinson's entry card. One thing at a time.'

'One way or another, it sounds like a decent lead.'

'It does. Vicky, follow this up. Take Sally and interview Trevor Robinson. Explore the issue of his missing entry card, and also try to find out how deep the victim's enmity was towards him.'

'You think it might have been him?'

'Joanna Woodford told us Turner and Robinson didn't get on; I think *thoroughly disliked* were the words she used.'

'It's a bit like pissing on your own doorstep, don't you think?' Harry Wallop said. 'I mean, if it was him, he must have known he'd be a suspect. One, because it was his security card that was used by the perp, and two, because he shared an office with our victim.'

'There's a number three, Harry,' Henderson said. 'He's also a defence lawyer and knows how these things work, but domestic murders pan out in much the same way. If a woman is found dead, the husband will be the first person in the frame. He knows this before he murders her, but he still does it.'

'I suppose so.'

'I can imagine another scenario,' Walters said, 'where Robinson is working late. Turner comes in pissed, they're both tired and irritable, and after an argument about something, Robinson snaps and stabs him. He then calls a mate to use his card and pretend there's been an intruder.'

'We've got a list of all the movements in and out of their building for that day and night,' Neal said. 'I'll go through it and track Trevor Robinson's, find out if he left work at the normal time or not.'

'Good. Let's move on and take a look at the criminals Martin Turner was responsible for defending.'

'The list they gave us,' Wallop said, 'was for cases over the last five years. They can supply other years if required. What we've done is compile a spreadsheet, listing the name of the criminal, the crime they committed, the outcome, and the criminal's opinion of their defence.'

'Okay.'

'We've split this into three: one for major crimes, that is, those facing an inordinately long or life sentence; intermediate crimes, a ten-year-plus sentence; and lesser crimes, fewer than ten years.'

'I like that approach,' Henderson said. 'Let's start with the bad boys.'

'First up is John Pope. Accused of murdering his business partner over a land sale. Turner could do little about compelling forensics, and he got life. Died of cancer in prison nine months back. We've looked at reports of the story in the media, and nowhere does he criticise his defence team, nor was he upset about the result. He expected it, he said.'

'Did his family or associates express any disquiet about the outcome at the time?'

'We couldn't find any evidence.'

'Okay, put him to one side for the time being.'

'Next is Bruce Nolan, a scrapyard owner from Newhaven. Blood dripping from a crushed car brought forensics into his scrapyard, and they found it belonged to a man who had tried to blackmail him. Nolan had been having an affair with his wife. He claimed he had nothing to do with the murder and that it was only the ineptness of his defence, in the form of Martin Turner, that had got him sent down.'

Henderson remembered the case now. *The Argus* enjoyed a field day with grisly headlines and puns about being left on the scrapheap.

'Is this the first chink in Turner's armour?' he asked.

'How do you mean?'

'I was wondering how a guy who drinks nearly every night, and on occasion sleeps on the floor of his office, manages to function in his day job. I imagine there are days when he doesn't, and maybe this was one of those.'

'Could be. I don't know if Nolan was bad tempered and irascible before being accused of murder,' Wallop continued, 'but according to prison reports, he was like a bear with a sore head behind bars. He constantly berated his lawyers to launch an appeal. Eventually they did, and he won.'

'Put him on the interview list, Harry.'

'With pleasure, gov.'

'Who's next?'

'Dominic Green.'

'I don't think anyone in Sussex will forget him,' Henderson said, 'although I think it was before your time here, Vicky. A top drug baron with a network of smaller dealers all over Sussex. Owned a manor house near Horsted Keynes and was, by all accounts, untouchable.'

'He was facing life for kidnap, drug importing, and being an accessory to murder,' Wallop said, 'but good work by Turner got this reduced to six years. As we know now, he's a free man, and running a food business close to where I live in Shoreham.'

'As much as Green should feel thankful to Turner and his barrister, I don't trust him one bit. Put him on the interview pile.'

'Righto. Next up is Raymond Schofield.'

'I remember this one,' Walters said, 'it was in all the papers at the time.'

'No wonder,' Wallop said, 'he's a multimillionaire who, at the time, ran a company called Raybeck Leisure Plc, an international business with hotels and coffee shops, six marinas, and a chain of health clubs. To try and sweet talk Allan Blake into selling his health clubs, Schofield took him on a trip aboard his yacht. While off the coast of Bretagne in France, they hit a storm and Blake disappeared over the side. His body has never been recovered. When Schofield returned to port and reported the incident, Blake's blood was found on the deck and in the main cabin. Schofield was accused of murder, the CPS claiming Blake was reluctant to sell, but now with him out of the way, his widow had agreed to do so.'

'He can't have any complaints against Turner, can he? If I remember right, he was acquitted.'

'You're right. He heaped praise on his barrister, and on Turner in particular for all the detailed work he had done to counter the impact of the prosecution's forensic information.'

'Put him on the aside pile with the first guy,' Henderson said. 'Even though we're dismissing them now, they're gone but not forgotten. If anything comes up in the investigation to connect them, we'll haul them back out.'

For the next couple of hours, with the help of coffee and some sandwiches brought over from the staff restaurant, they ploughed through the rest of the list. It wasn't a large number of individuals, as they were looking only at those represented by Martin Turner. The firm had a large team of other criminal lawyers and paralegals who would have dealt with many more cases.

Before setting out to review the client analysis, the logic behind it had been thrashed out. They expected the motivation to kill Turner would have come from a serious criminal who believed it was their lawyer's fault they served time in prison. By the end of the review, several people fell into this category: Bruce Nolan from the life sentence group, and six others from the ten-years-plus group. With the addition of Dominic Green, it gave them eight persons of interest. What Henderson and his team needed to do now was track them down and have them answer some serious questions.

SIX

A loud *beep-beep-beep* resonated around the yard as the car transporter reversed. The noise brought Bruce Nolan out of the Portakabin that served as the office, a resting place for his workers, and a place where they could eat meals.

He looked around but couldn't see Pedro. He cupped his hands. 'Pedro you motherfucker. Where the hell are you?'

A flushing sound came from the Portaloo away to the right. The door was flung open and the man in question came out, hauling his trousers up while trying to stop his copy of *The Sun* flying off into the wild blue yonder in the folds of a whipping wind.

'Can't a man have a sheet in peace around here?' Santiago Rodrigo González,' said, his hands trying to add emphasis to his words, but lost inside flapping pages of newspaper.

Pedro, which they called him for short, had arrived in the UK over ten years ago, but still hadn't lost his Bilbao accent.

'Not when there's a truck needing unloading. Get your arse moving.'

The transporter contained twelve car wrecks. It wasn't possible to determine where one started and another one finished in the untidy tangle of mangled plastic and metal, but Nolan had seen the invoice.

The delivery was a mix of cars that had been involved in bad smashes and written-off by insurance companies, and those that had come to the end of their useful lives. To those in the scrap business, a new car wrecked in a serious crash was a goldmine. Often, parts of the engine were still intact, and so were fuel and oil pumps, alternators, and sometimes even radiators could be extracted and sold.

In addition, the catalytic convertor, containing valuable palladium and platinum, could often be salvaged, as well as some of the electronic gear inside. He knew a guy on the lookout for any decent ECU, the Engine Control Unit, the electronic circuits that controlled most of a vehicle's systems. What he did with them, Nolan didn't know; all he cared about was that he paid top dollar for any still intact.

The old bangers were good for nothing, other than putting them in Big Daddy, the crusher that could turn them into a cube of metal. These were sold for a reasonable sum, but nothing compared to a good insurance write-off.

Nolan returned to the office wondering where Jake had gone now there was work for him to do.

He was about to sit down at his desk when he heard a noise behind him. Jake was lying on the settee at the back of the office, reading a novel.

'Jake, what the fuck are you doing in here?'

'Taking a break, boss. I spent a couple of hours this morning stripping copper out of all those thick wires we got from that old power station in Essex. I'm knackered.'

'You can sleep when you're dead. Get out there and help Pedro. A transporter's just turned up.'

With reluctance he got up, bitching about his job and his shitty boss in Serbian. Nolan was no linguist, but he had heard the words so often he knew what the insolent sod was on about.

'You're lucky to have a job, you lazy bastard.'

Jake slammed the door in protest. Nolan went back to what he'd been doing. He took a seat behind his worn and scratched desk, rescued from a skip, and opened up the lid of his laptop. He loaded the couple of websites he used most often to sell scrap metal to see if he could get a good price for the six kilos of copper he now had in the store.

Ten minutes later the door swung open. He didn't look up from his computer. It would be Pedro wanting to cadge a fag or to tell him his tired old joke: *Hey boss, come and see, there's a body in one of the cars.* Nolan was sure he would see the funny side too, if he hadn't spent three years inside one of HM shitholes.

'Howdo, Bruce.'

He looked up. It wasn't Pedro, but the rough-hewn features of Tod Hardcastle, his friend and handyman. The scrap business was a tough place to make a living. Most of the time he, Pedro, and his two Alsatians could handle the majority of chancers, those who thought nothing of breaking in to steal nickel and copper, dump their old crap, or try to twist his arm into doing something illegal. If they didn't take a telling: a kicking from Pedro and him, or a mauling from Crash and Bang, there was Tod.

Tod was a former steelworker, built like the side of a ship, and frightened of nothing. He was capable of charming himself inside most people's houses, before grabbing the offender and thrusting their hand into a blazing fire, or sticking their head down the toilet. He never failed to get results.

Tod reached into his bulky Parka jacket, needed today as it was bloody cold, and extracted a small sheaf of papers. He handed them to Nolan, who flicked through them, checking the detail on each.

'It's all there, Tod, good job. Did you have any trouble?'

'Nothing I couldn't handle.'

This was Tod's stock answer. Nolan didn't need to question him. What he would do if he was interested was buy *The Argus* for the next few days and see what heat his actions had generated. It was a difficult path to tread for a former convicted murderer, overturned on appeal, but in the eyes of the cops a guilty man running free. They were waiting in the wings for him to make a wrong move, and when he did every cop from here to Worthing would descend on the scrapyard, and start to pull his life apart.

Nolan reached into a drawer and pulled out a thick envelope. Inside, a bundle of twenty-pound notes. He handed it to Hardcastle, who flicked through it before it disappeared into the folds of his Parka.

'Anythin' else for me, Bruce?'

'Not at the moment, Tod. I'll call if anything comes up.'

'Fair dos. Be seeing ye, pal.'

'See you, mate. Thanks for doing this.'

The door closed. He wanted to take a closer look at the information supplied by Tod, when he noticed a car drive into the yard. This was an unusual occurrence, as scrapyards were not on the list of the *Ten Best Places to Visit in Sussex*.

There were two people in the car, a man and a woman. They parked in front of the office and stepped out. He knew at once they were cops, and they had obviously been to a scrapyard before, or they were just plain lucky. Parking close to the office meant neither of the lads would be tempted to use the industrial magnet attached to the crane to lift their car, by accident or on purpose, and drop it into the jaws of Big Daddy.

The guy was tall and slim with a mop of light-brown hair, worn in a side-parting. He was dressed in a suit with no tie, and wearing a black overcoat to counter the cold. His companion was smaller, up to her colleague's shoulder, and for a moment, mesmerised by the activities of the large magnet. She was good-looking, although with a serious resting face that suggested she frowned a lot.

The door opened and in they walked.

'Bruce Nolan?' the man asked.

'Might be. Who might you be, barging in without an appointment?'

'I'm Detective Inspector Henderson, Surrey and Sussex Major Crime Team. This is Detective Sergeant Walters. Are you Bruce Nolan?'

'I am.'

'Can we sit down?'

He indicated a couple of chairs lying in the corner. 'Help yourself.'

Henderson lifted the plastic chairs and placed them a metre or so away from Nolan's desk. The detectives sat down.

'What do you lot want wi' me?'

'Early on Wednesday morning, Martin Turner, a solicitor at Jonas Baines in Brighton was found murdered.'

Nolan gave a slow clap. 'Thank fuck for that. A result, and I didn't have to lift a finger.'

'Why do you say that?'

'Why the fuck do you think? He's a drunken bum and a shit lawyer. His inept handling of my case put me in jail for three years. The three worst years of my life, in case you're interested. It was only when I changed to a guy recommended by a lag I met inside that an appeal was lodged and I got out.'

'Where were you on Tuesday night?'

'You think I did it?' he said, pointing at his chest. 'Do you think I'm that stupid? I've criticised the fucker in public every chance I got. Now I'm on social media I can do it from the comfort of my home. If you look at his phone and computer and see any abusive emails or texts, I admit it, they're mine. Save you the trouble of having your IT people tracking me down. Why would I be so stupid as to go and top the bastard when I had so much fun rubbishing him on social media?'

'Why do you blame him and not your barrister?' Henderson asked. 'It was the barrister who presented the case to court.'

'My barrister was a top man. He did all he could, but he was like a poker player dealt a crap hand. I'm telling you, Turner didn't do his job. He should have talked to all the people who saw me that night, and taken a look at my home computer and spotted that I'd sent an email around the time of the murder. If he did, I would never have been convicted; maybe the case would never have made it to trial. If so, you lot would have forgotten about me. As it is, here's a murder, let's go talk to Bruce.'

'Nevertheless, Mr Nolan, we need to know where you were on Tuesday night.'

'Let me think,' he said, pausing for a few seconds. 'I worked here until seven. Went to a pub called The Pilot, along the docks, with Jake and Pedro, the two guys who work here. I stayed for about an hour, then went home.'

'Do you live alone?'

'Used to. Fucking bitch of a wife left me when I got convicted, didn't she? When I came out, I started dating the barmaid at The Pilot, a woman who visited me a few times in prison. We've been living together ever since I came out. She was at home when I came back from the pub. She'll tell you. I was at home all night.'

The coppers left ten minutes later. He was unperturbed; they didn't have a clue. He would put a call through to his girlfriend in a minute or two and tell her to back up his story, which she would. Despite the grimy job and the scum he often had to deal with, she still thought the sun shone out of his arse.

He couldn't tell the coppers where he really was that night. He didn't like prison, and no way was he going back.

SEVEN

'Oh, hi Angus. Come in; take a seat. I'll be finished in a minute.'

Henderson walked into Chief Inspector Sean Houghton's office and sat down facing his desk. The CI was busy reading reports and appending his signature to a number of letters and memoranda. Looking at the size of the pile, Henderson reckoned he would be at it for the rest of the afternoon. This was further evidence, if any was needed, that he would be too tied-up to join in with any of Henderson's investigations.

He got on well with Houghton, but he was the boss, and Henderson didn't want him looking over his shoulder. In any case, the senior investigating officer on any murder investigation came under enough scrutiny from the press, public and the families of victims. If they screwed up, there was a long list of people and organisations they would have to answer to: the IOPC – Independent Office for Police Conduct, PCC – Police and Crime Commissioner, and if any illegality was involved, the criminal courts.

With a flourish, Houghton appended his signature to another large report, before it was placed on the 'read' pile, a tad smaller than the 'to be read' pile.

'Right, finished for now. Can you hang on for a few minutes more Angus? I'd like to organise some coffee. I haven't had one since about nine this morning. You want one?'

'Yeah, why not?'

'Good man. I'll be back in a jiff.'

True to his word, the CI was back soon; but as he had a secretary working for him and not a shared Administrative Assistant as Henderson did, he didn't have to make his own coffees.

'So, what did you want to see me about, Angus?'

'I wanted to bring you up to date on the Martin Turner case.'

Houghton gave him a blank look.

'The lawyer murdered in his offices in the early hours of Tuesday night, Wednesday morning, at Jonas Baines in Linden House, Trafalgar Arches.'

'Ah yes. The criminal lawyer who defended Raymond Schofield.'

Henderson wondered why he'd mentioned Schofield specifically, but he said, 'Yes, him.'

'I didn't realise what a big noise Schofield was in Sussex until I had lunch with the Assistant Chief Constable yesterday.'

'Oh?'

'Yes, he supports a number of victim support charities, and he's on the board of several organisations who put on five-a-side football tournaments, run races, and manage food kitchens for disadvantaged kids.'

'I didn't realise.'

'As a result, he's friendly with the Chief Constable, the heads of east and west Sussex County Councils, and a number of local MPs.'

The door opened and Houghton's secretary walked in bearing a tray. While the coffee and cups were being unloaded, he considered Houghton's comments.

It was perhaps a brain-dump, passing on information he'd heard at a meeting which related, albeit indirectly, to the Martin Turner case. On the other hand, it might be a veiled warning not to go near Schofield as it would ruffle too many feathers.

When Houghton's secretary departed, Henderson took a sip of coffee before continuing what he came here to do.

'We've gone through Martin Turner's life and family and, despite an ex-wife who seemed calmer than usual to hear of her former husband's murder, no one has stood out so far.'

'Tell me what you've found.'

'According to his ex-wife, his two closest friends are Stephen Bradshaw and Will Slater. Bradshaw was with him during the early part of Tuesday evening, the night he was killed.'

'What does he do?'

'He's an accountant working in his father's practice. They have offices near the Theatre Royal.'

'Okay.'

'He and Turner met for a drink after work. A drink with Turner often turned into six, he said, but at around ten o'clock, Bradshaw decided he'd had enough. He offered to walk with Turner to Brighton Station to put him on a homeward-bound train, but

47

Turner refused, saying he wanted to continue drinking. Bradshaw departed.'

'The last time he saw him?'

'Yes.'

'How did he take Turner's death?'

'Devastated, as Slater was when he found out.'

'What about Turner's family?'

'We're still going through the list, but they appear rich, comfortable, and middle-class, with no black sheep. Not one of them has a bad word to say about our victim.'

'What about CCTV?'

'Bradshaw told us they had been drinking in The Tap House in Brighton town centre. From the pub's CCTV cameras, we see the victim and Bradshaw drinking together. They were having a good time with no animosity present.'

'Okay.'

'Bradshaw knew Turner was heading to the Palm Club on the seafront, and we see him walking there. Around two in the morning, he comes out and walks towards Brighton railway station. It's clear he's the worse for wear, staggering and not walking in a straight line.'

'No one following him?'

Henderson shook his head. 'Queen's Road was more or less deserted. He entered the Jonas Baines building alone, then we have CCTV of the perp entering the premises about an hour later.'

'Okay. Go on.'

'There is nothing distinctive about the perp, with the exception of a branded woolly hat. The majority of our focus now will be on the criminals Turner defended.'

'Let me think about this for a moment.' Houghton paused, drumming his fingers on the desk. He stopped drumming and looked at the DI intently. 'If he was defending criminals, why would any of them want to kill him? A prosecuting lawyer from the CPS, absolutely, but not one trying his best not to send them to jail.'

'In the majority of cases, I would have to agree with you. Several of his clients were given reduced sentences, others had various charges against them dropped. In a few cases, such as Raymond Schofield's, they got off with no jail time. However, Turner was wrestling with a few personal demons.'

'Like what?'

'He was always very fond of the booze, according to his ex, but ever since their divorce two years ago, he'd stepped it up a couple of notches.'

'Hence the reason for sleeping in the offices of Jonas Baines the night he died?'

'For sure. Logic dictates he couldn't keep all the balls in the air, what with drinking, hangovers, dealing with clients. Something had to give, and now and again, a client would surely be given a sub-standard service.'

'Which would result in a number of unhappy clients?'

'We've found a few.'

'Hold on a minute, Angus. It's perhaps natural to be pissed off with your legal team when you receive a life sentence for killing a rival drug dealer when you were under the impression you might get off. However, it would take a lot more to think of murdering your lawyer just because once or twice he had an off-day, or came to a meeting smelling of stale beer and yesterday's aftershave.'

'I realise that. What we did was also review newspaper reports at the time of their trials. Then, with feelings raw, it became clear from statements made by friends and family, those who had a genuine grievance and those who were just having a moan at the severity of their loved-one's sentence.'

'I suppose it adds another layer of intelligence, but it sounds to me a bit rough and ready.'

'It's all we can do with the information we have and the time available.'

'How confident are you that the murderer will be included in that pile?'

'I have to say completely, otherwise I wouldn't see much point in doing it.'

'What if the perp isn't among them? What will you do then?'

Henderson shrugged. 'I suppose we would have to move from thinking the perp broke into Jonas Baines to kill Martin Turner, to believing he was there for some other purpose. What that was, at the moment, we don't have a clue. If it doesn't become obvious, it will mean grilling all the partners at Jonas Baines until we find it.'

Houghton screwed up his face. 'Bloody hell. I don't like the sound of that at all. They're one of the region's top legal practices. They could make life difficult and sue us for harassment.'

Henderson was tempted to laugh, but didn't. 'Let them. If this is how they would treat one of their own, by suing those who are trying to find his killer, the public will judge them harshly. In any case, what choice do we have? A perp enters the offices of Jonas Baines and commits murder. It can only be for one of two reasons. He went there with the express aim of killing Martin Turner, or he had some other motive, and our victim became collateral damage.'

EIGHT

Vicky Neal, accompanied by DC Sally Graham, parked the pool car in a visitor's space at Linden House. They didn't dawdle but walked briskly towards the building. It was a bitterly cold morning with a chilly, swirling wind, and it didn't pay to hang about.

Only last month, Neal moved into a new flat in Brighton. It didn't take long for her to discover the 'recently renovated and updated, converted flat' in Portland Place was smart in every respect, with the exception of the gas boiler. Brighton was experiencing a Siberian cold snap and last night, despite having the boiler on full blast, the flat was still chilly. This morning, her shower had run cold.

She had made friends with the elderly lady who lived downstairs and she had agreed to let the boiler engineer into her flat today. Neal was annoyed that she couldn't be there in person when he called. She knew enough about human nature to realise when someone was talking bullshit or trying to fob her off with a substandard or expensive solution.

It was the third time they had been to the offices, and the security guy on the door was starting to recognise them. After checks, they took the stairs and made their way up to the second floor. They passed through the new security measures installed at Jonas

Baines, now with their own makeshift reception, overhead CCTV camera, and a new, reinforced entry door, and were shown into a conference room.

Unlike the skanky meeting rooms they were often ushered into at industrial sites and dilapidated office blocks, this one emanated luxury. It was equipped with soft padded seats, a freshly vacuumed carpet, and a tray containing a coffee pot and a plate of pastries. They had been instructed to help themselves and they didn't need to be told twice.

A few minutes later, Trevor Robinson walked in and closed the door. When interviewing some of the other lawyers at Jonas Baines, such as Alex Vincent, they almost burst into the room, giving the impression every minute they spent in here was time wasted. Robinson, by way of contrast, exuded a casual air.

After introductions, he moved to the coffee pot and filled a cup. He placed his cup on the table and more or less slumped into a seat. Now, was this relaxed manner his usual modus operandi, or was it affected behaviour, designed to deflect them from suspecting him?

'Mr Robinson, we are members of the team investigating the death of your colleague, Mr Martin Turner, on these premises in the early hours of Wednesday morning, 8th February.'

'I know.'

'I see you're still wearing a temporary badge,' Graham said.

He sighed. 'If you lose your entry card, they give you one of these. It's only supposed to be for a week, by which time you've either found the missing card, or if not, they'll replace it. I've had this one longer, but then everything is a bit strange at the moment.'

'How well did you know Mr Turner?'

Martin Turner was forty-five and, despite his penchant for chasing young women when drunk, in the office when dealing with clients he apparently behaved like a sensible, middle-aged lawyer. Robinson was thirty-three, over ten years between them, and it showed. He had gelled, styled hair, and although he wore a smart shirt like the rest of them, his bore the logo of the tailor, and the tie didn't quite meet the collar. On closer inspection, the suit looked tired, as if it had been worn many times. She would make allowances in his case, as being a criminal lawyer he would often be called upon to visit clients held in a police cell or in prison.

'I knew Martin as well as anyone. I shared an office with him for three years, and often we'd socialise together.'

'What sort of things did you do socially?'

'Oh, we'd go to the races at Brighton Racecourse, the Goodwood Festival of Speed, the Test at the Oval, barbeques at his house, all sorts of stuff.'

'We know at times Martin liked to drink to excess, and I assume you were aware of this if you were socialising with him. Did you ever join him?'

He laughed. 'Sometimes I did, just to be sociable. I didn't really enjoy it as it would often get out of hand. I know my limits, but Martin didn't. I think, in truth, he was an alcoholic, although he would never admit it to himself.'

'Did you ever try to speak to him about it?'

'He wasn't an easy guy to talk to,' he said, giving a remorseful look, as if he regretted not doing more, but it didn't quite come off.

'In what way?'

'I mean, when he was drinking, which was about any time he wasn't working, if you tried to say, *hold on a minute, mate, I think you've had enough*, he would shrug you off and tell you to mind your own business. If you persisted, he'd tell you to go and fuck yourself. If you went that bit further, I don't know what he would do. He used to box, about four or five years back. He was a big man, so I wouldn't want to chance it, if you see what I mean.'

'One of the lines of enquiry we are pursuing is that he was killed by one of the clients he represented.'

'A natural course to follow in the circumstances, I would imagine.'

'Did you work on the same cases?'

'Hey, hang on a minute, what are you saying? If one of our clients killed him, he might come after me as well. Am I in some kind of danger?'

The air of casualness might have been put on, but the fear in his expression wasn't.

'If I gave you that impression, I apologise. As far as we know, you are not in any danger.'

'How do you know for sure?'

'As I said before, this is only one of the avenues we are exploring.'

'What are the others?'

'I'm not at liberty to say, but please take comfort from the fact that at this stage of the enquiry we are only fact-finding. We don't know for certain why he was killed.'

He didn't look at all reassured, but he said, 'Okay.'

'So, did you and Martin work many of the same cases?'

'We used to.'

'Not now?'

'Not for a while.'

'Why not?'

'I have my own clients.'

'Did something happen between the two of you?'

'What makes you say that?'

'Call it intuition.'

In fact, it was body language. It was just as well he was a solicitor and not a barrister performing in front of a jury. She could read his guilty facial expressions like a book. It was also based on feedback DI Henderson had received from Turner's former wife.

'I suppose our relationship had sort of cooled off.'

The detectives sat in silence.

'Okay, we fell out big time.'

'What about?'

'It was stupid, really. We were all at a barbeque at his house, when he was still married, that is. I got talking to his daughter who then was about eighteen. I'd had a few drinks and maybe I'd let her come on to me a bit more than I intended, but cutting to the chase, he caused an almighty scene and punched me.'

'Why?' Sally Graham asked. 'Did he catch the two of you in a compromising situation?'

'God no, it didn't go that far. She was hanging on my arm, and laughing at all my jokes, that sort of thing, which was nice. I think in Martin's mind it was only a matter of time before we started searching for an empty bedroom, but that wasn't my intention. It was only a bit of fun. No way would I do anything with a colleague's daughter, or their wife or sister for that matter. It's out of bounds as far as I'm concerned.'

'What happened in the end?' Neal asked. 'Did the police become involved? I'm sure I didn't see anything on the system.' She looked at Sally who shook her head.

'No, the police weren't involved, Haldane saw to that.'

'He was at the barbeque?'

'Yep, him and most of the senior people in the practice.'

'How did the incident pan out?'

'Officially, Turner received a severe telling off, but it was agreed that he had been provoked. The fact that he was half-pissed at the time seemed to have been overlooked. When they talked to me about it privately, they said it was all Turner's fault. If I didn't go to the police or the newspapers, they would pay me five thousand pounds and move me out of his office. I got the money, but it was decided that because we worked together a lot and seemed to be getting along in a professional capacity, I should remain where I was.'

'Did that annoy you?'

'Definitely. Turner was okay with the arrangement, as his memory of the day was fuzzy on account of him being on a bender for the three days prior to the incident. I wasn't happy about the situation, but being the junior member of the criminal defence team, I had no choice but to suck it up.'

'Going back to the question I asked earlier,' Neal said, 'and now with the caveat of your soured relationship, you used to work together on some cases?'

'Yeah, on a few of the big ones. He needed someone to cover the groundwork. You know the sort of thing: interview witnesses, talk to you people, review dates and times. All the time I'd be looking for errors and angles, as we call it.'

'What would you call *the big ones*?'

'I'm sure you've heard the names before as they've been in the papers: Raymond Schofield, Bruce Nolan, Dominic Green, John Pope. All murders, all high profile.'

'One final question: did you resent the fact that Martin as the senior man, got most of the credit? It's his name that's prominent in newspaper articles.'

'Too bloody right. I worked day and night on the Schofield case. Everybody in the practice knew I was doing it, but to Schofield it was Martin this, and Martin that. All calls were answered by him, all the papers were sent straight to him.'

'Why did you work so hard on the case?'

'I'd met Schofield several times, and he was impressed with my knowledge of the Raybeck business and the research I was doing on the facts of the case against him. He said if he ever got off, he would employ me as his personal counsel. You see, it was me who thought of introducing a round-the-world sailor as an expert witness. This guy described why, in the middle of a vicious storm, Allan Blake was standing in the position on the yacht where Mr Schofield said he was, before being swept overboard.'

'What happened? You're obviously not working for Mr Schofield at the moment.'

'Martin Turner happened. That bastard claimed all the credit for work done by me, and in the end I was eased aside. When Schofield got off the murder charge, I was expecting a call, but it never came.'

NINE

Following a private flight to Faro in Portugal, Raymond Schofield and Clare Mitchell climbed into a limousine. Ray didn't like travelling in cars for any distance, especially as they had been in an airport where many helicopters were available. However, as their destination was only ten kilometres away, Clare managed to persuade him that such additional expense was an extravagance.

Clare had come from a solid upper-working class background. She had attended a decent state school, had a reasonable wardrobe of clothes, and lived in a nice house, but money, for the most part, was tight. When she went to university, the first in her family to go to Oxbridge, her folks couldn't afford to subsidise her, so she took a job and borrowed the maximum student loan she could.

Over the years she had worked at a senior level in two international organisations, both of which were profligate with corporate largesse, but she had never got used to wasting money. Ray, on the other hand, wouldn't think twice about hiring a helicopter to avoid travelling on busy roads, paying for first-class airline travel so he didn't have to talk to other businessmen, or renting a speedboat so he wouldn't have to queue with a group of tourists at a ferry port.

'Drink?' Ray asked.

'Something soft. It's too early for anything stronger.'

Ray opened the minibar and poured himself a whisky, before opening a can of Coke Light and emptying it into a glass.

'Cheers,' he said, clinking his glass against hers.

'What are we celebrating?'

'I dunno. Us.'

'To us.'

'In a way,' he said, 'I'm just pleased to be away from Sussex for a spell. I swear to God, Rebecca's hired a private eye. A couple of times in the garden I've felt someone watching me and sometimes in the distance I can see a flash or a glint, making me think it's a telephoto lens or binoculars in the light.'

'You might be right, Ray, or maybe you're just paranoid.'

'There's nothing wrong with a bit of paranoia; look what happened in Scotland.'

'That was a different situation, but you're right, Clachan Foods were a rum shower.'

'They were trying to outbid me when I tried to buy that Glasgow coffee chain. I had to sweep the rented house in Newton Mearns for bugs three times.'

Clare nodded. She remembered the incident fine as she was the one who had organised the sweeps. She hoped Ray wasn't losing the plot. She knew it was a comedown from running a large international company with over three thousand employees, to starting a new investment vehicle with only her as a partner.

She liked to think he saw it as a new challenge and would throw all his considerable energies and business acumen behind it. The alternative, a dotty and forgetful Ray, keen to sink a couple of G&T's before eleven, his afternoons spent on the golf course and evenings in a restaurant downing several bottles of expensive wine, would be no use to anyone, least of all her.

'Why would Rebecca engage a private eye? It's not as if she needs more evidence of our relationship than she already has.'

'No, it's not that. She's got all the reasons she needs all sewn up; she's determined to get her claws into all my assets.'

Clare looked at him, a questioning expression on her face. 'She's got that. You've given her a statement of assets already, haven't you?'

'Yes, all three hundred and fifty million quid of it. You'd think half of that would satisfy ninety-nine percent of the people on the planet, but the greedy bitch wants more. She thinks there's more and she's determined to find it.'

'She employed a private eye to do what? Follow you and hope it would lead him to a pot of gold buried at the bottom of the garden which you didn't tell her about? Could this person have followed us here?'

He laughed. 'I'd like to see anyone try. As you know, Quinta do Lorenzo is a gated community; they don't let just anyone in.'

It was true. They were heading towards an exclusive resort where villa prices started at two million euros and didn't stop until they reached twenty. Neighbouring properties to Ray's had been snapped up by Premiership footballers, pop stars, movie legends, and successful businessmen. They came to enjoy the sunshine, play golf and tennis, enjoy the well-appointed gym and spa, and not be bothered by the paparazzi, or stalkers.

If Ray wanted to play a round of golf, he was welcome. She could find plenty to do on her own, but it would be for one day only. She had explained to him that no way was she coming to Portugal to sit in the villa for four days alone while he enjoyed himself with his golfing buddies. He knew she was serious, and if he broke their agreement she would be in the back of a taxi on the way to Faro Airport before he had reached the second tee.

'What's happening to the Portugal house in the settlement?'

'She never liked it here and says she doesn't want it. All she wants, it seems, is money. Not the apartment in London, the house in Warninglid, the villa here, or the one in St Lucia. She wants a couple of paintings, but I don't mind, she can take them all if she wants. You know my opinion on art.'

She did indeed. Ray was a non-practicing Catholic but he had ecclesiastical tastes in art. If he had his way, the house wouldn't be adorned by watercolours by local artists, paintings and drawings by Ronnie Wood and Bob Dylan, and sculptures by Antony Gormley. He would happily trade them for large, garish oils by Hieronymus Bosch and Bruegel the Elder, and, knowing Ray, he would somehow lay his hands on the originals.

At last, the gates of Quinta do Lorenzo appeared. She had been twice before and recognised the amiable security guard with the sidearm who relaxed at the sight of the limo, presumably thankful it wasn't a couple of street punks instead, high on crack. He waved them through.

Ray's villa was at the upper end of the property scale and looked like something James Bond would buy, or more likely wreck in an attempt to rescue a kidnapped girl. It was modern, with large sheets of smoked glass and everywhere sharp, straight lines. The glass offered spectacular views of the coast, less than a kilometre away. However, in order to block the relentless sun from superheating the villa and blanching the furniture all through the summer months, heavy blinds had been fitted, and Ray had an app on his phone to activate them.

The villa was equipped with an eight-seat cinema, a small gym with a treadmill and exercise bike, and a pool table. Outside, there was a large pool, a jacuzzi, a barbeque area, a tennis court, and loads of seating areas where they would often enjoy a glass of wine while watching the sunset.

The limo driver removed their bags from the boot of the car and not only took them into the house but, as he had been there before, carried them up to their respective bedrooms. If he was surprised at the sleeping arrangements, he didn't show it. On her first visit, Ray had been CEO of Raybeck and married to Rebecca. The three of them were at the villa, Clare accompanying Ray as his Financial Director, there to discuss a takeover in private, away from the prying eyes of competitors and FT journalists. Then, Clare had been given the use of a suite of rooms at the top of the house.

When Ray divested himself of the business and separated from Rebecca, Clare decided to leave the room arrangements as they were. Ray was a fitful sleeper, up at three to look at his phone or laptop, and often again at four to make a cup of coffee. She was a sound sleeper and needed a good seven hours, or she could be a grouchy bugger. If he wanted sex – and Ray, despite his copious wine consumption and advancing years, could be a randy sod – he had to show willing by first climbing the stairs.

After the limo driver departed, and with the door closed, she lay down on the king-sized bed. When she was a student, she had travelled to Portugal with three friends. They had battled through crowds at a busy airport, been squashed like sardines on a packed, package holiday flight, and endured a stifling, un-air-conditioned bus ride to a ropey two-star hotel.

Then, she'd slumped down on the lumpy single bed, exhausted from the journey, and could have gone to sleep but for the screeching of her roommate, Ella, ogling at all the gorgeous guys around the pool. A private jet followed by a cool limo drive didn't compare. She had arrived refreshed, and was tempted to head over to the resort's main gym and see if there was a HIT or spin class she could join.

Instead, she pulled out her phone and texted the real man in her life, Jamie Davidson.

Arrived safe, villa splendid. I'll call you later. Love you always, Clare. xxx. She added a few sun and beach emojis, just to make him feel jealous.

She unpacked, and after a quick shower, changed into a summer dress before heading downstairs. Ray was sitting outside, talking to someone on the phone. He had a fresh drink in his hand, and they hadn't eaten lunch yet. It was going to be one of those holidays.

She walked into the kitchen, opened the door to the fridge, and was taken aback by all the food and drink on the shelves. The villa was managed by a local woman, Maria, who organised cleaners and gardeners and acted as housekeeper whenever Ray was in occupation. She imagined the same thing happened to several of their neighbours, a clutch of Premiership footballers. From a very young age until they retired at around thirty-five-years-old, every whim was taken care of by the club. Wherever they went, fresh clothes, food, and clean rooms appeared as if by magic. She imagined it would come as a severe shock when it all was taken away.

She poured some lime cordial into a glass, topped it up with fizzy water and added some ice. She picked up the glass and walked outside.

'Hi babe,' Ray said, looking up from his phone. 'You look lovely. New dress?'

'Yes, do you like it?'

'Yes I do. Come here.'

She walked over to where he was sitting. He scooped her up into his large arms and sat her on his knee. Ray was a good kisser, passionate and engaging. It was the rest of it he needed to work on.

'Don't get any ideas, girl,' he said pulling away. 'I've just been on the phone to Marco's; they've found us a table.'

'Good. What time?'

'In twenty minutes.'

'We'd better get a move on. It will take us that long to walk over.'

Marco's had two Michelin stars, and in her book the restaurant deserved both just for how good the food looked. Dishes were presented, not merely served, and laid out in such a way that if any Instagrammers were about, and this lunchtime she could see a few, it would have them reaching for their phones in a bid to make their followers jealous.

She wasn't a big eater. She valued her trim figure, something which took considerable self-discipline for a woman pushing forty, more than any desire for food. However, she did like Marco's as the dishes not only looked lovely, they tasted amazing, and weren't served in large portions. Ray often had a moan about it, despite him eating dessert and tucking into all the petite fours served with coffee.

This type of lunch suited her, as Ray would wash it down with an expensive wine. The way he drank, slurping it down like a builder's first pint of the day, would have him comatose for most of the afternoon. It was also a good excuse for him to get out of the heat, as it was too much for a Northern lad, as he liked to say.

Clare would be awake, rifling through the safe in the lounge. She had already searched the safe at Warninglid, leaving this one, the one in London, and the one at the villa in St Lucia. She hoped she would soon find what she was looking for, as she couldn't bear to spend another holiday with Ray Schofield.

TEN

'What's wrong, darling?' Anita Vincent asked, walking into the marital bedroom and taking a seat on the bed beside the prostrate figure of her husband. 'Aren't you going into work today?'

Alex turned to face her. 'I feel listless, completely lacking in energy.'

She leaned over and playfully nipped his cheek with her fingers. 'You were a bit of a tiger in bed last night. I thought we were going to wake the boys. Perhaps you overdid it.'

'No, it's not that.'

'No? What then? The murder at the office?'

'You make it sound like the title of one of those books you're always reading.'

'Obviously, with something so vicious happening so close, in your actual office, it's bound to affect you. However, you said it yourself, you didn't like the man much.'

'It doesn't mean I wanted him dead,' he said curtly.

'No need to be so snappy, I'm only concerned for your welfare.'

'I know you are, darling. I'm sorry.'

'Mummy! He's hitting me!' came a cry from downstairs.

She sighed. 'I stupidly left them eating breakfast together. No doubt I'll go down and find there's more Rice Krispies on the floor than in their bowls. I'd better go or they'll never be ready for school. Get up if you're going in to work, or if not, phone and pull a sickie.'

'I'll go in, don't worry.'

Ten minutes later he was showered and dressed, and walked downstairs into the kitchen. Ben and Thomas were nowhere to be seen, no doubt upstairs making an attempt at putting on their uniform for school while their noses were buried in a book, or in Tom's case, a comic.

His usual breakfast was Shredded Wheat with whatever fruit was around, or if Anita could be bothered and the boys were behaving themselves, eggs. In winter, it was often something warm, usually porridge or Weetabix with hot milk. This morning nothing appealed.

He poured a cup of coffee and took a seat at the kitchen table. Sweeping the floor, Anita had been right, there was enough cereal in the pile of debris to feed another child. It was just a shame the dog didn't like Rice Krispies.

'Do you want me to make you something?'

'No. Anyway, you haven't time. You concentrate on getting the boys out the door. I'll sort myself.'

'You can't go to work on an empty stomach.'

'There's a sandwich bar near the office. If I get hungry, I'll buy something there.'

She was saying something about not knowing what rubbish ingredients were included in shop-bought food, but he wasn't really listening. The murder of Martin Turner had shaken him. He should have felt reassured by the interview he'd had with the two detectives from DI Henderson's team, who told him it was either a random act, or his colleague had been specifically targeted. There was no need for other members of the legal practice to feel threatened.

The reason this didn't make him feel safe was that he had known people like Martin Turner at the private school he'd once attended. While they were rarely academic, they dominated the sports field, whether in rugby, cricket, or tennis, were popular with many teachers, and a hit with all the girls. In his mind, people like this were bulletproof, able to withstand and bat away the trials and problems that life threw at them as easily as a bouncer from a West Indian bowler.

If Martin Turner could be stabbed to death so easily by some low-life, what did it say about his own chances? How could he protect the house, his wife, the two boys? He was thirty-eight, but starting to believe his adverse reaction to Martin's murder was in part due to the early onset of a mid-life crisis.

He'd been feeling this way for several weeks, one question continually popping into his head: Is this all there is? Would he always be trapped in a box marked, 'divorce lawyer, married to Anita, father of Ben and Thomas?' What had happened to his dreams of inventing something, of climbing Everest, taking a year out to sail around the world?

With considerable effort, he said goodbye to his family, picked up his briefcase, and walked out to the car. If there was one aspect of his life that didn't mark him out as a staid, washed-up, middle-aged lawyer, it was the car. Jonas Baines operated a leasing scheme, offering him a sum of money to lease any car of his choosing. The other partners drove status symbols: Jaguars, Mercedes, Range Rovers, while he opted for a BMW 8 Series, a stunning-looking coupe with a top speed of over one hundred and fifty-five miles per hour. When he was feeling blue, he knew a quiet stretch of road where he could open the car up and let it fly.

He completed the drive from the house in Henfield to Trafalgar Street in a dream. It was often said that sophisticated cars like the BMW could almost steer themselves, making the driver feel refreshed when they arrived, as if they had barely left home. To him, this was advertising flim-flam. However, he couldn't have told an enquirer if traffic on the road was light, if the weather was windy or wet, or what the presenters on the Radio 4 Today programme he had been listening to were talking about.

Vincent approached Linden House, and climbed the stairs. He was more awake now, his mind in his usual professional lawyer mode. He needed to be, as despite having worked there for years, he would not be allowed to enter unless he used his key card to open the door, signed the Security Book, and had his photograph taken by the camera. He imagined the other partners would soon tire of this imposition, but for him, it offered a modicum of reassurance.

At the back of his mind, his reluctance to come into work this morning was in part due to his move back into his office. It had been a week since the murder and the police had finished with what they were doing a few days before. Since then the firm had employed a team of contractors to deep clean the crime scene: replacing the blood-stained carpet, removing the police tape, and cleaning all surfaces of fingerprint dust.

He had been presented with the gleaming, finished article the previous night by Robert Haldane, and told to take as much time as he needed. He had been working in one of the meeting rooms for the last week, and despite not having access to all his files, had coped admirably.

None of his divorce clients would have noticed much difference. It was tempting to carry on in this way indefinitely, but to the other partners in the firm, many cut from the same mould as Martin Turner, it would show him up to be, in their terminology, a wuss. He would be forever tagged as a yellow-bellied, spineless coward who could never be trusted.

He placed his briefcase on the desk, removed his jacket and hung it on the coat stand. He stood at the desk, thinking. There was a decision to make. A paralegal appeared at the door, but without saying anything he waved her away.

Summoning up resolve he didn't think he possessed, he walked into Meeting Room 2, the place where he had decamped, and began the process of moving his papers and boxes back into his office. No one offered to help, perhaps feeling they would be tainted by walking into a former crime scene, or maybe his stony expression was repelling them. Plus, he didn't want any assistance. The demons he was wrestling with were his and his alone.

By nine-thirty, the move back to his office was complete. He sat down at his desk and let out a long sigh. He reached over to the piles of papers and began to put them back where they belonged. His more relaxed demeanour must have been noticed, as one of the secretaries walked in and placed a cup of coffee on his desk.

'I thought you might need this,' she said.

'Thanks, Alice, I do.'

'If you need anything else just shout.'

'Have I got any meetings today? I'm not sure where I put my diary.'

'You've got Mrs Russell at eleven-thirty and a partners' lunch at one. There's nothing in the diary for this afternoon, but I expect you'll find it by then.'

'Great, Alice, thanks. You're a lifesaver.'

'I aim to please.'

He was often asked if divorce work was depressing, picking over the dead bones of what used to be a thriving marriage. In some ways, and in some circumstances, it was, particularly when children were involved, but there could be a bright light at the end of the tunnel. Years later, when the wounds had healed, he would occasionally meet one of the previously warring parties, and often they were flourishing in a new relationship and happy to be exploring new opportunities.

If the questioner still harboured doubts, he would compare it with the crime team in the office next door. There, clients could be heinous criminals facing life behind bars for a brutal murder. Martin and Trevor had no choice but to put a brave face on it and try to secure the best deal they could for their client. Often there was no light or anything at all bright at the end of that particular tunnel.

By eleven, with the majority of his paperwork now in its place, he pulled out the Russell file to prepare for his next meeting. Due to the reputation of the firm and the high fees charged, the majority of divorces crossing his desk involved substantial amounts of capital. Most couples in the end would come to some sort of arrangement over the children, but the division of those assets caused more rancour than anything else.

The Russell divorce was, for the moment at least, an amicable one. Mrs Russell was rich, the chief executive of an office cleaning company, while her husband was a part-time web designer and prime carer of their three children. The couple were in agreement that he would receive the sum of ten million, and a monthly salary which would be used to look after the children.

The two parties hadn't yet come to an agreement about the amount of the husband's monthly salary, as they had to take into consideration his earnings. He was self-employed and his earnings fluctuated greatly, so they had decided to take the average over three years. Vincent had asked her husband for the information, and he was sure Roberto had sent it, as Vincent could recall seeing it. Now, where had he put it?

He kept many current files close to hand in a drawer in his desk, but he searched there without success. He then turned to the bookcases behind his desk. He found the box file containing the Russell family information. He removed it and lay it on his desk. He took a seat and opened it. The Russell folder was there, but when he looked inside, it was empty.

ELEVEN

At eight-thirty, Henderson pushed through the double doors and entered the Detectives' Room. At the far side, he joined his murder team for the morning briefing. The group of fifteen or so present were quiet, a common trait part-way through an investigation when many leads had been chased down with no discernible result, and with few others appearing on the immediate horizon.

On the whiteboard behind him were three main headings, the key prongs of their approach for finding the killer of Martin Turner: family and friends, work colleagues, criminal clients.

Henderson perched on the edge of a spare desk. 'Phil,' he said to DC Philip Bentley, 'I think we've exhausted the family and friends file. Are we in a position to close it?'

'I think so, gov. On the family side, I don't think I've ever met such a level-headed and well-adjusted bunch of people in my life. They were all proud of his achievement at becoming a partner in Jonas Baines, even if for some, defending scumbags railed against their morale code.'

'What about friends?'

'He had a wide group of friends, the closest, I came to realise, the people he met at school. As has been said before, his best friends were Stephen Bradshaw and Will Slater.'

'Bradshaw. This is the guy who was with our victim earlier on Tuesday evening?'

'Yep, and his story checks out. CCTV confirms he left the bar around ten and went home.'

'No animosity between the two men?'

'We've got CCTV of them sitting in the bar. It was all joking and laughing. A typical blokes night out if you ask me.'

'Bradshaw went straight home?'

'He did. Confirmed by his wife and grown-up son.'

'What about Slater?'

'He was devastated to hear about Turner's death, probably more than Bradshaw. He had arranged to meet the victim about a week before his murder and was forced to cancel at the last minute. He was beating himself up about it.'

'Where was he on Tuesday night?'

'At home with his wife and kids. She confirmed it.'

'Okay. Nothing else?'

'That's it.'

'Right, the family and friends line of enquiry is closed. Let's move on to the victim's work colleagues. Vicky, your call.'

'Right, gov. We've met a number of people at Jonas Baines, and two people stand out. There's the guy the victim shared an office with, Trevor Robinson, and his neighbour from the office next door, Alex Vincent.'

'No one else?'

She shook her head. 'Nope.'

'What about Haldane?' Walters asked. 'I didn't take to the man.'

'He thinks of himself as a wheeler-dealer, a big noise in Sussex society. As much as I wouldn't want to be stuck in a lift with him, as he gives off a creepy vibe, his grief following Turner's death seemed genuine. From a business perspective, he's lost out big time. Turner was a big earner for the practice and not an easy man to replace. Not to mention, Haldane and the victim were best buddies. Several people said so.'

Henderson considered this for a few moments. 'Yes, I tend to agree with you. If Haldane had fallen out with Turner, or he hated the guy, I'm sure he could have found a way to lever him out of the practice before it came to this.'

'It wouldn't be hard,' Neal said. 'Smelling of booze is enough to get you suspended in many businesses.'

'There's no one else working at Jonas Baines,' Henderson asked, 'or anyone flagged by someone else; a temp, intern, or the security guard?'

'No. We've interviewed a large proportion of their staff, and nobody can think of any reason why Turner was murdered.'

Henderson was alarmed to see the number of 'persons of interest' dwindling to a dangerously low level. 'Tell us about Vincent and Robinson.'

'Let me start with Trevor Robinson, the guy who shared Turner's office,' Neal said. 'He's worked with the victim on crime cases, and apparently they were the best of friends at one time.'

'This is what Turner's ex-wife told us.'

'They would go out drinking together and, as Robinson likes a flutter, sometimes to the races.'

'They fell out?'

'They did, big time. Robinson told us it was because Turner believed he was coming on strong to his eighteen-year-old daughter at a summer garden party. In retaliation, he smacked Robinson on the nose.'

'Not a good move to promote good working relations. You've corroborated this story with other attendees?'

'The consensus from those who were there was that an incident did happen, but not as Robinson describes it. They say Turner was getting annoyed not with Robinson's behaviour, but with his daughter, who was tipsy and flirting like mad with Robinson. He went over to remonstrate, and in the process of hauling her away, accidentally, and for that read, drunkenly, elbowed Robinson in the face. He apologised for it afterwards.'

'So, what caused the big falling out?'

'Robinson doesn't just like a flutter, he's a serious gambler.'

'Is he?'

'Yes, from what we've been told, more and more when the two men went out together, it wasn't for a good drinking session as Turner wanted, but to a place where Robinson could place a bet. He did this at rugby games, horse races, casinos, you name it.'

'What caused the relationship to sour? Surely Robinson's a grown man and free to do whatever he likes with his own money?'

'In most forms of life it wouldn't be an issue, but just as we in the force don't tolerate heavy gamblers, as it might make them susceptible to taking bribes or stealing from drug hauls, it seems Turner felt the legal practice offered similar temptations. They have access to people's wills, they deal with criminals who might use it as a lever, and so on.'

'Did Turner report him?'

'Haldane had been made aware of the situation, but declined to do anything to rock the boat. Turner and Robinson, in his view, were a great team and making more money for the practice than anyone else. Turner wasn't appeased, and warned Robinson if he didn't mend his ways he would make sure he would suffer.'

'I've known several serious gamblers,' Henderson said, 'and it's hard to change them without help, and only then if they want to do it themselves. All the same, does a soured relationship give Robinson enough reason to kill Turner? If things were coming to a head, all Robinson needed to do was resign from Jonas Baines, maybe with a decent reference in his back pocket as Turner would be glad to see him go, and find a job somewhere else.'

'I suppose as a motive it borders on the weak,' Neal said.

'Keep your eye on him, Vicky, he sounds a problematic character.'

'Will do.'

'What did he have to say about his missing security card, the one used by the perp to get into the building?'

'He said he had no idea how he lost it. It was in his jacket pocket at all times. When I asked if he always wore his jacket, he admitted he took it off when he arrived in the morning, and put it back on at night when he went home. Draw your own conclusion.'

'If we assume someone took it out of his pocket, it wasn't one of the employees of Jonas Baines, as none of them, as you said earlier, bore Martin Turner any malice. It had to be someone visiting their offices on that day, or is it days? Does Robinson know when he lost it?'

'He didn't notice the card was missing for 3 days. During this time, he was giving an intern a lift, a friend of the family, apparently. When they arrived at the office, the intern's card was used to open the door.'

Henderson sighed. 'How many visitors are we talking about?'

'Including window cleaners, sandwich sellers, job interviewees, and clients of Jonas Baines, we're looking at about fifty people.'

'My God, this is all we need.' He thought for a moment. 'Vicky, compile the list of names. I'm not sure it will tell us much, although if any of their names come to the fore in the course of the investigation, it will give us another piece of evidence to throw at them.'

'Will do, gov.'

'What about the other lawyer you mentioned, Alex Vincent?'

'He works in the office next door to Martin Turner, in the place where the body was found. We asked him if he thought the victim or the perp had been in his office for a reason. He handles divorce, and while he admits the people who come to see him are rich, he didn't think there were any grounds for believing his work was in any way connected to the incident.'

'Why?' Henderson said. 'Divorce generates as much hate and anger as any other issue in life. Maybe more.'

'He said if one person in a relationship hated the other enough to kill them, they were doing the right thing by coming to him and initiating divorce proceedings.'

'We'll park that thought for the moment,' Henderson said, 'because it leads us down a different path, a place I don't want to go at the moment.'

'Just a random thought,' Carol Walters said. 'Do we think the perp was in Vincent's office and Turner came in to see what he was doing, or was Turner in Vincent's office when the perp showed up?'

Henderson thought for a minute. 'In the former scenario, it suggests Turner heard a noise, came in and confronted the perp. Given the undressed state of the body, I think this is the more likely. In the second...I'm not sure it hangs. It implies Turner was in his colleague's office in the middle of the night, wearing only his underwear, rummaging through his files. If he wanted to, all he needed to do was find an opportunity during the day when Vincent was out at a client meeting, or at lunch, don't you think?'

'I suppose, it was just a thought,' Walters said.

'Vicky,' Henderson asked, 'how did Alex Vincent get on with our victim?'

'Very well by all accounts, although not enough to socialise together. It was Vincent's concern for the welfare of the former Mrs Turner that came to our notice. As we've discussed before, Joanna didn't seem too upset to hear about her ex-husband's murder. Despite this, Vincent's been over to see her several times. To comfort her in her hour of need, we were told.'

Vicky Neal's words had switched on a light bulb in Henderson's head. All the pieces slotting into place like a child's shape sorter toy. It would be easy for Vincent to steal Robinson's security card, and he would know when Turner was going on a bender, forcing him to sleep on his office floor, probably down to the day. In addition, he knew the layout of the Jonas Baines offices, and would have no trouble finding his way around the place in the dark.

'Have other staff mentioned goings-on between Vincent and Turner's ex?' he asked Neal.

She shook her head. 'No, they haven't.'

'Sorry, Vicky,' Henderson said, 'now I think about it, it's a stupid question. If they were engaged in a clandestine affair, why would anyone else know?'

'You're right,' DC Sally Graham said, 'and don't forget, lawyers are noted for their discretion.'

'Good point, Sally. Vicky, anything else to say about Vincent?'

'Nothing more, gov.'

'This sounds like a good lead. The next step is we'll bring Vincent in here to discuss it.'

'I agree.'

'Harry, where are we with the rest of Turner's criminal clients? From memory, six people from the ten-year-plus category are still to be tracked down.'

'We've made contact with four. Two are back in jail and were there at the time of the murder.'

'Okay. What about the other two?'

'Neither of them had any real qualms about Turner's performance, other than to complain that he didn't get their sentences reduced far enough.'

'I can imagine. So, apart from your missing two, Harry, that leaves Nolan, Green, and Schofield. DS Walters and I have talked to Bruce Nolan, and I'm still convinced he's hiding something. I think we'll be speaking to him again at some stage. Green hasn't been around, so we'll catch up with him when he returns. As for Schofield...'

He tailed off, thinking of Houghton's veiled warning and Schofield's highly public acquittal. There didn't seem to be any point in talking to him, as he had been extremely satisfied with Martin's Turner's work. Then again, he was someone who knew Martin Turner well. '...we'll put him on the back-burner for now.'

Henderson left the room ten minutes later, all attendees with follow-up instructions, including the job of producing typed-up transcripts of interview notes. Normally, he would take a detective's word for it when they said the people they'd interviewed didn't bear any malice towards the victim. Now, with so little to go on, he would spend this evening and the one following reading the transcripts, looking for a single chink of light.

TWELVE

It was bitingly cold when Trevor Robinson stepped out of the offices of Jonas Baines. He buttoned up his coat, cursing the firm's stuffy dress code which didn't allow him to wear his puffy skiing jacket, a thickly quilted garment designed for conditions much colder than this. It would have done a better job of keeping him warm than his smart-looking coat, but then again, it was bright yellow and people often mistook him for a council worker.

He walked down Queens Road. At the Clock Tower, he took a right and headed along Western Road in the direction of Hove. He walked everywhere as he didn't own a car despite a generous contract scheme being offered by the firm. He was no ecowarrior, he just didn't like them much.

He didn't like things he couldn't understand, and one thing he didn't understand was cars. His father was a sales rep for an industrial pipe-making business, and he used cars as anyone else would use a bus. He dumped rubbish on the floor, didn't care if the windows were smeared, and only put the thing in for a service after receiving a terse email from the firm's vehicle manager.

It was a cold evening, but despite this Churchill Square Shopping Centre was busy with eager shoppers. He liked it busy, as he often walked past when everything was locked up, making it appear abandoned, desolate. He lived in a flat close to Palmeria Square, but hadn't resided in the town long enough to remember when Brighton and Hove had become a unified city. In an argument between gentrified Hove or bohemian Brighton, his apartment was definitely in Brighton.

It was located on the top floor of a building in Lansdowne Place. It had been converted about eight years before, and as nothing much had been done in the way of updating by the previous owners, he bought it at a discount. He'd spent money he couldn't afford installing a new kitchen and having the whole place painted magnolia, and now it exuded a fresh, clean look.

He wasn't the tidiest of people, but he couldn't bear to live in a slum. Despite not washing, ironing, or vacuuming as often as he needed to, after each meal he tried to leave the kitchen tidy. Today it looked neat, with only this morning's breakfast dishes to sully the worktop.

For a couple of hours he watched some TV, made a meal, drank a few beers, and called Miranda Moss. He had been divorced for six years and despite being a modern man and understanding enough about computers and social media not to make a dick of himself online, he couldn't get along with internet dating.

There was something sad about seeing his modest achievements and shallow characteristics in black and white. It didn't take long, only a few dates, for him to discover he was the one being honest, while most of his companions not only embellished their profiles, some had downright lied about them.

He'd met a 'thirty-two-year-old' woman who didn't look a day less than fifty, a 'vivacious and outgoing party goer' who hauled him into Waterstones to listen to a dreary author talk about diversity, and an 'intelligent and ambitious actress' who worked in a dingy hairdressing salon while awaiting her big break.

He'd met Miranda this way. She was the first person who hadn't lied about her lack of success or the insecurity she felt when meeting new people. She was warm and smart, and he was helping her come to terms with life after a difficult divorce from her childhood sweetheart.

When he finished the call, he headed into the bedroom to change. The business suit he wore to work was smart enough to wear into most places, but to be still wearing it while out in the evening smacked of a hapless office worker with nothing much to go home to. For casino night he liked to adopt the rich, smart-casual approach, much like the Middle-Eastern guys did. Difference was, they bought theirs in stylish boutiques in Brighton and London, had a Lamborghini parked outside, and a penthouse flat overlooking the sea to back it up.

Robinson left the house and walked towards Hove. He was a member of four casinos in Sussex, but the Belgravia Casino in Hove was his favourite. Not because it didn't require him to hop on a bus to get there, as the one in Brighton and the other in Worthing did, or a train like the one in Haywards

Heath, but he often had more success there. He needed it tonight, as late on Saturday night, after a date with Miranda, he had become engrossed in an online poker game. He'd been trying to learn the game for a while and had wagered too much on his overrated ability.

Robinson nodded at the doorman before pulling out his membership card. He took it and wiped it across the slot in a card reader and his details popped up on the tablet he was holding. They must have checked out, no reason why they wouldn't, although there was always a flutter at the back of his mind in case they didn't. He handed the card back and said, 'Have a successful evening, Mr Robinson.'

'Thanks, I'll try to.'

He loved the buzz that walking into a casino generated: the soft music, plush carpets, and the *clack-clack* of dealers as they shuffled cards and scooped the counters from the roulette table. He'd been in casinos as far apart as Las Vegas and Macau, where gambling was brash and genuine billionaires mixed with ordinary punters. He preferred the British model, a touch of opulence and class, with the faint whiff of a gentleman's club, a fixed point in an ever-changing world.

Gambling was in essence, a male-dominated activity. If he ventured into the poker room he would find perhaps no more than four or five women sitting at the five tables, and looking across at the roulette table, blackjack, and one-armed bandit room, there was a clear prevalence of men. A woman he'd met on a Bumble date had explained it thus: men were more stupid than women. Women, she'd explained, were nest builders, while men were hunter-gatherers, risk-seekers, and predators. Needless to say, she didn't make it to a second date. In his mind, and he suspected in the minds of many of his fellow punters, it was because men enjoyed taking risks and were able to focus on one subject for a considerable period of time without distraction.

He walked to a cashier and handed over his credit card to the vivacious brunette in the low-cut dress behind the screen. He felt flush, for reasons he couldn't understand, so he asked for fifty pounds in chips instead of his customary thirty.

He was a novice at poker, so he didn't plan on heading into the poker room any time soon, but reckoned he was a top-dog at blackjack. As a kind of warm-up before playing blackjack, he would spend around twenty minutes playing roulette.

Four rounds later, he was doing all right. Years back, he would bet on a single number; now he was doing splits – two vertical numbers, and streets – three numbers in a line. A woman he had never seen there before was giving him her best smile as his winnings were pushed towards him, but he vowed never to go out with anyone he met in the casino. One gambler in a relationship was bad enough, two was a car-crash waiting to happen.

For the final five minutes of his warm-up session, he lost. He stayed on an extra five to try to recoup his losses, but Lady Luck had deserted him and the smiling woman had moved off. He took his depleted pile over to the blackjack tables and sat down.

Blackjack was a posh name for a card game he'd played as a kid. His father called it Pontoon, he Twenty-Ones, and sweets would be used as chips. The principles of the casino game were the same, only the value of the chips was different. In essence, he would beat the dealer if his cards added up to more than the dealer, and they didn't exceed twenty-one.

He played for an hour and slowly his chip pile went down. The losses sustained at roulette had left him with less to play with, and as a result, he was playing with caution. He left the table and headed over to the cashier's office. He handed over his credit card and asked for another thirty pounds' worth. She gave him a beautiful smile that on another night, and in another situation, would have stirred hormones, encouraging him to switch on his charm. Tonight, however, it was adrenaline not testosterone rushing through his veins, and it was taking all his resolve not to tap his fingers irritably on the counter, or shift nervously from foot to foot as they waited for the little machine to respond.

'I'm afraid this card's been rejected, sir. Do you have another you'd like to use instead?'

'Rejected? How?' His mind didn't compute. He was thinking about cards, the playing variety, not credit, and wondering why his oft-used strategy of counting the royal cards wasn't working.

'Do you have another card, sir?'

He took the proffered credit card back and looked at it, as if there had to be some obvious explanation written there. Had he given her his building pass by mistake, or was there something covering the chip? He had a five-thousand-pound credit limit and couldn't believe he had spent that amount in a month. He pulled out his wallet, put the useless credit card away, and handed over his debit card. This one sailed through without issue. He had been paid about a week before, and the only large payments coming out of there were the mortgage on his apartment, and council tax.

The cashier passed back his card, chips, and receipt. This time, she didn't crack her 'come up to my room' smile, instead it was a neutral expression, probably thinking, 'what a loser'. He headed back to the blackjack table double-determined to show her what a great player he was.

Trevor walked out of the casino at midnight, chastened and cursing Lady Luck under his breath for deserting him in his hour of need. For reasons he couldn't explain, a sharp dealer, loaded cards, or his cavalier approach, he was down nearly two hundred. Despite his best intentions, he had gone back to the cashier several times throughout the evening, convinced his luck would change.

He walked along New Church Road eastwards, in the direction of Brighton. He passed a bank and decided to stop and check his cards at the ATM. His credit card had no trouble being accepted here, but his balance was up to the limit. How the hell did that happen?

Thinking back, he recalled a Saturday some weeks before when he and a friend had spent the day drinking and placing bets at various bookmakers, before entering a casino in Shoreham in the evening. He had no idea how much money he went through, but he didn't have a better explanation for his baffling level of expenditure.

His cavalier use of the credit card annoyed him, but when the debit card was inserted into the machine, the result rocked him. He had less than two hundred pounds to last him until the next payday.

He walked back towards his apartment angry, believing this wasn't his doing, but thieves filching money from his bank account. Turning into his road, he resolved to call his bank first thing in the morning and give them a piece of his mind. Then, it slowly came back to him. An evening at a dog track in East London, courtesy of a client.

He'd drunk too much and, ever the big shot, had used his debit card to withdraw money for the night, and did it again when he needed more. He knew he'd spent more than he'd intended, but at this rate he would be living on bread and water for the rest of the month. He didn't care much about food, but he couldn't go a week without feeling the buzz of cards between his fingers, his concentration fully focused on the dealer's hands.

He needed money desperately. His family couldn't help, and even if they could, they wouldn't. He didn't have much in the way of savings. What was he to do?

THIRTEEN

'Good morning, darling,' Anita said mid-yawn when she appeared at the kitchen door.

'Morning,' Alex Vincent said, from his seat at the kitchen table, barely looking up from yesterday's newspaper.

She walked over to the kitchen table where he was sitting and wrapped her arms around his neck. She stayed there for a few moments, before giving him a kiss on the cheek and breaking free. She started a series of stretching exercises, something she did every morning.

'You were up early. Couldn't you sleep?' she asked, taking a break from stretching to fill the kettle from the water filter. He preferred coffee first thing in the morning, Anita tea.

'I slept fine. I've got a lot on today.'

'Have you?' She laughed. 'Since when did the world of divorce become so demanding it needs you to go into the office at seven in the morning? I know the warring parties want it over quickly, but this is ridiculous.'

Anita had dedicated herself to the care and upbringing of their two boys, and as such, most people treated her as a housewife. This suited her fine, as she could attend coffee mornings and bring-and-buy sales, without intimidating people, which usually happened when they found out she was once a top mergers and acquisitions specialist. This also made her a difficult woman to lie to.

While working, she earned three to four times his salary, and often was awarded an equally large bonus to boot. He wasn't a dinosaur who believed a woman's place was in the home, but he felt emasculated by her huge earning power, and in the high circles she coasted through, dealing with chief executives, government officials, and top civil servants with consummate ease.

It had been her decision to take care of the boys when Thomas was born, and even though Alex had supported her decision, they didn't half feel the jolt when her salary was removed from the family finances. With him now the principal breadwinner, he felt the weight of responsibility like a rucksack filled with rocks on his shoulders. Be careful what you wish for, his father had said to him at the time, and now he understood what he meant.

'No, it's Robert. I mentioned to him about the missing files, and far from taking it lightly as I expected, he fears litigation and has asked me to determine the risk to the firm.'

'You?' she said, taking a seat opposite him at the table, a mug of tea cupped in her hand, and looking at him with unflinching, piercing green eyes. 'You don't know anything about business risk.'

'He trusts me.'

He stood and moved his plate and cup to the sink, not keen to meet her steely gaze. He opened the dishwasher and began putting the items inside.

'Leave it, Alex. I'll do it. You know I don't like anyone else loading the dishwasher.'

'I'll go up and get ready,' he said, walking out of the kitchen quickly before Anita decided to probe further.

When his wife had got the bit between her teeth she was more effective than any of the Radio 4 *Today* programme presenters he listened to on the way to work. She would repeatedly ask the same question until she had received what she regarded as a satisfactory answer. When meeting someone for the first time, she would know more about them in five minutes than he would from spending an afternoon chatting to them.

The journey to Brighton was more pleasant than normal. Less traffic for a start, and fewer holdups at the usual choke points. He was on the road before school traffic, most office workers, and almost all retail employees. It was so easy, he wondered why he didn't do it all the time; there was certainly enough work on his plate to fill the extra hours he would gain.

When he reached the outskirts of Brighton, the junction between the A23 and A27, instead of driving straight into town he took the bypass and headed east towards Lewes.

Malling House, the Headquarters of Sussex Police, wasn't the bland sixties office block he was expecting. To his surprise, it looked like a manor house with a variety of different sizes and shapes of office blocks located directly behind it.

He parked and, after entering one of the buildings and informing the uniformed policeman behind the desk of his name, was led into an interview room. He liked coffee, but refused the offer of a cup from the young constable. He couldn't bear coffee from a machine, and he knew how bad police coffee could be from stories told to him by Martin Turner.

Minutes later, two people walked into the room. It was DI Henderson, and DS Walters, both of whom he'd met at the Jonas Baines offices. Henderson was clean-shaven, an unusual occurrence nowadays if any of the clients he met on a daily basis were anything to go by, and dressed in a suit. It wasn't an expensive suit. His own were handmade and looked and hung better.

'As I'm sure you're aware, Mr Vincent, I am the Senior Investigating Officer in the hunt to find Martin Turner's killer.'

'Yes, I was aware.'

'You have already been interviewed by two of my officers—'

'So why do you need to see me again? I've had to make this appointment early so no one in the office, or even my wife, would know I was coming here. If people knew I'd been seen by you people twice they'd think I was a suspect.'

'You didn't tell your wife?' Walters said. 'Why not?'

'If my wife suspects I am hiding something, Sergeant, she is like a rottweiler with a piece of gristle in its mouth. She would gnaw at me for as long as it took to wheedle the truth out.'

'Why, do you have something to hide?'

He realised he'd said something he shouldn't. 'No, that wasn't what I meant. I was using the metaphor to illustrate a point. If she knew I was coming here, I would have been bombarded with questions; that was all I meant.'

'When you talked to my officers,' Henderson said, 'you said you and Martin were friends.'

He sighed. 'In the past, we were and I would have admitted it without hesitation. We'd often go to each other's houses for a dinner party, or a barbecue in summer, but in the last couple of years, less so.'

'Did Martin's drinking habits annoy you?'

'Why, because I'm teetotal?'

'Are you? I didn't know.'

'Yes, I am. It's not for any religious reasons, or because I'm an ex-alcoholic. Suffice to say, I had a bad experience with alcohol as a teenager and I never want to repeat it. Plus, I like driving too much to risk losing my license over something as inconsequential as a drink.'

'As police officers who have seen our fair share of tragic accidents as a result of drink-driving, we can only commend you.'

'Thank you.'

'Going back to my question, Mr Vincent. Did Martin's drinking bother you?'

'It did. It would turn an intelligent and interesting man into a boorish lout who behaved no better than an overgrown schoolboy.'

'Did things change following his divorce from Joanna?'

'That's a good question, Inspector, and I have to say yes. He drank much more after the divorce, when it wouldn't just result in high jinks where he would drench everyone with his kid's super-soaker, or throw bread rolls in a restaurant. He became a more morose individual who, if we were in a pub together, would bore me witless with his troubles, or be eyeing up every woman in the place.'

'Would you say you were still friends at this point?'

He thought for a moment. 'I didn't socialise much with him at this time, but we still saw each other at work functions, or when dealing with the same client.'

'There's crossover?'

'Some women can't wait to get divorced if their husbands are charged with a serious offence. Gone are the days of standing by your man.'

'Hallelujah to that. It makes our job so much easier.'

'Even though Martin and I didn't socialise together, it didn't stop my wife and his. Their kids are older than ours, although they still have Seb at Hurstpierpoint College, the school where our two go. The two women meet for coffee once a week, and they're both on several of the same committees at school.'

'Mr Vincent, my officers have noticed you seem to have a personal interest in Joanna Woodford.'

'Is this in reference to my visiting her house after her former husband was found murdered?'

'Yes, although going once in the last week wouldn't bother me, but I think three times requires some explanation.'

'I have a right to be concerned; she's a good friend. I'm appalled at your lack of sensitivity. In fact,' he said, standing, 'I will say no more on the matter. This meeting is finished.'

'Sit down,' Henderson said sharply.

'Or what?'

'I will arrest you.'

'On what grounds, pray tell?'

'On suspicion of murdering Martin Turner.'

'What?' he said in a strangled, high-pitched voice. 'I haven't murdered anyone. Where is your evidence?'

'Sit down, Mr Vincent.'

Vincent sat down slowly, but with the speed of an electronic news feed he saw the implications of this accusation as it raced across his brain. At the first whiff of a scandal, the firm would suspend him despite the often-quoted mantra of 'innocent until proven guilty'. Anita would kick him out and the information would zip around his boys' school with the alacrity of an Australian bushfire, not blackening the landscape, but his reputation. He needed to be careful here, or all thoughts of a ten o'clock client meeting followed by lunch with Joanna would become a distant and gut-twisting memory.

'Mr Vincent, and remember, this conversation is being recorded, are you and Joanna Woodford involved in an affair?'

His first instinct was to lie, a little white lie in the scheme of things, but the light on the recording device glowed red. He knew from personal experience and working with divorce clients how lies, even little white ones, often came back to haunt.

'Yes,' he said, 'but only after Martin left.'

'Are you sure?'

'It may have started,' he said waving a hand dismissively, 'I don't know, a few months before he was chucked out, but the writing had been on the wall for two, maybe three years before.'

'So we understand.'

'Good, so you'll know how bad the situation was.'

'On the night of Martin Turner's murder, you were where?'

'I told all this to your officers. Don't you people talk to one another?'

Shit! He didn't mean to sound so aggressive. If he did it again, the murder charge would surely make another unwelcome appearance.

'Yes, we do talk to one another. I have their report right in front of me. I want to hear you say it.'

He sighed. 'If you wish. I arrived home around seven. I changed out of my work clothes into sportswear, had something to drink, then drove to my badminton club. It's held at the community hall in Henfield, if you want to check. I came home around ten, feeling pretty shattered having played three hard matches. I had something to eat while watching television with my wife, and we both went to bed at eleven. I didn't get up again until about seven the following morning.'

'Can you see why this new information interests us?'

'No, tell me.'

'I would have thought, with you being a divorce lawyer, it would be obvious. If Martin had found out about your relationship with Joanna he would have had a hold over you. Perhaps he threatened to tell your wife, or tried to intimidate Joanna into discontinuing maintenance support.'

It hit him like a steam hammer. He knew Martin's movements, how he drank heavily, how he sometimes slept in the office, the whole kit and caboodle. Now they were adding a reason as to *why* he would want to do it. He felt his grasp of reality slipping away. He wanted to say it but couldn't face the embarrassment, that often-heard staple of many popular television crime dramas: *I need a lawyer.*

'No,' he said weakly. 'I didn't kill Martin. Ask my wife, she'll tell you.'

Walking out to his car, with instructions not to leave the country still ringing in his ears, Vincent felt like he was stepping on quicksand. Yes, Anita would back up his alibi, but when she found out about his betrayal, and with her best friend, one careless word or a feigned lapse of memory on her part, and the quagmire would become real.

FOURTEEN

Henderson drove along Brighton seafront, a mirror of his earlier morning run. It was a dull winter's day, with no sign of the sun, and the sea the colour of gun metal. Not surprisingly, there were no leisure craft on the water: no yachts, paddleboards, or windsurfers, only the slow-moving commercial ships on their way to one of the large ports on the Continent.

'You were saying about Alex Vincent,' Carol Walters said from the passenger seat.

'Aye, I was. He ticks all the boxes of a classic love triangle murder, but I'm not entirely convinced.'

'You mean, he doesn't look like a murderer? He does to me.'

'We've had this discussion before: what does a murderer look like? We talk about the loner who has a suffocating relationship with his mother, or conversely, one in which she rejects him. Alternatively, the con or ex-soldier with a chip on his shoulder. This before someone mentions genial, old Harold Shipman, everyone's favourite GP. I accept Vincent knew the victim's movements, didn't like him much, and would perhaps gain from his death, but in this instance it doesn't feel enough.'

'Well, the team back in the office will keep tearing his background and alibi apart until they find something.'

'His alibi hangs on his wife, Anita. As you know, husband and wife alibis are notoriously difficult to break down. Plus, who goes to their badminton club on a night they're planning to kill someone? It's a tough, exhausting game at club level. Most people, sitting in the dark at Jonas Baines waiting for Martin Turner to show up, would be fast asleep in a corner.'

'Ach, trust you to spoil it, I think he's such a good fit.'

'Let's see what the team come up with. Make sure he did go to the badminton club as he said, and speak to one or two members and find out if he played the games he said he did, and what frame of mind he was in. Also, check the time he left.'

'Will do.'

'Next, talk to Anita again, and see if she agrees with his timing, but don't mention the affair. There's no need to blow their relationship out of the water if we don't have other evidence to stack against him.'

'No problem.'

At Shoreham Harbour, Henderson turned into an industrial estate before pulling up outside a warehouse. The name Rema Foods was displayed prominently.

'Not bad for a man who's spent the last few years inside,' Walters said.

'A lot of illegal money was confiscated when he was convicted, but he must have had a lot of it salted away in order to start this, don't you think? I can't see him, with his track record, trotting along to his local Barclay's branch and asking for a loan, can you?'

They got out of the car and approached the door. It was locked, but he noticed the CCTV camera above his head and it didn't look like a dummy. Henderson pressed the bell and waited.

'Hello, this is Rema Foods. What can I do for you?'

The person talking was displayed on a small video screen. 'Detective Inspector Henderson and Detective Sergeant Walters, Sussex Police, to see Dominic Green.'

Henderson heard a click from the door's mechanism. He pushed it open and they walked inside. It was a typical warehouse operation with rows of racking filling almost the entire building, the shelves full of large sacks. As they walked in the direction of the office at the back, Henderson saw that some of the sacks contained tea, some pasta and others flour.

A man stepped out from behind a desk and headed towards them. He was small with grey hair swept back and a big gut hanging over his belt, as if concealing a car tyre under his shirt.

'Sussex Police to see Dominic Green,' Henderson said, holding out his ID.

'I'm the warehouse supervisor. Is he expecting you?'

'He is.'

'He said fuck all about it to me, but what the hell, it's par for the course in this place. Follow me.'

He led them past other shelves containing smaller packages, half-kilo and kilo-sized, presumably the shop-ready versions of the sacks he had noticed earlier. Through the glass panels of the office at the back, Henderson spotted the familiar bald pate of its sole occupant, Dominic Green.

To all intents and purposes, this looked like a successful and legit operation, but leopards didn't change their spots any more than serious criminals like Dominic Green decided to go straight. However, Henderson couldn't help but admire the attempt.

The warehouse supervisor stuck his head around the office door and said, 'Two cops here to see you, boss.'

'Thanks, Sid. Send them in.'

Henderson and Walters walked inside while Sid waddled back to his desk grumbling about something.

'Don't send your children to the same charm school as our Sid, that is, if you don't want them to come out more ignorant than when they went in. Inspector Henderson and Sergeant Walters, this is a pleasure. Please take a seat.'

No handshakes, no genuine bonhomie and there would be no offer of drinks. Henderson expected as much.

'It's an impressive place you have here, Mr Green,' Henderson said.

'What, for a former con?'

'No, I meant in comparison to the other businesses around here. You've got plenty of stock and it's obvious you're busy.'

'I started this business about eighteen months ago, importing bulk commodities such as tea and flour from contacts in India and Pakistan, and selling them in smaller quantities to local supermarkets and farm shops. I'm more than happy with the way it's turned out. Our White Knight brand is flying off the shelves.'

'I've seen it displayed in a supermarket near me,' Henderson said. 'I didn't know it was one of yours.'

'Now you do. Buy some and help an ex-con trying to make his way in the world.'

'Aye, maybe I will. I'm in charge of the team investigating the murder of a prominent local lawyer, Martin Turner.'

'I was distressed to read the story, I can tell you. It was Martin, after all, who prepared the groundwork in my case, and while I would give Giles Rayworth QC the bulk of the credit for his theatrical but magnificent performances in court, he couldn't have done it without Martin's help.'

Henderson was listening, but all the time looking round for any evidence to suggest this operation was a front. If so, to hide the trade in what? Green was a career criminal who specialised in importing and selling drugs, and while this could be more of the same, he wouldn't put it past him to be dabbling in something else: gunrunning, art fraud, laundering or forging money.

'Have you had any contact with Martin since the trial?'

'Other than trying to lodge an appeal, do you mean?'

'Yes.'

'I should have had. It's quite remiss of me. You know as well as I do I was facing serious charges and a possible twenty-year stretch. In the end, I received four, and was allowed out after eighteen months. I'm not trying to rub your noses in the mud, it's just how the wheels of British justice turn.'

'We know.'

'The reason I fared so well was entirely due to Martin's tenacity in getting to the truth. It's only when you're out that you realise this. All the time you're inside, all your energies are focussed on doing your bird and getting out. I should have taken Martin out to the pub for a drink or a meal and thanked him in person.'

Henderson had never seen Green quite so sentimental about anything before. In fact, in many respects he would have said he was a classic psychopath, lacking any capacity to be empathetic to anyone.

'Do you know any of Martin Turner's other clients? Anyone who might've wanted to kill him?'

'You think one of his clients killed him?'

'It's one of the strands of our investigation.'

'The other strands being, what? His private life and his work colleagues. Am I right?'

'Very perceptive of you.'

'When you've been around criminals for as long as I have, you tend to pick up such things.'

'I bet you do.'

'I don't know if I can be of any help here. I know plenty of cons, but I couldn't be sure if they were one of his clients.'

'You must know some. Turner was probably recommended to you by some other con; he might have let slip the odd name during a conversation with you, and don't tell me cons don't chat about the performance of their lawyers while they're inside?'

'We talked about them, right enough, and I admit some were desperate to get out and do their briefs some damage. Mind you, most of them are still inside, serving longer sentences than me.'

'Does anyone come to mind?'

'No, and I'm not saying this because you people are the forces of law and order. Martin was a decent guy, a bit posh for my taste, but a bloke who believed everyone was entitled to a fair crack at justice. I don't know anyone who didn't like him.'

Five minutes later Henderson and Walters were outside Rema Foods, walking back to their car. They climbed in and Henderson drove off towards Lewes.

'He's got a sophisticated security system back there,' Henderson said. 'It looks like a new alarm box with CCTV cameras and detectors all over the place. To justify it, I thought there must be something valuable inside, but as far as I could see it's only big sacks of flour, rice, and tea.'

'Maybe there's been a lot of burglaries in the neighbourhood.'

'Maybe, but I don't think so. I didn't notice many cameras on the other buildings nearby. Perhaps I'll have a word with Gerry Hobbs and his drug team. It might be something more valuable than tea and pasta he's protecting.'

'You could be right.'

'Do you remember Green saying he hadn't been in touch with Martin since coming out of prison?'

'Yeah, he made a point of it. He was looking wistful with a touch of regret, the lying toad.'

'He's got as much sincerity as a viper. Did you notice an untidy pile of paper, sitting on the small filing cabinet over to Green's right?'

'No, my view was blocked by him and the in-tray.'

'Sticking out, but not too far was a document bearing the Jonas Baines letterhead.'

'What?'

'It was definitely one of theirs.'

'Might it be an invoice for something they'd forgotten to send at the time of his trial?'

'I'd imagine if they found something un-invoiced it would have been sent to Green's wife at the time, and no later than a couple of months afterwards. I didn't see much but it didn't look like an invoice.'

'A statement of account, perhaps?'

He shrugged. 'Could be, but why now, so many years after the trial?'

'In which case, Green lied to us.'

'I wonder why. If it's got something to do with Martin Turner, I'd like to know what.'

'There are ways and means.'

'Not the formal route, as there's not enough for a warrant, but I'd normally be racking my brains to see if I could come up with a name, someone who could sneak inside Rema Foods and take a look, but no. I'm afraid Green's over-elaborate security is doing the job it was intended to do.'

'What's that?'

'Keeping nosey bastards like me out.'

FIFTEEN

He wound down the window and flicked out his cigarette butt. Despite a chaotic schooling where he ran with the wrong crowd according to his mother, but the right one if you wanted to have fun, Bruce Nolan had never smoked. It was hard at times, as his mates would light up whatever they laid their hands on: tobacco, weed, crack, but inside the nick his resistance had melted. Not because he wanted to look tough, or fit in with the crowd, but because of the sheer boredom of the place. Nothing to do all day but smoke and wonder why he had ended up in there.

It was around eight-thirty, and already dark on a chilly evening. Instead of being home and watching a football match on television with a cool beer in his hand, he was sitting in a cold car outside a terraced house in Elm Grove. It was a neat, trim little house nestling within a row of grubby companions. He didn't know much about Brighton. He had lived most of his life in Newhaven and only travelled into Brighton at weekends to drink, or if there was something he wanted to see at the theatre or the cinema. He imagined the scruffy houses were rentals, perhaps to students, as he knew some departments of Brighton University were located nearby.

Inside the smart house, Harvey Templeton had probably finished shagging the pretty thirty-year-old with the jet-black hair who had opened the door about a half-hour before. Templeton would now be lying on his back on her soft pillows, blowing smoke rings at the ceiling, thinking about his next business deal, or about going home soon to his equally pretty wife.

Bruce Nolan knew all about Harvey Templeton. His name had meant little before his incarceration, one of several property developers who had shown an interest in buying his scrap metal business. Companies would contact him now and again with tempting offers. The business was located on a large site beside the waterfront. Behind it, and across the water, were apartment blocks. The yard was the only industrial unit among a sea of the bloody things.

No matter if they decorated their offerings with tales of sculpted green spaces, affordable houses, and play parks, he was unmoved. He wasn't selling. He wasn't an obstinate man, but the scrap metal business had got him out of trouble as a young man and kept him going in the dark days of prison. It was one of the few stable things in his life, and no way would he give it up.

Among the myriad of property companies, developers, and chancers, Templeton had been the persistent one. He had tried every trick in the book, but now Nolan had proof that Templeton had been instrumental in sending him to prison. If things turned out right tonight, it would be Nolan's turn to behave badly.

He couldn't understand why the participants in an illicit love affair would do anything with the curtains open. He was unable to see them in flagrante delicto in the bedroom upstairs, but afterwards saw them walking into the lounge, him picking up his beer from the coffee table, and her most likely a vodka and lime. They both took a drink and kissed. The sloppy, languid movements of the après sexed.

They sat down out of sight. He wasn't some private dick looking for proof of his, or her, infidelity on the instructions of their other half. He didn't have a sophisticated camera fitted with a telephoto lens and a motor drive to capture multiple shots of their Kodak moment. He wasn't interested in her, or what they did together. His only consideration was Harvey Templeton.

At one time, he'd considered going through this woman, or Templeton's wife, to get at him, but it would have lowered Nolan to Templeton's level. He was better than him, and in his view the fewer people who suffered, the more he liked it.

The reason he was following him was Templeton was a hard man to get on his own. As a former estate agent and now property developer, he was gregarious and often surrounded himself with colleagues, friends, associates and on occasion, a minder who accompanied him to building sites. This was a tall black guy Nolan called Mr Muscle, who looked as though he packed not only muscle but something else too, as sometimes there an odd bulge in his jacket.

The lovers rose and walked out of the lounge. He imagined the time taken to exit the lounge and open the front door, which could be anything between one and five minutes, was not the time Harvey needed to button up his coat and tie his scarf. Judging by past episodes, when they'd both appeared at the door with dishevelled clothes and messed-up hair, they were indulging in a bit of last-minute fumbling.

For once, the coupling was brief, and with a tender touching of fingers, Templeton strode down the steps towards his car. Befitting a successful property developer, it was a convertible Jaguar F-Type. Nolan had made the mistake the previous week of borrowing his partner's car, a Vauxhall Corsa. Despite Harvey not realising he was being followed, his mind still in his trousers, the simple act of pulling away from traffic lights or climbing a hill in the Corsa had left him floundering some way behind.

This time he had brought his own car, a Tesla Model S. Despite working in an old donkey jacket and jeans, and driving a ten-year-old VW Golf to work, his business was a money spinner. He kept his eye on building developments and was the first to approach owners and demolition managers at power and sub-stations, telephone exchanges, and factory sites with a proposal to remove old cable.

Elements like copper, the main constituent of electricity cables, and titanium, found in the catalytic converters of cars, were continually rising in price. In fact, an Openreach project around Newhaven to strip out copper telecommunications cables and replace them with fibre optic had, in effect, paid for the Tesla.

Templeton lived in the Dyke Road area, a smart part of Brighton and befitted a property man, in a villa which wouldn't look out of place in the hills above Marbella: all white walls, large areas of glass, and the area in front of the house paved with decorative slabs. It was without question in the one-and-a-half to two-million bracket, way more than Nolan would ever be able to afford, no matter how many lengths of cable he managed to procure.

He turned down Elm Grove and when they reached the Lewes Road, took a left towards Brighton. At St Peter's Church, he did a U-turn and joined London Road, now heading north. His next manoeuvre, if the previous times he'd followed him were anything to go by, would be to take a left at Trafalgar Street. This would lead him past Brighton Station, to Dyke Road, where his wife would be waiting. Instead, he drove past the junction and carried on driving north.

Once clear of the roundabout where the A27 from Lewes joined the A23, the Jaguar moved into the outside lane and Templeton gunned the big cat's engine. The Tesla was no slouch and Nolan had no problem keeping up, but at a safe distance, while sticking to the inside lanes where possible to minimise the chances of detection.

He didn't need to do this for long, as Templeton wasn't going to London, or further north as he feared. Instead, he turned off at the Burgess Hill junction. Nolan knew this road well as a few metal dealers were located in the area. He also knew Burgess Hill was a reasonably large town, surrounded in the main by wooded countryside. What business Templeton had here at this hour of the night, he couldn't guess.

They climbed Clayton Hill. When they passed Mill Lane, leading to the Jack and Jill Windmills, the left indicator of the Jaguar flashed. Nolan was a couple of cars back, so he had time to slow and make the turn, making sure Templeton's car wasn't directly in front of him. In fact, when he did, the Jaguar was nowhere to be seen. The reason soon became apparent: the narrow track was heavily wooded with a tight bend up ahead. Nolan committed the track's layout to memory before killing the car's main lights.

He drove down a wood-shrouded incline hoping there would be a place to turn at the bottom; he didn't fancy having to reverse all the way up the narrow track to the main road. On a flat area about twenty metres from the bottom of the slope, he saw lights, and what looked like a farmhouse with a couple of barns, one behind the house and the other over to the right. He stopped the car and took in the scene.

Templeton's car had come to a standstill beside the barn to the right, which Templeton was walking towards. Seconds later, a man came out of the house. Templeton stopped and waited for the other man to catch up. They greeted one another like old mates.

Nolan felt deflated. He'd hoped Templeton was heading to a rural property for a more solitary purpose, perhaps to visit an elderly or infirm parent. If so, he would have confronted him outside. The guy who joined Templeton looked like his minder, Mr Muscle.

When the two men had disappeared inside the barn, he coasted the car down the remainder of the incline and into the clearing, and turned. Due to the Tesla's quiet operation, he had no fear of Templeton coming out to investigate the sound of a strange car. He parked it as close as possible to the access road, under the shade of some trees, hoping its presence wouldn't be too obvious. He also made sure the front of the car was pointing towards the main road, just in case he needed to make a swift exit.

He was undecided about what to do next. He couldn't confront Templeton with Mr Muscle present, unless he wanted to end up broken into little pieces, or on a mortuary slab. On the other hand, the rural location, the time of night, and the presence of the two men, piqued his interest. What was the conniving rat up to now: growing weed, making skunk, printing phoney credit cards?

Nolan kept his eye on the farmhouse windows for a few minutes to see if Mr Muscle was living there alone, or if others were in the house. He saw no movement: no shadows, no lights switching on and off, and with the car window down, no sounds of music or a television playing. He switched off the interior light of the car before opening the door and stepping out into the cold night. Crouching, he ran towards the barn, occasionally glancing over his shoulder at the farmhouse, making sure no one had spotted him or was trying to outflank him.

Reaching the barn, light flooded out from the part-closed entrance. He disappeared into the darkness at the side. From the spots and shafts of light spilling out from broken or warped wood panels, he could tell it was an old and badly maintained barn.

If this was a property owned by Templeton it hadn't been in his stable for long, as, in common with many property developers he knew, they had no regard for anything old or traditional. When he got round to it, this barn would be razed and replaced with a gleaming new one, or a small block of exclusive rural apartments.

Using the torch on his phone, he checked his footing to make sure he wouldn't slip, before positioning himself in front of a decent-sized crack in the wood panelling. The barn didn't contain much inside, save for a few bits of dilapidated farm equipment and a small stack of hay bales. In the centre and tied to one of the support posts, was a man. He was side-on to Nolan and he could see his face was a bloody mess; he looked barely conscious.

Templeton was asking the tied man questions. When he didn't like the answer, Mr Muscle stepped forward and gave him a smack. Nolan couldn't hear the Q&A as he was too far away, but he looked hard at his face when the head of the man flopped to one side. He realised he knew him. It was his number two at the scrapyard, Pedro.

SIXTEEN

The alarm sounded at six-thirty. Not exactly an alarm but the unbelievably cheery voice of the morning DJ on Heart Sussex. Carol Walters had always been a terrible riser and for this reason the volume was set loud.

'What the fuck's that racket?' Nick Something groaned beside her. At least she thought it was him, but she couldn't be sure; as all that was visible was a tousled mangle of hair. His voice sounded strange too, all raspy and rough, having lost much of its Dublin twang on account of having to shout over the loud music in the Kerrang! Club last night.

She reached over to the radio-alarm clock and reduced the volume, but didn't turn it off. To do so would be fatal. Suffering from a hangover and walking around a cold flat looking for clothes was no match for a warm bed and a hunky man to cuddle.

She worked up the courage to get out of bed, but her resolve almost melted when Nick Something's arm snaked over her stomach and his hand moved between her legs. Almost. She put his arm back where it belonged, got out of bed, and headed into the shower. She turned up the heat and soaped herself until the base of the unit was foaming with suds, then reached for the heating control again and this time turned it cold. She stood there shivering, counting down from sixty.

She stepped out of the shower gasping. It never failed as a wake-up cure. Sometimes it wouldn't manage to cut through her hangover if she'd drunk too much, but while last night she had been merry and in the mood for a good time, she had tried to be sensible. The team were in the middle of a murder investigation, after all, and she needed to keep a clear head.

She was so busy rubbing herself with the towel, trying to warm up, she didn't notice Nick was standing there until she felt a hand on her shoulder. He pulled her towards him and they kissed.

'We were good last night, you and me,' he said in a husky voice.

'We were,' she said. A few seconds later, she broke free. 'Now, I have to get to work.'

'Why so early, and on a weekend?'

'I told you last night, I'm involved in a murder investigation.'

'Oh yeah, a cop. I never realised you had to start so early, but I suppose it's all shifts and rotas. Me, I can usually go in more or less when I like.'

She left him in the bathroom while she walked to the bedroom to dress, racking her brains, trying to remember what he did. He was a web designer. No, she was thinking of Rob, the bloke she had been with the previous week. An interior designer? No, she was confusing him with someone else. She settled on something in IT. She vaguely remembered a story about a system developing a fault, resulting in twenty-pound notes being spurted out of ATM machines, although she couldn't remember if his company had caused the problem, or if they were involved in fixing it.

She walked into the kitchen, switched on the coffee machine and popped a couple of slices of bread into the toaster. She was sitting beside the kitchen table munching a piece of toast and drinking a mug of milky coffee when Nick breezed in. He had availed himself of her shampoo as his hair was clean and damp, but it was obvious he didn't fancy using her pink-handled razor as his face was still a mass of stubble.

'Tea or coffee?' she asked.

'No, nothing for me, thanks. I've just remembered, I need to go and collect my car. Last night I left it outside a mate's house and I forgot, I've got a conference call with a company in Dubai at nine, so unfortunately I've got to run.'

He leaned over and kissed her. Not the goodbye kiss of two acquaintances, but the deep, sensual one of two illicit lovers.

'I'll call you, okay?' he said, walking away.

'I'll look forward to it. Bye.'

'See ya.'

The door snapped shut.

This was how it often ended: the door closing, and silence. After a few days with no call or text, she would start again. In many respects, going out with the girls, enjoying a few drinks, meeting a guy, was a preferable way to go about things than online dating. Chancers in the past had lied about being single, and if they closely resembled their online picture, it was the exception.

Apart from that, online dating couldn't reveal much about a person's true character. She'd been out with guys who criticised what she had been wearing or how she looked, got annoyed when she took an opposing point of view, or became aggressive when someone else took an interest in her. Even when a guy was a close match for his photograph, and appeared to be a reasonably balanced character, there still remained the issue of compatibility.

She liked to party, but now pushing forty and looking ahead, at some point she wanted to settle down. Not the pipe and slippers beside a roaring fire type of settling down, but one with the occasional restaurant meal, concert, theatre outing, and trips to London to visit an exhibition or see a show.

She left the breakfast dishes on the worktop to be sorted later, and walked into the hall. She picked up a warm jacket and put it on. Scooping her car and house keys from the hall stand, she headed outside.

Walking to her car, she wondered if the warm jacket might be overkill. It was a mild morning, a sign of spring to come. No matter, she could leave it in the office. That said, by the time she left for home, often around seven, it would be starting to get dark and the outside temperature would plummet; she would need it then.

She reached the Malling House car park before the eight o'clock news on the radio, and with so many administrative staff working at the campus who hadn't yet arrived, there was a choice of parking places. She parked her Golf behind a Nissan Primera and as she got out, the driver of the Nissan also got out.

'Jan!'

It was Jan Allan, one of the women she had been out with the previous night.

'Oh, it's you, Carol. I didn't expect to see you this early. It's Sunday, for goodness' sake.'

'Why not? I didn't drink as much as you or Lena.'

'I thought you'd be up all night shagging that bloke Nick, and be well knackered this morning. He was hot. If you're not up to it, girl, pass him over to me.'

'It didn't work out with his mate, what was his name, Charlie, wasn't it?'

'Harley, as in bike, and about as interesting as one with a flat tyre. He was a crap kisser, and you know me, if they can't get that right, the rest will be bloody awful. So, it was an early night for me. Anyway, my love, I've got to go. The boss has got a conference call with his counterpart at the Home Office and he's shitting bricks thinking he's in for a bollocking. I'd better go and lend him some morale support. Catch you later.'

'Bye Jan.'

Carol walked towards her building and Jan to hers. Like Walters, Jan was divorced. In the DS's case, mainly due to her former partner, Rory, being such a useless prat: at finding a job, doing DIY, looking after her. In Jan's case, it was because he had been abusive. Not the hard-to-spot, drip-drip of the psychological abuser, steadily exerting his control over his partner, but the blindingly obvious punch-in-the-face type. They were easier for the police to prosecute, as photographs produced irrefutable evidence that could be put in front of a jury. Jan's ex was proof of this, as he was still inside, but the reasons and responses behind the abuse were often harder to comprehend.

After greeting her fellow detectives and other staff present, she took a seat at her desk. She woke up her computer and checked the serials, a list of all the crimes committed in the Sussex region overnight.

At ten, she and Sally Graham headed outside to the car park. DI Henderson wanted Joanna Turner, now Woodford, interviewed again, and for the subject of her affair with her ex-husband's colleague, Alex Vincent, to be raised. For this, he thought, and she agreed, the interview would be better conducted by two female officers.

Walters drove out of the car park and headed towards the A27.

'Did you see on the serials this morning, Sally? Harvey Templeton's been arrested.'

'The news report I read described him as a multi-millionaire property developer. I wish someone would call me that.'

'Do you know who he is?'

'Never heard of him before.'

'I have. A friend of mine bought a seafront property in Shoreham, one of his developments. She's had nothing but trouble with leaks, heating not working, wind blowing in the windows, you name it.'

'That's terrible. You can understand it happening in an old house, but not in a new development.'

At the A27 - A23 junction, she headed right at the roundabout and joined the A23 northbound.

'It sounds as though he won't be doing much property development for the time being,' Graham said.

'You think?'

'Don't you? He's been charged with serious assault and kidnap. Either one will give him plenty of jail time.'

'I wouldn't be so sure.'

'Why not?'

'He's rich and as slippery as an eel. He'll get his lawyer to argue it was all his accomplice's handiwork or something.'

Joanna Woodford's house was warm when they arrived. They were directed into the kitchen where a large Aga stove dominated the room, and where Joanna was baking.

'It's for the school, you know. You'd think we pay enough in fees not to need bake sales, but who I am to question it? Are you any closer to finding who killed Martin?'

'Our investigation is ongoing,' Walters said.

'That's cop speak for either *we don't have a clue*, or *we're about to arrest someone*. Which is it?'

'It's somewhere in between, if I'm being honest.'

'At least it sounds like progress. What would you like to talk to me about today?'

'We've interviewed Alex Vincent. He told us you and him are having an affair.'

She stopped what she was doing, the spoon used to mix the ingredients in the bowl hung in mid-air. 'Has he? Oh shit!'

'What went on between you and Alex in private is not our concern,' Walters continued, 'but the fact of the affair itself is. You see, if Martin had found out about it and confronted Alex, it could provide a motive for his death.'

'Oh yes, I do see, as it would put Alex in the frame. I can put your mind at rest. Our affair is no more than a dalliance between a lonely woman and a man who, somewhat prematurely, finds himself in the midst of a mid-life crisis. We don't love each other and I have never asked or wanted him to leave his wife for me.'

'Would Mr Vincent concur with your view?'

'You'll need to ask him, but I would be surprised if he said anything different. He's never made any demands on me other than those of a physical nature, and as for Martin becoming jealous and confronting Alex?' She shook her head. 'I just don't see it. The affair started around the time Martin left. If Martin did have any feelings for me and discovered our affair, he would be forced to admit he had no one to blame but himself.'

SEVENTEEN

Henderson poured muesli into a bowl and added some cold milk. He was feeling tired, not because he had been out the previous night and he had come home late, but he was unaccustomed to talking and concentrating for so long.

The previous night, he had gone to the cinema with a lady and afterwards, went to a pizza restaurant. It wasn't Sharon from upstairs this time, but for the last four weeks he had been dating Kelly Jackson, a Sociology and Criminology professor at the University of Sussex.

Kelly was one of the UK's foremost experts in offender profiling, and had spent time at the FBI's training base at Quantico, learning how they profiled serial killers. He had known her for several years, having attended a couple of her lectures and consulted her on more than one occasion. He hadn't considered asking her out, despite her being an attractive woman, as he had no idea about her personal circumstances and, in his experience, most of the good ones were already spoken for. While they were chatting, he mentioned he was moving house following the split between him and Rachel, and it had prompted Kelly to ask him out.

He drove to the office, his mind switching from the enjoyable time the previous night, to the hunt for the murderer of Martin Turner. He had spoken to Carol Walters after she had re-interviewed Joanna Woodford. While Joanna's assertion that the affair with Alex Vincent was inconsequential, not dissimilar to her nonchalant reaction when hearing of her husband's murder, it wasn't sufficient reason to put a line through Vincent's name just yet. Henderson would leave him on the 'persons of interest' list for the time being.

The team had now completed most of the strands initially identified at the start of the investigation: Turner's family and friends and his work colleagues, leaving only a couple of convict clients unaccounted for. If none of them were responsible, the only conclusion to be drawn was that Turner had been in the wrong place at the wrong time, and the intruder had been attracted by something in the place where he had found himself, Alex Vincent's office.

He had mulled this point over in his mind several times and still felt unable to cite divorce as a viable murder motive. If a couple hated one another so much that they were in danger of killing one another, wouldn't a separation and divorce solve the problem? Even if the sums of money involved were large and disputed, UK divorce law was robust enough to ensure the non-earning partner would be equitably compensated.

Henderson sighed as he drove into the Malling House car park. The thought of trawling through Alex Vincent's files: harrowing tales of humiliation, violence, misery and boredom, did nothing to fill him with glee. A filter could be added to the mix by cross-referencing it with the list of criminal clients developed by Harry Wallop, but even doing that wouldn't necessarily shorten the odds.

Walking into his office, he dumped his document case on the desk and headed straight to the coffee machine in the Detectives' Room. It was early and only a few of the team were about. He was heading back to his office with his mug when Carol Walters burst through the double doors.

'Ah, there you are. I've been looking for you. I need to show you something.'

'Good day to you, Carol. How are you this fine Monday morning?'

'I'm okay, gov, thanks for asking. How's yourself?'

'I'm good. Now, why were you looking for me?'

'Did you see this last night?' she said, holding up a printout.

'No, I was out.'

'Oh, how was it?'

The doors opened again and this time Phil Bentley walked in.

'Morning Phil.'

'Morning gov, morning Carol.'

'As I was saying,' Walters said.

'Hold that thought for a moment,' Henderson said. 'I think it's better we move, or everyone will think this is the start of a new Chief Constable initiative: greet the team as they arrive for work.'

They walked to Walters' desk. She sat behind the desk while he pulled over a spare chair.

'Now, where were we?' he asked.

'If we spin back to yesterday,' she said. 'In the serials, Harvey Templeton and Jason Tames were arrested for kidnapping and beating up a Spanish bloke.'

'I saw the story. The name Templeton rang a bell.'

'He's a big property developer, based in Shoreham. Has a reputation for playing fast and loose, mainly with other people's money.'

'I remember. He's a bit cavalier in the way he deals with objectors and protestors who are against his developments, but his investors all seem to get paid in the end. So, he was arrested for kidnap and assault, but I take it there's more?'

'As much as I'd enjoy a slimeball like Templeton spending a night in one of our cells–'

'You mean he didn't?'

She shook her head and pointed to the printout, still in her hand. It was from a news website, probably the *Mail on Sunday*. 'He was released last night, but his bully-boy Tames wasn't. Templeton claimed that when he turned up at this farm, a place he was allowing Tames to use, Tames was beating up the suspect. He was trying to stop the assault when police arrived.'

'Believe that and you'll believe in the tooth fairy. It's a likely story to save his skin and blame the other guy. What's the relationship between the two of them?'

'It says Tames is an employee of Templeton's company.'

'There you go, then. The employee is taking the rap while his boss goes free. I wonder how much he's paying him. What does the victim say?'

'He's unconscious.'

'Oh, is he? Nevertheless, what's it got to do with us? I know many property developers sail close to the wind, but Templeton isn't on our radar.'

'No, but Bruce Nolan is. The victim works for Nolan. The victim's name is Santiago Rodrigo González.'

'He works for Nolan? Now that puts a different slant on things.'

'What do you think we should do about it?'

'Do scrapyards open early?'

'I assume so.'

'Ach, by the time we negotiate the morning traffic and get to Newhaven, it'll be after nine. Grab a jacket and we'll go and talk to the irascible Mr Nolan once again. Maybe he's a morning person.'

'I wouldn't bet on it.'

Henderson had been right about the traffic. They'd hit Lewes as everyone was dropping their kids off at school. They crawled around the periphery of the town and things only speeded up when they had cleared the Southerham Roundabout, and even then, the car didn't travel faster than forty miles an hour.

'There's something I meant to say earlier,' Henderson said, 'and it's just come back into my head.'

'What about?'

'The Templeton assault,' he said.

'What about it?'

'If I've understood the story right, Tames was beating up one of Bruce Nolan's employees in a barn, on a farm, many miles from anywhere.'

'Yep.'

'Assuming they're not overlooked, who made the emergency call?'

'You're right, they aren't overlooked, I looked the place up on Google Maps. It's an interesting question. When I get back, I'll check with the 999 Operations Room and see if someone left a number.'

'The plot thickens.'

When they arrived at Nolan Base Metals in Newhaven, Nolan was driving a forklift truck. This wasn't surprising as he was one assistant down. He pointed towards the office as he continued driving the truck.

They walked in and, as expected, it was empty. Henderson pulled over the two chairs they'd used in their previous visit and both detectives sat.

'There's a laptop lying there,' Walters said, nodding. 'Is it worth giving it a go?'

He shook his head. 'While a large proportion of laptop users never change their passwords and still use 123456 or admin, it will be protected by something. Most operating systems keep pestering you until you create one. That said, it wouldn't take the Digital Forensics team more than five minutes to find out what's on there, but as we don't live in a police state, we'd need a warrant first.'

It was just as well they didn't, as through the window they saw Bruce Nolan stop the forklift and jump from the cab. He shouted something to his companion before striding towards the office.

The door burst open and Nolan stomped in. He slammed the door behind him, which did little to dampen the loud noise of some other machine operating outside.

'What the fuck is it this time? I've told you all I know, and now I'm a man down and that big truck over there with a load of pipes won't unload itself.'

'We won't keep you long, Mr Nolan. We know how busy you are. How is Mr González?'

The question threw him. It was if he wanted to vent more anger on the next thing the DI said, but couldn't.

'He's as well as you would expect after being given a good kicking by that bastard Tames.'

'Still unconscious?'

'He is, yeah. Thanks for asking.'

He took off his hard hat and jacket and hung them on a peg before taking a seat behind his desk. 'What did you want to see me about?'

'It was Mr González we wanted to talk to you about.'

'Everyone calls him Pedro, it's easier.'

'Fine. What was he doing at the farm?'

Nolan sighed as if he had made a decision. 'I suppose I can tell you, there's no harm in it. Harvey Templeton has been wanting to buy this place for ages.'

'It's a big site.'

'It's almost an acre and most of it is on the waterfront. Templeton wants to do what they've done

133

at the side of canals in other places like Manchester and Norwich; build blocks of flats with shops and cafes underneath, places for people to sit, eat and drink.'

'There's certainly a market for it. It doesn't interest you?'

'I'm not against progress, and God knows, Newhaven is in need of a lift, but this business is my life. I don't know what I'd do without it.'

'With the money he's offering, surely it would be enough for you to start afresh elsewhere, or do something else?'

He shook his head. 'I left school with nothing, not a single piece of paper to my name. Now, thanks to my missus, I can just about read and write. What else could I do?'

'So, Pedro's beating was, what? An attempt to bully you into submission?'

'I don't know for sure until I can talk to him, but yeah, that's what I think.'

'If it is, did it work? Do you feel bullied into selling the business to him?'

'Do I hell. No way would I give in to a little shite like Templeton.'

'I don't know if you've heard, he's been released from custody.'

'I hadn't, but I expected as much. He's a greasy bastard, nothing sticks to him. What about Mr Muscle, Tames?'

'He's still in custody and will remain so. He's been charged with a number of serious offences and from what I've heard, there's strong evidence against him.'

'Good. He deserves what's coming.'

'I hope this doesn't mean you're considering taking the law into your own hands, Mr Nolan.'

'Don't you worry, it would take a lot more intimidation than he's able to muster to make me think of doing that.'

EIGHTEEN

Alex Vincent said goodbye to Anita and closed the front door. The house had been quieter than normal this morning. The boys were at a stage now where they talked to each other instead of trading insults and blows as they did when they were younger. He suspected they had stayed up later than normal last night doing just that.

His usual route to work was along the A281 through Woodmancote, joining the southbound A23 at Muddleswood, or if time was on his side, remaining on country roads and driving over Devil's Dyke. This morning was different. He drove slowly as he knew Joanna would be dropping Seb off at Hurstpierpoint College, the same place where Anita would be going.

The BMW was not a happy motor to be driving at this reduced speed. The big engine was at its best sailing down the outside lane of a motorway at eighty. Tootling along the stretch between Henfield and Woodmancote, he felt it wanted to do more than the regulated forty to fifty; like a thoroughbred horse it wanted to gallop off into the distance. In addition, he wasn't making any friends with the irate drivers behind, who all had obviously important places to be.

Woodmancote wasn't much of a village, more of a hamlet, as it didn't have a pub, shop, or community centre, unlike Henfield which bustled with shops, a garage, and numerous pubs. That said, Woodmancote wasn't far from Brighton and the south coast, giving residents a taste of the country without leaving them isolated or out of touch.

Vincent turned into Blackstone Lane and on arriving outside Forest House, got out of the car and keyed in the gate code. He drove in, switched off the engine and turned up the radio. The relationship between him and Joanna was familiar enough for her to have given him the gate code, but not so intense it included a spare key to the house.

He was listening to a government minister on Radio 4, whose face he couldn't recall, blathering on about how we all needed to 'tighten our belts' to help reduce the deficit caused by the UK's exit from the EU. *We would*, he could imagine all the listeners saying to their radio sets, *if people like you stopped stuffing your faces on big meals in the subsidised House of Commons canteen, and claiming expenses for your second and third homes.*

He must have dozed off as he didn't notice the gates of Forest House opening and was only aware of Joanna's arrival when her large 4x4 crunched noisily over the stones in the driveway. He got out of the car and stretched.

'Hello, Alex, this is a pleasant surprise. You look tired,' she said as she stepped out of her car. 'Late night, or problems sleeping?'

'Hello Joanna, it's good to see you. No, nothing so mundane. I think it's my reaction to all the issues at the office.'

'Come on in and I'll make you a nice cup of coffee.'

She unlocked the door and walked inside. He followed. Despite not having neighbours, and with few people living nearby, they had decided, although not in so many words, never to show any affection outside. Once the door was closed, she wrapped her arms around his neck and kissed him warmly.

'You poor thing,' she said, her mouth next to his ear. 'It must be so hard for you. Would you like to go upstairs and forget about it for a while?'

'It wasn't the reason I came, but you make such an irresistible offer.'

Three-quarters of an hour later, they were seated in Joanna's large rustic kitchen: flagstone floor, pots hanging from a wooden frame, and an Aga pumping out welcome heat. Her two red setters loved him, and after giving them both a clap and rubbing behind their ears, they settled down and were now lying close to his feet.

Joanna liked to chat in bed after sex, the place where they usually shared thoughts, issues, and problems before he dashed off to his badminton club or home, depending on what excuse he was using. This time, he wanted to be dressed and sitting across from her.

'I've been interviewed by the police,' he said as he sipped his coffee. Joanna had a knack of making great coffee. If he could bottle the recipe, he would have sold it to Raymond Schofield for use in his Crema Coffee chain. He was handling the divorce between him and Rebecca which made him think of her, as she had left him a voicemail earlier.

'I have too,' said Joanna brightly, as if talking about a new jumper she'd bought. 'Twice.'

'You have?'

'Well, perhaps not interviewed exactly, more chatted to. The first time to tell me about Martin's death and to take a look at my fit for their suspect profile.'

'Are you a suspect?'

'Don't be soft. When Martin went out of my life, that was it, he was gone. I don't have, and never have had, any residual affection for him.'

'I know. I was only kidding,' he said.

'The other thing they asked about was if I knew of anyone who might have killed him.'

'Do you?'

'Yes. I said you.'

'What? How could you?'

'Calm yourself. It's my turn; I was only kidding too.'

'Oh really? Touché.'

'Why did you mention the subject of the police interview? Have you said something you shouldn't have in yours?'

'No. Well, yes I...I did.'

'What?'

'I told them about our affair.'

'I know.'

'What do you mean, you know?'

'Two detectives came to see me yesterday and asked me about it. I knew it had to have come from you as I'd never mentioned it.'

'Right.'

'How could you, Alex? We both agreed we had to keep it secret. For the sake of Anita, the kids, the school.'

'I know, I know. I had no choice, it sort of tumbled out.'

'You're a lawyer, for goodness' sake. Words and secrets are your stock in trade. Nobody knew anything, not Haldane, not Robinson, not even the police.'

'They said they suspected something as they knew I'd come round to see you a couple of times after Martin's body was found. They thought my interest was, I don't know, unusual.'

Her face grew animated. 'Yes, and they're probably now thinking you or I killed Martin, and you coming here was to ensure we both stuck to our stories. Alex, how could you? If I get arrested, who's going to look after Seb?'

He reached over to take her hand, but she pulled it away. This wasn't the stoic, sensible, logical Joanna he knew.

'That's not the way they're thinking.'

'How do you know what the police do or don't think? You're a divorce lawyer, Alex. I've maybe got a better idea than you, and I think the worst.'

He left Woodmancote ten minutes later. The drive into Brighton, the time when he usually listed in his head the activities for the day ahead, so he could hit the ground running when he arrived in the office, was replaced with thoughts of doom. His anxiety was hard to rationalise, as he knew he hadn't killed Martin, and he was one hundred per cent confident Joanna hadn't done so either.

The thing he'd wanted to say to Joanna but hadn't, was that he wanted to protect Anita and the boys from any fallout. He could do this if the police investigation didn't intrude further, but not if he or Joanna were arrested.

NINETEEN

Before he realised what was happening, the car turned into the car park at Jonas Baines and slotted itself into his reserved parking space. Alex Vincent knew it was infused with all sorts of smart electronics, but for it to behave like a lost dog finding its way home in a snowstorm was beyond his comprehension.

He sat for a moment and tried to shift his thinking into work mode. Slowly, it worked. By the time he walked into his office, he looked and behaved like Alex Vincent, Sussex's top divorce lawyer.

His assistant had left two new instructions on his desk. He always looked at them first to get a flavour of how the next few months would pan out. Inevitably, a new case coming into the office today would be his total focus in about three weeks from now, and for the following two or three months.

One case looked straightforward, while the other was anything but. A woman's husband had been indicted for fraud over a bogus scheme to establish a palm oil plantation in Malaysia. Hundreds of people had invested significant sums of money, often by raiding their life savings and pension pots, keen as they were to carve a rich slice from this crop-of-the-moment juggernaut. However, no land had ever been purchased and most of the money raised had been plundered by the directors.

The problems he foresaw were that the couple owned a large house, their four children all attended private school, and they employed five staff to maintain their sprawling acres. It would be hard placing a value on their marital assets with a guilty verdict most likely in prospect, and the Fraud Office patiently waiting in the wings, ready to grab a sizeable slice of their ill-gotten gains.

He put the new instructions to one side and set about today's first task. Ten minutes in, he remembered the voicemail he received this morning when his phone was switched off. He had listened to the beginning to hear who called him, but when he realised it was about work, he stopped.

'Hello, Alex, it's Rebecca. Sorry to bother you at such an early hour, but I've been up half the night thinking about the case. I wouldn't be so pushy, but my new man wants it all to be settled, so we can make a start on our lives together. Can you call me with an update ASAP? Talk to you later. Bye.'

He cradled his phone thinking about Rebecca. She had been the driving force behind Raymond Schofield's rise to prominence as one of Britain's most successful entrepreneurs. It was she who had come up with the idea for a chain of themed hotels, which in time became a hugely successful one-hundred-and-twenty-strong European-wide business. She was also the driving force behind the Crema Coffee business, developing the ten Italian-themed coffee restaurants they'd bought for £2 million over ten years before into a two-hundred outlet goliath. This wasn't her idle boast, but the distillation of numerous articles published in the *Financial Times*, *Daily Telegraph*, and *Wall Street Journal*.

Having now sold all his business assets, Raymond wanted someone to share his new life. Most people's money was on Clare Mitchell, his finance director at Raybeck and now his constant companion. However, Rebecca's heart had been broken, and her marriage irrevocably damaged by Raymond's earlier affair with Sylvie Goss, her former best friend.

A little warning light went off in Vincent's head about Rebecca's new man. He hadn't met him yet and it wasn't his place to say, but she needed to be made aware of the danger from gold diggers. She was high-profile and anyone with a laptop could see she was a very rich woman. Yes, her new man might want the slate wiped clean to woo the woman of his dreams without impediment, but equally he might want the divorce settled so he could get his greedy mitts on her loot. And what a pile of loot it would be.

According to the financial press, Raymond's sale of all his business interests had realised somewhere in the region of eight-hundred-million pounds. He was declaring a personal wealth of three-hundred-and-fifty-million in the divorce papers, of which Rebecca was claiming half, but she also suspected him of hiding a lot more.

Before returning Rebecca's call, he needed to dig out her file and examine a financial document she had given him. By surreptitiously entering Raymond's office when he wasn't around, she had discovered details of a variety of Caribbean bank accounts not declared in his statement of assets, totalling over five hundred million pounds. To date, Raymond had denied having any more cash, telling anyone who would listen that he'd paid a sizeable sum on advisor's fees and repaying bridging loans.

Vincent had only given the schedule a cursory glance at the time; now he wanted to see if the details looked authentic and verifiable, and to assess whether it could stand up in a court of law. He swivelled his chair and stared at the box files behind him, arranged alphabetically. He reached for the 'S' box and laid it on his desk.

He knew the Schofield file was thin, but growing, so he would need to search for it. He found it, removed it from the box, and laid it on the desk. He opened it, but there was nothing inside. He searched through the other folders in the box, in case the papers had been misfiled. He still couldn't find them.

A few minutes later, he pulled out his phone and dialled.

'Hello Rebecca, it's Alex. Can we talk?'

'Oh, hi, Alex. Thanks for calling back. Yes, we can. How's it going? Any idea when the hearing might be?'

'I don't know how I can say this without alarm bells ringing, but when I looked in your file, it's empty.'

'How do you mean?'

'The folder with your name on the front is empty. All the papers I had in it, the schedules, the forms, the statements, everything is missing.'

'How can this happen? Has it been misfiled, or maybe someone else is using it?'

'I've looked all over, Rebecca, it's gone. If you remember the—'

'What about the schedule I gave you of Ray's hidden money?'

'It's gone too.'

'Oh my god! That was a one-off, I can't recreate it.'

'Rebecca, keep calm. Remember what I've been telling you, there's always...'

'I know, I know. There's always another option.'

'Right. If you remember, we had a break-in the night Martin Turner was murdered?'

'How could I forget? The poor man.'

'You might not be aware, but the incident took place in my office.'

'My God, how awful. How can you still work there?'

'I'm stronger than I look. The only thing I can think of, is when the intruder was in here, he must have removed a number of files. Last week, I was looking for a file and couldn't find it, but I didn't think anything of it. With your file missing it points to something more serious. I'll have to raise it with Haldane.'

'Why would they do that? Any thieves I've heard about are after money, jewellery or electronics, not stuffy legal papers.'

'Don't ask me as I haven't a clue; perhaps it was to confuse the police.'

'You should know me by now, Alex. I don't dwell on problems, I focus on solutions. What can we do to move this forward?'

Rebecca had been head of HR in Raymond's organisation. She was empathetic and a good listener, but she took no prisoners when she wanted something done, and didn't stumble if she found an obstacle in her way.

'I can recreate a few of the missing papers and notes from memory, I think,' Alex said. 'We have some of the blank forms here and others were sent to me by email. The only one that doesn't fit into any of those categories is the schedule of Raymond's secreted money. I know you said it was a one-off, but did you, by any chance, keep a copy?'

'Damn, damn, damn. No, I didn't. I assume the details are hidden somewhere in his laptop, but he'll never let me into that house again to look. Even if he did, he wouldn't leave me alone long enough to access his laptop.'

Alex was kicking himself. If only he had examined the schedule in more detail: authenticated the bank details, verified the amounts, certified the dates. It would have given him the basic material to help reconstruct it.

'What I could do,' Vincent said, 'is employ a firm of forensic accountants to access and analyse his finances.'

'Ray wouldn't be best pleased, as I'm sure you are aware. Is something like that allowed?'

'Not without showing a judge prima facie evidence of his wrongdoing. Some proof, on the one hand that he opened those Caribbean bank accounts, or that he had access to those additional funds.'

'I'm not sure I can give you anything like that. You know Ray, he's as slippery as Teflon and doesn't leave that sort of stuff lying around.'

'Give me some time to think about it, Rebecca. See if I can come up with something.'

TWENTY

This was an interview Henderson was reluctant to conduct. Raymond Schofield was one of the few criminals from the 'serious' list who shouldn't have had a beef with Martin Turner. Schofield had been charged with murder, but due to Turner's diligent research and his thorough briefing of Schofield's barrister, the accused had been found not guilty, surprising the press and police alike.

Every newspaper at the time was convinced Schofield had killed Allan Blake. This was supported by Blake's repeated statements about his unwillingness to sell his chain of health clubs. The fact that Blake's widow sold them to Schofield's company a few months after the trial only succeeded in encouraging them to vent their spleen one more time.

'Quite a nice area this,' Walters said from the passenger seat. 'Lots of green space and some very large houses.'

'Fancy a move to the country, do you?'

'I would at some point. Cities are all right when you're young, but they're not a place to bring up a family. It's all concrete, dog mess, and crazies hanging out on street corners.'

'Plenty do.'

'I know, I see them in their school blazers and little shorts standing at bus stops, but they have to walk past the said crazies and drug users on their way home.'

'Liberals would argue that it toughens them up for the hard knocks ahead. If the kids are too soft, they'll be taken in by smooth-talking fraudsters and online scammers.'

'Trust you to burst my bubble.'

'What will really put a pin in your dreams are the house prices. I reckon around here you wouldn't get much change out of three or four million.'

The house where Raymond Schofield lived was in another category altogether. Once the metal gates had swung open, they could see a huge place with perfectly spaced trees and a flawless bowling green-standard lawn, giving it the air of an up-market conference venue. Judging by the number of upstairs windows, it probably had eight or nine bedrooms, with space downstairs to accommodate all manner of facilities. To one side, he could see a tennis court and a pool, while the border of trees that appeared to mark the boundary of the property looked a long way off in the distance.

Henderson rang the bell and a small, portly woman opened the door.

'DI Henderson and DS Walters, Sussex Police, to see Mr Schofield.'

'Ah yes, he is expecting you. I'm Lyn Malone, Mr Schofield's housekeeper. Do come in.'

Outside, the house was as traditional as any in the neighbourhood, but inside the hallway it was light wood, minimal furnishings, and pieces of modern art on the walls, giving it the feel of a trendy art gallery.

They were shown into something Mrs Malone called a 'study' to wait for the big man, but it was the size of a small ballroom in a lesser establishment. In keeping with the minimal theme, two walls were lined with bookcases, while the rest of the room only contained a large desk and chair, with two visitor's chairs in front. A settee was sited close to a floor-to-ceiling window overlooking the garden. All in all, a large room with not much in it.

Walters took a seat on the settee while Henderson walked over and stared out of the window.

'What a view,' he said. 'I don't know what I'm looking at other than the South Downs in the distance, but the slope of the valley and the trees is nothing short of stunning.'

'I suppose it's all included in the price.'

'Officers,' Raymond Schofield said, breezing into the room. 'I'm sorry to keep you.'

Henderson turned. It was a surprise to see Schofield in 'civvies': casual trousers, yellow V-neck, check shirt, and loafers without socks. In pictures he'd seen on the web, he was inevitably clad in a smart two- or three-piece suit, often with a handkerchief poking out of the top pocket. At one time, he had been voted Britain's best-dressed businessman by several men's fashion magazines.

Following introductions, Schofield took a seat behind the glass and metal desk while the officers settled into the two visitor's chairs.

'It's good of you to see us, Mr Schofield.'

'If I was still running Raybeck Leisure I wouldn't have been able to see you so soon, and you would have been forced to go through my old secretary, Sonia, who at times, could be a bit of a battle-axe. Now that I've sold everything off, these days my work is done at a more easy-going pace.'

'Not if the article I saw in *The Financial Times* is to believed.'

He smiled, but it wasn't warm. 'You're right. In partnership with Raybeck's former financial director, we've set up a vehicle to invest in emerging high-tech companies. We're focussing mainly on sustainability: technologies to reduce an organisation's carbon footprint, and in making existing processes work more efficiently. It's a serious venture and involves targeting suitable companies and providing funding for those we think will succeed. As you can imagine, it's very different from corporate life.'

Despite the casual attire, Schofield looked and sounded as sharp as a knife. Henderson had watched a YouTube video of him being interviewed by a dogged presenter on the BBC 2 programme, *Newsnight*, and not once did the presenter get the better of Schofield. He had clearly come on the programme with an agenda and several points to make, and make them he did.

'I'm in charge of the team investigating the murder of Martin Turner, two weeks ago in the early hours of Wednesday 8th February,' Henderson said.

'I'd heard about it. In fact, Robert Haldane called to tell me, just as I was watching the story on the local news. It was a terrible thing to happen to Martin, really terrible.'

'You knew Mr Turner well?'

'I liked and respected him, and I never imagined he would die in such dreadful circumstances. Although, it just shows you the mark of the man. So dedicated was he to his work, he didn't have time to go home; he was sleeping in his office. I know people in your line of work are often forced to do such things, but it never occurred to me lawyers would be so snowed under they would be required to do it as well.'

'We're here to find out more about Martin and ask if you knew of anyone who might have had reason to kill him.'

'You probably know, but I first met Martin when I was accused of the murder of Allan Blake, the owner of Blake's Health Clubs. I liked the business but not the name. When I bought it, I changed it to what it is today, Premier Fitness.'

Henderson nodded.

'The case against me, brought by Kent Police not Sussex, or I wouldn't be giving you guys the time of day, was founded on his reluctance to sell the business. Plus, traces of his blood were found in the cabin and on the deck of my yacht. The prosecution couldn't provide a body or murder weapon, and couldn't show malice on my part. I was stitched up.'

'What happened at sea?'

'A big bloody storm blowing up from the Bay of Biscay is what happened. We were sailing off the north French coast after visiting Jersey, the place where Allan was born, when we ran smack into a storm. I don't know if you know anything about yachts, but if you see a storm on the satellite feed it's not like being in a plane where you can detour around it. A yacht moves too slowly, so if you can't get out of the way, all you can do is batten down the hatches and hope to ride it out.'

Henderson did know about yachts and storms, as his own yacht, 'Mingary', was berthed at Brighton Marina.

'Was Allan Blake a keen sailor?' Walters asked.

'That's an interesting question, and I don't think it was raised by anyone at my trial. Perhaps they assumed he was. He was a keen sailor, used to smaller boats than mine, but he knew enough not to be a liability in a crisis.'

'How did Mr Blake die?'

Henderson wasn't listening too closely, instead he was looking at Schofield's face. The former chief executive was an animated speaker, his facial expressions and the movement of his hands being used extensively to emphasise various points. A big wave sweeping someone overboard was a common enough occurrence in sailing. With the conditions as bad as Schofield described, it would be near-impossible to conduct the 'man overboard' manoeuvre with the sea pitching and rolling so violently, and he would imagine visibility would also be impaired.

However, ignoring the intensity of the storm for a moment, it was the perfect place to stage a murder. Even if the person was harnessed, as an experienced sailor would be if moving around the deck, a sharp knife could take care of it, and with visibility marred by mist or driving rain, who would notice someone disappearing over the side?

'Did his widow not have any reservations about selling the health club business to you, despite you being accused of her husband's murder?'

'No, not at all. She didn't believe I played any part in Allan's death. She knew how well we were getting along. In any case, she believed he was involved in an affair with Clare Mitchell and was on the point of divorcing him. She wanted the money from the sale to start a new life.'

'Clare Mitchell, your former financial director at Raybeck?'

'Yes. I'd been trying to buy Blake's Health Clubs for many years, and when I first approached Allan with an offer, she was FD there. It didn't take me long to realise how good she was, and when my existing FD retired due to ill health, I poached her.'

'Were Allan Blake and Clare Mitchell having an affair, as Mrs Blake believed?'

'God, no. He was much older than her, by about fifteen years, and anyway, she didn't fancy him. She saw him more as a father figure, a substitute for the one she didn't have. Her father died of cancer, you see, when she was about seventeen. Blake's widow mistook Clare's affection for something sexual. It wasn't.'

'It was the work done by Martin Turner that got you off, I believe.'

'He was excellent. He questioned everything the CPS threw at me, and the round-the-world sailor he brought in to explain how the accident could have occurred, was brilliant. His unquestionable knowledge about yachts and the vivid way he described one of his own crew being swept overboard in a storm in the Southern Ocean had some of the jury members weeping.'

'What do you think happened to Martin?'

Schofield's hands were still for the first time, now placed in front of him like an American Evangelical preacher engaged in a TV broadcast.

'I've read newspaper reports and seen television broadcasts, but unless you can tell me any different, no one seems to have a clue. I think a druggie broke in, thinking there was money and valuables to be had, and Martin got in the way. He was that sort of person, you see. If he ever saw a homeless person being berated by a couple of youths, he would go over and remonstrate. He wasn't the type to sit idly by and let someone else deal with it.'

TWENTY-ONE

Yes, there was a touch of spring in the air. Trevor Robinson walked out of the Jonas Baines offices in Trafalgar Street and, for the first time in ages, felt the sun on his face. Even now, around five-thirty in the evening, the air was warmer than it had been the previous week when he had worn a scarf around his chin. It wasn't temperate enough for him to take off his coat, or more importantly, for the lovely girls of Brighton to remove their shapeless jumpers and jeans and change into summer dresses, but all that would happen in the fullness of time.

If he was feeling a bit more sprightly than usual it was because he had just been paid. It wasn't his normal salary either, it had been topped up with a discretionary amount, which he would continue to receive for the following six months or so. It was in compensation for the anxiety suffered at the loss of his work partner and for taking over many of his duties and cases.

He knew in the months to come he could be replaced. Once Haldane had recruited a person to take over from Martin, and when they had found their feet, Robinson's bargaining chips would turn to dust in his fingers. He would therefore play the anxious and indispensable card to his advantage, but not so much that Haldane would get rid of him at the first opportunity.

His improved finances had warmed his heart, as tonight was casino night. It was also the night to pay some debts. He walked in the direction of home in the fading sunlight, Brighton looking resplendent in the yellow glow it created. He decided his developing paunch wasn't a becoming look for a successful criminal lawyer, and so even if the weather was inclement he resolved to walk home.

Before reaching Waitrose on Western Road, he opened the door to Romario's Coffee House and walked in. Miranda Moss was seated at a table, staring into her latte glass as if it held the solution to all of the world's problems.

'Hello, love,' he said.

'Oh god, I was miles away.'

She tilted her head and responded to his kiss.

'What were you thinking about?'

'Oh nothing, just about that dick, Fran. I wasted most of the afternoon fixing a problem he created.'

'Can I get you anything?' he asked, nodding towards the counter.

'I just got this,' she said, tapping her latte glass.

'A refill, or something to eat?'

'Maybe later.'

'No problem.' He walked to the counter and ordered a latte. As usual, he took a good look at the goodies behind the glass: chocolate cake, brownies, cherry tart, and was about to order a chocolate muffin when he remembered the paunch issue.

The company Miranda worked for was located in the centre of Brighton, so it was easy for the two of them to meet for a coffee on evenings when they weren't going out together later. She was a computer programmer, a coder in modern parlance, working for an outfit involved in the design of bespoke solutions for telecoms companies.

Why they decided to locate their offices in an area where it was a nightmare to park, and druggies could be hanging about in the evening hassling staff for money, was anyone's guess. The few IT companies he knew about were based in shiny new estates on the edge of Brighton, or in Crawley, in a suite of purposely designed offices.

He carried his coffee to the table and took a seat opposite Miranda.

'What, no muffin?' she said, an astonished look on her face. 'Stock markets will collapse, the price of pork bellies will fall to the floor, market traders will slash their wrists.'

'Yes, yes, enjoy mocking me. It's not as if I don't get enough of it at work.'

'Difference is, I've got your best interests at heart. Who wouldn't want to be with a man with a beach-ready body?'

This was good. Miranda didn't often talk of the future, but here she was, suggesting they'd be together in a few months' time.

'How was your day?' he asked.

'I didn't do much of my own work. I spent the morning in a meeting about a new productivity tool, and in the afternoon, after I fixed the problem I mentioned earlier, yet another meeting, this time with our biggest client.'

'Openreach.'

'Very novel, a man who listens to me. Are you still okay for Sunday?'

'Meet the folks? Can't wait.'

'You might not be so enthusiastic after you've met them.'

It was the end of February, and easy to commit to something at the weekend. In a couple of months' time it would be the start of the flat horse racing season; if she asked then, he would first need to get out his phone and check to see if he could fit her in. He would then find out if this curbed her enthusiasm for the summer to come.

They talked for another fifteen minutes before leaving the café. He walked Miranda back to her flat in Brunswick Place, before carrying on to his own street. With the time they'd spent talking, he couldn't dawdle, so he changed his clothes, had something to eat, and then left his apartment. His commitment to improving his physique was undimmed, but he'd done enough walking for one day. He walked to a stop on Western Road and waited for a bus heading in the direction of Brighton Station.

The Regency Casino in Church Street wasn't his favourite, but he liked to vary his routine by never visiting the same casino twice in a row. He couldn't say why, as he hadn't experienced a lot of bad luck there, wasn't intimidated by some of the strange people who frequented it, and the staff seemed friendly enough. Casinos for him had a vibe. He'd been to others in Nevada and Macau and hated them instantly. There, he could feel the hunger of the gamblers, their love of money subverting any love they had for the game: the noble art of pitting their skills against the dealer and Lady Luck.

He stood for a few minutes watching players on the roulette table. Their behaviour would change depending on the time of day or night. Early on, betting was modest, the chips on single numbers or spread across two numbers. Later on, around ten o'clock when the careless had downed too much booze from the bar and the high rollers had made an appearance, it would become more daring. Piles of chips would be spread across multiple combinations, and chips would be placed at the 'odd and even' and the 'red and black' stations. He often wondered how the croupiers kept track of the winnings.

One of the gamblers at the table swept up his modest pile of chips and vacated the seat. Robinson sat down in his place. Within twenty minutes, he had several stacks of chips in front of him. He had barely lost any spins, but he knew luck could be a fickle mistress. Therefore, as playing cautiously had reaped dividends, he decided to continue in this vein.

Five minutes later, and still on a winning streak, he was watching the wheel spin when he felt a hand on his shoulder. He looked up to see the perfectly formed features of Hassan Khouri.

'Hello Hassan, it's good to see you.'

'You too, Trevor.'

'Black twenty-two,' the croupier called, before sweeping a pile of chips towards Robinson.

'You seem to be doing all right tonight.'

'I am, but I think I'll stop there. I know my limitations.'

He scooped his chips into his hand and stood. 'Fancy a drink?'

'Why not? Seeing you're so flush.'

Hassan walked over to sit at a table while Robinson cashed in most of his chips. He kept some back for the blackjack table later.

When Robinson headed over to join Hassan, his wallet bulging with cash and his expression satisfyingly smug, a waiter was already at the table taking Hassan's order. Before sitting, Robinson added a whisky and soda to the order. He usually made a point of consuming no alcohol while gambling in a casino, but tonight he would make an exception, as he liked Hassan.

He had come to the UK from Syria as a child when his family had been wiped out by a terrorist bomb explosion. He stayed with his uncle, a former university lecturer in Syria, and did well at school, gaining a place at Birmingham Medical School. He trained as a doctor, eventually specialising in reconstructive surgery. Ten years ago, he left the NHS and started his own practice in Hove, called Cavendish Body Sculptures, specialising in cosmetic surgery for the rich and famous.

He was tall, early forties, with handsome, chiselled features, a neat quiff of thick dark brown hair, and a perfectly proportioned nose and mouth befitting a man in his profession. His naturally light-brown skin gave him a permanent tan, in common with many of his rich clients, who got theirs on the deck of a yacht or around the pool at their foreign villa.

The ladies loved him and he was never short of beautiful companions. He occasionally brought them to places like this, but Robinson knew what Hassan meant when he called them a distraction; he didn't mean their beautiful faces or voluptuous figures. Gambling was a pleasure that could only be savoured alone.

The drinks were served.

'Cheers, Trevor,' Hassan said, picking up his drink.

'Cheers Hassan.'

'Thanks for the drink,' he said, a moment or two later. 'Perhaps I can do something for you. Do you like rugby?'

'No, I'm not really into any particular sport.'

'That's a shame, as I can lay my hands on several tickets for the England versus Scotland game in a couple of weeks' time. If you change your mind, just let me know.'

'I will. Thanks for the offer.'

'So, tell me, what's going on in the legal world?'

To hear his plummy southern English accent, a stranger would never guess Hassan's origins. If not practising cosmetic surgery, he could easily read the BBC evening news, or voice-overs for top-of-the-range car adverts.

'Since the last time I saw you, and as part of my new, broader role, I attended my first senior management meeting.'

'You were taking Martin's place?'

'Yes, but it seems the meeting was more subdued than normal, due to recent developments.'

'That's understandable. Did you discuss anything of note?'

'We mainly talked about the fall-out from the break-in, you know the sort of thing: staff counselling, security, visitors to our offices, and so on, but then what Alex Vincent said topped it all.'

'Oh?'

'He's convinced that as a result of the break-in, a number of his files have gone missing.'

'My goodness, that is interesting. Why would the killer do that?'

'We all thought the same and treated it as a bit of a joke, until we realised he was being serious. Haldane's so concerned he's instructed Vincent to engage our auditors to make an inventory of all that's missing. He fears litigious clients.'

Khouri reached for his drink and took a sip. 'I can understand his concern. If one of your people was to mess up something like a serious fraud case due to the absence of an important schedule, you could be tied up in litigation for years. Do the police have anyone in the frame for the murder yet?'

'If they have, they haven't said anything to us.'

'I certainly haven't seen anything in the papers.'

'You would know, as I suspect you have them all delivered to your surgery every day.'

'Yes, we do,' he said, smiling, revealing perfectly even, white teeth. 'What's happening with Raymond Schofield? Do you know if the police have spoken to him yet?'

'I don't know.'

'If they haven't, they should.'

'I'm surprised to hear you say that, Hassan. Why would Ray be involved? It was Martin, and myself, of course, who worked on the case and got him off. With all the money he has, he should be erecting a statue to Martin, not stabbing him to death.'

'He's a very bad man, Trevor, you must have seen that when you were dealing with him.'

'I realise he didn't get to his exulted position by being nice to people. Many of his dirty dealings were exposed during the trial, something we and a PR agency had to spend a lot of time trying to counter.'

'It's worse than you can imagine. I've dealt with at least two people in my surgery who've been battered by his thugs.'

'What? I thought his next business venture was investing in high-tech start-ups. What's that got to do with strong-armed bully boys?'

'It's not the new business he's protecting. It's his women.'

'Women? I thought there was only one, Clare Mitchell?'

'Oh, no. I've counted at least three. He owns various properties around Sussex and his women live in the houses rent-free. He visits them from time to time. If he finds some guy's been sniffing around, he sends in his thugs to sort them out. Mind you, I'm only seeing the casualties who go private. Who knows how many others he's maimed who are now being treated on the NHS?'

TWENTY-TWO

Clare Mitchell stepped out of the villa and jogged in the direction of the beach. Despite the late hour, seven-thirty, and the season, early spring, the heat was oppressive. She ran down the steps and through the garden. She knew, on Ray's property at least, she wouldn't trip on a rogue stone or branch, as he paid gardeners and maintenance people to work all the year round.

She liked St Lucia. It was hot, but it wasn't the dry, oven heat of the Middle East that enveloped your body as soon as you stepped outside, leaving you panting and your t-shirt soaked after running half a kilometre. Here, there was more moisture in the air, making it easier to breathe, but in time, it crept up on you. By the end of a five-mile run, she often felt ten years older and totally drained.

She had no desire to spend another holiday in the company of Ray Schofield, but when he suddenly suggested a short break in St Lucia she jumped at the chance. It was one of the two places she hadn't yet searched; the documents she was looking for could possibly be there.

The timing of the holiday bothered her for a reason she couldn't fathom. In no shape or measure could Ray be considered an impetuous man. No one running a large international company with over a thousand employees ever did anything spontaneous. Corporate types lived by plans, strategies, and budgets, devices designed to tell staff what to do, how to do it, and provide a measure of their performance.

Two things might have spooked him. First, the home visit from two Sussex Police detectives. She wasn't there at the time, but had gone out to a restaurant with Ray in the evening and he'd been jumpy. She'd met him many times in business after delivering a speech at the CBI, talking to a room full of fund managers, or being interviewed on radio or television. Then, she would have described his behaviour as high and excited, never jumpy.

He would want to know if he'd looked smart, sounded confident, covered all the things he had on his checklist, but he wouldn't be listening to her responses. He was too hyped-up with adrenaline, like a footballer at the end of a gruelling match. After his chat to the police, he seemed nervous, preoccupied, as if going over each of his answers, trying to determine if he'd said something wrong.

Second, he had received a call from his wife. To the tabloids, Rebecca was the blonde bimbo on the arm of leisure supremo, Raymond Schofield. She was smaller than him with an hourglass figure, large boobs, and athletic legs, courtesy of the days spent in her youth as a fringe player with the England hockey team.

Rebecca was anything but a bimbo, although Clare knew she didn't mind being characterised as such. It gave her license to do things in the business which people didn't see coming, giving them less time to organise their defences. The Crema Coffee shops were her idea, as was the way they were set up. She'd resisted all attempts by Ray to make them as efficient and functional as possible, and instead, she allowed them to develop a casual, bohemian style. All were supplied daily with fresh flowers, the female toilets were equipped with complimentary nappies and tampons, the men's with an aftershave dispenser, and she ensured the female-to-male ratio of staff in the business was maintained at fifty-fifty.

A day before he'd suggested going away, Clare knew Ray had been talking to Rebecca on the phone in the car when he arrived to pick her up from her flat in Hove. He'd appeared so agitated she had taken a step back into the hallway of her building to watch. In the main, conversations between the divorcing couple were amicable, if a bit business-like; you take the microwave, I'll have the coffee maker. She assumed all divorces progressed in this way, although she had never experienced one close up.

It was a common enough occurrence at Raybeck Leisure; one of the unintended consequences of Rebecca's desire to have an equal split of the sexes, was an increase in the number of shop floor romances and affairs. Clare, as financial director, often saw the fall-out: numerous 'Change of Beneficiary Forms' for the pension fund, increases in maternity pay, more dispute resolution dubbed, lovers' tiff resolution, and more severance payments; the whole nine yards.

Despite her initial reluctance to join Ray on yet another holiday, she had to admit, it was a fantastic villa sited in a spectacular spot. It was located high on a cliff at the midpoint between two sweeping, curved bays, each filled with soft, pale sand. Ray claimed he had spotted the villa, but if Rebecca hadn't found it, she had certainly played a major role in how it was furnished. In common with the house in Warninglid, the villa furnishings were minimal, but exuded great taste and style.

In this part of the island, few tourists knew the bays existed, or if they did, they didn't have the transport to negotiate the rugged access roads. On such a beautiful evening as this, there was no one lying on the beach or running along the hard sand near the shore as she was doing.

Clare hoped she was never part of the acrimony between Rebecca and Ray. She knew Rebecca well and had talked to her on a number of occasions since the split, and didn't detect the least trace of rancour. That said, people with less sense than Rebecca would resent Clare's presence in Ray's life.

She had a clear conscience as it wasn't her who had driven a wedge between Ray and his wife. It was Sylvie Goss, Rebecca's former best friend and a regular visitor to Mayfield Manor in Warninglid. She was similar in age to Rebecca, fifty-six, but unlike her friend, looked and acted ten years younger. She had a figure to match, with larger than average boobs, a slim waist and extraordinary long legs that could grace hosiery and shoe adverts, which at one time, they did.

Clare had been Ray's constant companion for the last seven years. He ran Raybeck on strict cost-conscious lines and deferred to her judgement on all things financial. She had accompanied Rebecca and

Ray to numerous conferences, trade shows, meetings, holidays at the villa in Portugal, and once to St Lucia.

To their eternal frustration, the tabloids were unable to capitalise on her presence. If a journalist called the press office because they'd seen Ray and Clare together in a London restaurant, they would be told Ms Mitchell was Raybeck's financial director and accompanying Mr Schofield to discuss a business matter. It never failed to fob them off, because if there was one thing designed to bore readers and have them turning over to the TV pages, it was an exclusive story about an accountant. In the public's view, they were slightly more popular than an undertaker or actuary, but less than an estate agent or fund manager.

Returning to the villa after completing her run, she began a series of cool-down stretches on the patio, in an attempt to reduce the build-up of lactic acid in her system and avoid muscle pain later. Facing the beach, she watched as the track of her footsteps in the sand across the bay vanished under the lapping waves, while the big orange disc of the sun slowly sank below the horizon. Since childhood, sunset had left a feeling of melancholy. The sun seemed to disappear so completely into the ocean she couldn't be persuaded it would return the following morning.

'Did you have a good run?'

Ray was standing outside the patio doors, a bottle of Wadadli beer in his hand. He was drinking more now that he no longer had a big business to run. Then, he had his fair share of management dinners and retirement lunches, but he would drink little, as he often had to make a speech afterwards, or he intended returning to the office once the event was over.

'Excellent,' she said. 'I think it's cooler in the evening than in the morning, and the views with the softer light are spectacular.'

'You should be a photographer or painter with an eye like that.'

'You know me, I don't have the patience.'

He walked over and kissed her.

'You're taking a risk,' she said.

'I know, but despite your top being soaked through, there doesn't seem to be the usual rancid hum of sweat. It must be something in the air back home. Pollution, I shouldn't wonder.'

'You've got a lot to learn about women, Ray Schofield,' she said, tapping him playfully on the nose. 'Rancid hum indeed. I'm off for a shower before you say something you might regret.'

The bathrooms in the villa were every bit as big and as well-appointed as those in Portugal. Not only was there a range of shower soaps, moisturisers, and night creams, all leading brands, there were also huge, thick bath towels to wrap herself up with.

She would never call herself a keen runner, subscribing to running magazines and scouring athletic shops for the latest gear. In fact, she didn't enjoy doing it, but instead used it to fulfil two specific purposes. She had always been a confident businesswoman and thought nothing of walking into a meeting room full of men, but now and again depression would strike. It was rooted, she believed, in the untimely death of her father and her mother's inadequate attempts to try and fill the void.

Running had been suggested by a coach at university, and whenever she spotted a black cloud on the horizon, she would lace her trainers and head outside. The abundance of fresh air and the surge of adrenaline would usually do the trick and push the clouds away. When she started work at the sumptuous offices of Raybeck Leisure in Leadenhall, her secretary soon became accustomed to her boss walking into her office in a smart business suit, only to appear a few hours later decked in a garishly-coloured tight top and clingy leggings. This, and her ability to bring clarity to Ray's often scattered thought processes, was the reason her staff called her Superwoman.

Running was also used to organise her thoughts. Her day would be filled with meetings, phone calls, interruptions by Ray, and emails, some requiring an immediate response. Pounding the pavements around Leadenhall was often the only time she could be on her own, her phone on airplane mode and set to playing upbeat music.

After drying off, she opened the wardrobe. She flicked through the dresses, rejecting the pale pink as she didn't yet have much of a tan, and instead, selected the navy. They were dining in the Calico Rose restaurant this evening, one of the Island's most exclusive establishments. The great and good of St Lucia would be there, even on a midweek night, with the added bonus of any visiting dignitaries.

She enjoyed a bit of celebrity spotting as much as the next girl, but this wasn't Ray's aim; he went there to be noticed. Even in this far-flung corner of the Caribbean, a long way from Fleet Street and Wapping, Ray had his eye on a photo opportunity and the flattery that a column inch or two would bring.

After selling the business, Ray promised he would leave all the hullabaloo associated with corporate life behind. There would be no more press conferences, meetings with the London Mayor, drinks with journalists, or meals in the latest 'happening' London restaurant, all in an attempt to shoehorn his picture into the paper. He was kidding himself, but she wasn't fooled. The level of adoration he once enjoyed would be difficult for anyone to give up; near impossible for a man like Ray with an ego bigger than any diva pop star.

She stood in front of the full-length mirror and did a twirl. Despite this being a holiday, she didn't want to look like a tourist, but as Ray's business partner. So, the earrings were small with diamonds, the dress knee-length, and the shoes were smart sandals.

Satisfied, she headed downstairs. At the mid-point landing, she stopped. She could hear Ray on the phone. If there had been any neighbours, they would have been able to hear him too.

'Just fucking do it!' he hollered. 'I don't care what you have to do!'

There was silence for a moment; Ray listening to the caller, or had he walked off towards the garden?

'Pete, listen to me. They know nothing. You're in the clear. Just fucking get rid of him, right?'

TWENTY-THREE

He reached into his briefcase and picked out the Tupperware box Anita had packed for him. Alex Vincent had told his wife on several occasions not to bother as she had the boys to deal with, but she had grown up in a household where her mother insisted a wife had to look after her husband. In his family, things were done differently, but having a discussion with his wife and trying to get her to change her mind, was about as fruitful as sticking his head down the toilet.

He opened the box and, as usual, a little note lay on top.

To Alex,
The most wonderful man in the world and the best father our two boys could ever imagine.
Love always,
Anita xx

He pulled the drawer open and added the note to the pile Anita had previously penned. When he explained her behaviour to friends, they found it hard to reconcile this with the high-powered Mergers and Acquisitions expert she once was. In those days, she lost no sleep over decisions to close factories or to sell companies to foreign rivals, and would happily raise millions of pounds to allow corporate raiders, asset strippers, and land hoarders to do their dirty work.

She was on a kick to try to reduce his burgeoning gut, another issue reinforcing his feelings of impending middle-age. It wasn't as if he didn't take any exercise: he played badminton at club level, football with two lively boys in the garden, and at weekends the family often went out for long walks. His affair with Joanna had admittedly curbed the amount of badminton he played. If there wasn't a league match, he would often leave the session a half-hour before the end, and tell Anita he and a few other players had gone to a pub in Henfield for a few drinks afterwards.

This allowed him an hour or two with Joanna. Her lad, Seb, was at the age when he would rather stay holed up in his sweat-infested room playing FIFA online with his mates than talk to adults, a bunch of boring old farts according to him. In fact, Joanna's house was so large they could be prancing around naked in one of the bedrooms in the west wing, and if Seb came downstairs for a can of Coke and a biscuit he wouldn't have a clue what they were up to. In addition, Vincent's excuse of going for a drink after the game didn't present a problem, as he was teetotal and had no need to fake alcohol on his breath.

Today, there was no flatbread or a sandwich, but chicken with couscous. He shook his head but realised it was all in a good cause. He didn't know how Anita did it. He supposed all the experience of working for a demanding German bank had honed her organisational skills to a very sharp point.

His lunch didn't look the least bit appetising, and he was about to shove it to one side and head down to the coffee shop in Trafalgar Street, when he decided to sample a piece. She had added a herb or two; he thought he could detect coriander and chilli, and it tasted delicious. He was halfway through devouring it when Trevor Robinson walked in.

'Sorry to interrupt your lunch, Alex.'

'No problem, it's not as if it will get cold if I leave it for a few minutes.'

Robinson took a seat. Vincent's view of the man had improved in the three weeks since Martin's death. He had made a good fist of stepping up to the plate, and was starting to sound and behave like the leading man, and not like the bit actor he once was. Everyone knew, Robinson included, that Haldane would be advertising soon to fill the vacant post, but like a football manager looking to buy a new striker, only to find that his current one can't stop scoring, Haldane had a difficult decision to make.

'Have I told you about the Fenwick case?' Robinson asked.

He shook his head and couldn't resist forking another mouthful.

'Brian Fenwick, Baz to his mates. He owns a big central heating business in Shoreham and is accused of stabbing a West Ham fan about three weeks ago, following their match with Brighton.'

'I remember reading about it. I didn't know the accused's name.'

'If you think he sounds like a typical teenage football thug, you'd be wrong. He's fifty-five, with a wife and three kids, but there the difference stops. He's a lifelong football hooligan with a list of previous convictions as long as your arm: for affray, assault, and carrying an offensive weapon.' He gave a mirthless laugh. 'I think it will be a hard sell to a jury.'

'I agree; he can't claim youthful petulance or the inability to control a testosterone-based temper,' Vincent said.

'I could suggest it's the result of a midlife crisis or a rocky marriage, and that's what I wanted to talk to you about. His wife, Valerie, has now had enough and wants a divorce.'

'Not a problem. When do you want me to meet her?' Vincent pushed his meal to one side and activated his pc. He clicked on the diary app.

'She's sitting in my office at the moment.'

Vincent shook his head. 'Sorry, Trevor, no can do, I'm afraid. After I finish this,' he said, glancing at his half-finished Tupperware box, 'I'm off to London. I'll be there all afternoon.'

'What's this, a new client?'

'Not really. You obviously know Ray Schofield from the criminal trial, but I'm representing his wife in their divorce.'

'At the time of the trial I knew Ray well, and I've met Rebecca a few times. She's a good-looking woman, even now.'

'You might remember I flagged the issue of missing files at the management meeting?'

He nodded.

Well,' he said, 'I've noticed Rebecca's file is missing too, including one very important schedule.'

'After you flagged it, I hear that Medical Negligence, and Business and Commercial have also reported missing files. Have you lost much?'

'Information on about eight or nine clients.'

'You're assuming Martin's killer took them?'

He shrugged. 'There's no other explanation.'

'Why would they? Trying to fool the police into believing it was a burglary or something?'

'Your guess is as good as the next man. The upshot is, an important financial schedule given to me by Rebecca Schofield is missing. It can't be recreated and she didn't keep a copy, and the only way I can think of getting the information is by employing a firm of forensic accountants to run a fine-tooth comb over Ray Schofield's finances. I'm meeting them this afternoon to discuss how we go about it.'

'Schofield won't like that one bit. In fact, I'd go as far as to say he will actively resist it. He's a narcissist with an ego the size of Texas, and goes all secret-squirrel if anyone tries to probe his personal life and finances, but he'll come out with all guns blazing if you call him a liar. Which in essence, is what you're doing.'

'So I've heard. We are talking about a large sum of money.'

'I can imagine, if it's anything to do with Schofield.'

'You might also recall, Haldane's very concerned about the missing files, and now as you say with MN and Business to consider as well, the situation has become more serious. He's asked me to meet with our auditors and have them make an inventory of what's missing. He fears we might be exposing ourselves to some expensive lawsuits if any of the parties involved accuse us of negligence. I'm meeting them later today to discuss what I'd like them to do.'

He laughed. 'Lawyers suing lawyers. The press will have a field day.'

'Quite,' Vincent said, standing and slipping on his jacket. 'So, if you can ask Mrs Fenwick for another date, I would be happy to meet her.'

'No problem,' Robinson said. He got up and headed for the door.

'Oh, Trevor?'

'Yeah?' the younger man said, his hand on the door frame.

'I don't know if you are still in contact with Mr Schofield, but as this issue is a somewhat sensitive, I'd rather he knew nothing about it.'

'No need to worry, I don't speak to him nowadays in any case. Your secret's safe with me. See you later, Alex.'

Vincent walked out of the office. He left the car in the car park, as Brighton Station was only about one hundred metres up the hill. Usain Bolt could cover the distance in under ten seconds, but Vincent would take longer; he wasn't as fit as the Jamaican and not in a blinding rush.

He purchased a ticket and scanned the departures board for a soon-to-depart train. There was a train at nine minutes past two, in eight minutes' time, and no delays were being displayed. He pushed his ticket into the barrier and walked along the platform. It always surprised him to see how many people travelled outside what was regarded as normal commuting times. Mid-morning, students would be heading to colleges in Crawley, Croydon, and London, and shoppers to Oxford Street. Mid-afternoon, it was shift workers off to clean or secure office blocks in London, and students, retail assistants, and office workers returning home after a busy day.

He stood approximately halfway along the platform where he expected the six-carriage train to stop, beside a gaggle of girls on one side and a smaller group of older boys on the other. In the distance, he could see the train heading towards the station. The girls were trying to grab each other's phones, while the boys were playing some game involving smacking one another on the arm and jumping back. He was fearful one of them might fall from the platform onto the rails.

The train rolled down the platform. He looked left and right to make sure the kids were behaving themselves. The train was close enough for him to see the driver's face, and he tensed slightly as the platform vibrated with the weight of the lumbering giant as it trundled closer. Seconds later, he felt a hard shove in the back.

The last words he heard before the huge wheels bore down on him was a voice screaming, 'A guy's jumped! A guy's jumped!'

TWENTY-FOUR

Henderson finished the morning briefing with the Martin Turner murder team, but he didn't return to his office. Instead, he stood looking at the series of whiteboards being used to flesh out the main issues in the investigation: Family and Friends, Work Colleagues, Criminal Clients. All were coming to a close.

The loose ends, which he hoped would offer them a decent lead, had all been more or less tied up. Jonas Baines security cards were not marked with their name, leading them to believe it had been taken inside the building. They had also examined Trevor Robinson's movements on the day of the murder, and he had left work at his usual time. It was his card that had been used by the perpetrator, but the CCTV pictures of the intruder did not match the physical characteristics of the young lawyer.

They had gone through the list of visitors to the offices for the days that Robinson's card had been missing before being reported, but no one stood out. It was nevertheless, on the criminal defence side at least, a roll call of the bad and worst of Sussex society: suspected rapists, arsonists, murderers, and fraudsters. Any one of them could have been working with the perpetrator and stolen Robinson's security card.

Robinson was a strange character. He was a well-respected criminal lawyer but wasted big money on casinos and racetracks. In some respects, the DI knew he should be offering the guy some sympathy. Most detectives had seen some awful things while doing their job: bodies shoehorned into chest freezers and suitcases, children beaten black and blue, rape victims so traumatised they were unable to speak. Some dealt with it by gambling, drinking heavily, taking drugs, or involving themselves in criminality. If detectives saw the results of heinous crimes at first-hand, lawyers like Robinson saw it second-hand, but it was often in the same level of detail and, in most cases, the impact would be no less disturbing.

It seemed the only option left was to trawl through Alex Vincent's divorce files. The danger was, they would end up with a large list of names, much like the security card list, with no evidence to hang on them.

'Gov, you've got to see this.'

He looked around. Carol Walters was calling him. He walked over to her desk.

'You know part of Brighton Station was closed yesterday afternoon, and only opened at ten this morning because of a body on the tracks?'

He screwed his face up. 'It's a gruesome way to do it, don't you think? Plastered over the wheels of a locomotive.'

'Poison's much better. Anyway, the reason I called you over is the victim was identified about an hour ago. It's none other than Alex Vincent.'

'The same Alex Vincent?'

She nodded.

He sat down. 'Bloody hell.' He paused. 'The first question that comes into my head is, did he jump, slip, or was he pushed?'

'I've read all the news reports and eyewitness accounts; they all say he jumped.'

'However...'

'However, we do have another dead lawyer at Jonas Baines. The first might have been a burglary gone wrong, but two? Not a chance.'

'C'mon, let's go and take a look at the crime scene.'

Henderson wasn't in a talkative mood in the car. He hadn't got clear in his mind the reason for the murder of Martin Turner, and now with his colleague also dead, it added another layer of subterfuge.

'Do you think he might have done it out of grief?' Walters asked.

Henderson considered this. 'Guilt, more like, because he was screwing Turner's ex-wife, but no, I don't. It would only work if Vincent and Turner had been close friends, or lovers even, but I don't see any evidence to support either premise.'

'No, me neither. Could it be, she says, thinking out loud, part of a vendetta against Jonas Baines?'

'It's certainly worth considering. Perhaps a rival wanting to muscle in on their business, or a disgruntled former employee seeking revenge.'

'The first reason makes them sound like a bunch of drug dealers.'

'Lawyers sometimes behave like them.'

'The second one sounds more of a goer.'

'Let's see what happened here before we add any more scenarios to our list.'

When they arrived in Brighton, Henderson headed for the big car park at the rear of Brighton Station. It was a long walk to the station, but he didn't mind. He needed the fresh air to clear his thoughts.

The station was open and functioning, but the platform where the incident had taken place was roped off with police tape. They were allowed through by a uniformed cop.

A railway employee saw them approach and walked over. He offered to talk them through what he believed had happened.

'The incident occurred about here,' their guide, Robert Lowe, said. They were standing at the edge of an empty platform, clean steel rails in front of them. By Henderson's reckoning, they were about sixty to seventy metres from the ticket barriers.

'The train is no longer here, as you can see,' Lowe said. 'Before it returns to service, it will be steam-cleaned, just as the rails down there have been.'

'The trains don't move very fast when they come into the station,' Walters said.

'I know what you're thinking. How can a slow moving train kill someone? But these things weigh about two hundred tons, and by the time they pass this point here, they're decelerating but still doing about twenty miles an hour. If the driver fails to brake, it will crush everything in its path, including the buffers you can see over there, and most of the front section would end up in the concourse of the station.'

'I see.'

'There are a couple of cameras up there,' Henderson said, pointing to one attached to a girder. 'Is it possible to see the pictures?'

'I think some of your people are up there now. I can take you if you like.'

'That would be helpful.'

'Is there anything else I can tell you while we're here?'

'It was the 14:09 train to London Victoria, I understand.'

'That's right.'

'Is the platform busy at that time?'

'Yes, and it would surprise you the amount of people moving about when everyone else is usually back at their place of work after lunch.'

Henderson looked at Walters. 'I don't think we have any more questions.'

She shook her head.

'Thanks for taking the time and letting us visit the scene, Mr Lowe,' Henderson said.

'No problem. I do what I can to help the police. My son's a constable in Lowestoft. If you've seen all you want, follow me.'

'How long have you worked here?' Henderson asked as they walked towards the ticket barriers.

'Twenty-two years,' he replied.

'I suppose you've seen your fair share of suicides?'

'Including yesterday's, I guess there's been about ten or twelve in my time.'

'That many?'

'Yes, and we've had a couple fall off the roof, and perhaps about a half-a-dozen killed trying to dodge over the tracks, or train surfing as the kids call it, lying on the roof of a moving train, the idiots.'

Lowe led them to the offices at the back of the ticket hall and up a set of stairs.

They walked along a short corridor before Lowe opened a door. 'They're in there.'

Henderson nodded his thanks and the detectives headed inside. An operator was sitting at a desk working the CCTV picture feed while a uniformed cop looked on.

'Afternoon, gents,' Henderson said.

'Afternoon. Can I help you?' the cop asked.

'DI Henderson and DS Walters, Major Crime Team.'

'Pleased to meet you, sir. I'm Constable Graham Jennings from John Street. What brings you here?'

'The victim of this incident was helping us with a murder investigation.'

'Oh, I see. So, I take it you want to take a look at the CCTV pictures?'

'If it's okay with you?'

'No problem,' he said, backing off. 'Can I interest you folks in a tea or coffee?'

'That would be good. White coffee for me,' Henderson said.

'Same for me,' Walters said.

The constable departed, glad to be out of it, Henderson surmised.

The officers pulled up seats beside the CCTV operator.

'I'm trying to find the period ten minutes before the incident,' the operator said, 'as the constable asked.'

A few minutes later, he said, 'Done,' and pushed his chair back. 'It's all yours. You can just leave it running and it should be fine. If you want to pause, press here,' he said, pointing, 'to play, press here, and fast forward and back, press here and here. Any questions?'

'No problem.'

'Great. I'm off for a slash. I'll be back in ten if you need me.'

'My, that sounds like a very long pee,' Walters said as the door closed and she moved her chair closer to the screens.

'It must be something to do with the coffee they serve here.'

The picture was good, as the camera didn't suffer from any impediments like weather, dirt on the lens, or a pillar in the way. Also, at this time of day, around two in the afternoon the light was bright, helped by the glass dome of the station. The only issue was it was sited a distance away from the people standing at the platform.

Five minutes later, the tall figure of Alex Vincent stepped into view.

'There he is,' Walters said.

Even in a crowd, Vincent would be discernible. He was tall, and walked like a former sergeant major, his back straight and arms at his side, one of them carrying a briefcase.

'The part of the platform where he's standing looks busy compared to further up,' Walters said. 'Why are all those kid's not in school?'

'Perhaps it's a school trip, and maybe their teacher's not in shot.'

They had a reasonable view of Vincent, a group of six girls to his left and five older boys to his right. The boys were larking about and the girls were high-spirited, causing Vincent, on occasion, to glance left and right.

Their view of the victim was now blocked by another man who had moved behind Vincent. He was around the same height as the lawyer, but better built, and didn't appear distracted by the ebullient youngsters around him. He was well-dressed in a suit with a coat draped over his shoulder and a trilby on his head. A bit old-fashioned for the more dressed-down look adopted by many banks and commercial businesses of today, but Brighton people could buck trends as well as set them.

The train came into view. Its appearance was sudden as the camera was static and they weren't viewing down the platform, but across it. There was a subtle movement of feet from the man behind Vincent before the lawyer tipped over the platform. Problem was, the guy had a coat draped over his shoulders and it was difficult to see if an arm or hand had moved.

'Play it again,' he said to Walters. 'Focus this time on the guy standing behind Vincent and on his upper body. I was watching his feet and I think he moved moments before the train came into view.'

They watched the replay three or four times, but the results were inconclusive. The arm might have moved, then again, it might not. People tended to move whenever a train came into a station. They were preparing to board while holding on tighter to their stuff in case it got caught in the train's air displacement and was sucked under the wheels.

Walters stood. 'I guess it's back to the drawing board.'

'Hang on a second.'

She sat down again.

He pressed 'play' at the place where they had previously stopped.

'I want to see what the guy standing behind Vincent does.'

Following the fall on the tracks, and the shocked reaction from all those on the platform, the guy standing behind Vincent strode back towards the ticket barriers and passed under the camera.

They watched the same segment three or four times, Henderson surprised at the cold, casual way the man made his exit and the blank look of his features. When they found the best view of the guy's face, he paused it.

'Our man showed us how to fast-forward and pause,' Henderson said, 'but he didn't tell us how to print.'

TWENTY-FIVE

Henderson decided to put the work of examining the divorce clients of Alex Vincent on hold for the time being. Despite Vincent not working on his own, there were about five solicitors, a number of paralegals and various admin staff who were also familiar with the client list, it wasn't a good time to be stomping around the offices of Jonas Baines and questioning staff.

Instead, they were focussed on the death of Alex Vincent. Henderson had looked at the CCTV and felt sure the man had jumped, despite not knowing any reason why he would do so. This came with several caveats: Henderson had conducted a trial incident in the office using chairs, and it was hard to differentiate the reaction of a jumper from someone being pushed. With a jumper, there would be less flailing of arms, but the leg action, almost as if trying to reach for a step, was similar.

The lack of flailing arms in Vincent's case could also be discounted to a degree. His officers were doing it because they expected to be pushed. Someone who had been pushed with no notice wouldn't be anticipating it, and they would have no time to react. It was all so inconclusive, but he wouldn't rest until he was one hundred percent convinced Alex Vincent had committed suicide.

'Vicky, I want you and your team to pull as much CCTV footage as you can from Brighton Station. See if we can get another angle on the incident.'

'Yes, sir.'

'I'm thinking here about one where we might get a decent view of the victim's face. A look of shock or surprise should tell us lots.'

'Will do.'

'Harry, I want you to track our man,' Henderson said, jerking his hand to the screen behind him showing the best view of the man who was standing behind Vincent on platform eight, 'on town cameras. We might not get an idea where he's going, but what I want is a better picture of his face.'

'No problem.'

'Carol, you and I will go and see Anita Vincent, and Sally, I want you to pay a visit to Joanna Woodford. I'm not interested to hear if she exhibits more emotion about the death of her lover than her husband, but I'd like to hear her take on his possible suicide.'

'Okay.'

Henderson fielded a couple of questions before grabbing his jacket, and with Walters beside him, headed out to the car park.

'It's one of those weird cases,' Walters said.

'In what way, weird?'

'All the evidence points to suicide, but everything we know about the man suggests otherwise.'

'They say you don't know what goes on behind closed doors, but even then, many women and men don't have any inkling what's really going on inside their partners' heads.'

'It's scary,' she said, as they drove out of the car park, 'but true. I've seen documentaries on Netflix about women living with serial killers in America, and they didn't have a clue what their husband did in his spare time. In one case, a guy worked in an abattoir, so it was common for him to come home with blood splatters on his clothes. Problem was, it didn't always belong to the animals he killed.'

'I don't know why you watch that stuff. I would have thought you see enough of it at work.'

'I do, but sometimes I just need it to give me some sort of perspective.'

'Whatever floats your boat.'

'Talking of sailing, have you been out in your boat with your new woman?'

'I haven't been out on the boat full stop. However, last Sunday she and I went down to the marina and gave it a spring-clean.'

'I can't imagine you with a duster in your hand, a can of Pledge in the other.'

'When you live on your own, needs must.'

Fifteen minutes later he guided the car through the pillars at the Vincent house in Henfield. It was an imposing house, nowhere near as large as Schofield's, he doubted many were, and smaller than Joanna Woodford's, but substantial nevertheless.

Anita Vincent opened the door following his knock. She was tall, slim, with shoulder-length hair and a petite nose. It was hard to tell her eye colour or the state of her complexion as she had been crying.

'DI Henderson and DS Walters, Sussex Police. We called earlier.'

'You did. Please come in.'

They walked into the lounge. The furnishings were a mix of old and new. The sideboard and bookcase were wooden and looked substantial, while the large flat-screen television hung from the wall and a sophisticated-looking hi-fi system with two huge speakers were more modern.

'Can I get you both a drink?'

'No thanks, we won't keep you.'

'Would you like me to make you a cup of tea?' Walters asked. 'It looks as though you could do with one.'

She looked at the sergeant, an expression of gratitude on her face. 'Would you? I would really appreciate it.'

The words were appropriate, but their delivery was monotone, lacking emotion. He was sure it wasn't her normal way of speaking.

'First of all, Mrs Vincent, please accept my condolences for the death of your husband. I've met Alex on several occasions and found him to be honest and forthright. Mr Haldane speaks highly of him.'

'How could you... Oh, yes, Martin's murder.'

Henderson had chosen his words with care. There was no point in telling her about Alex coming to Malling House for an interview, or what he had said during their discussion.

'How are you keeping?' Henderson asked, taking a seat. 'Is anyone looking after you?'

She slumped into an armchair. 'My neighbour along the way, Beth Falstaff, has been brilliant, as has a family friend who you probably know, Joanna Woodford. I've also had a visit from a Family Liaison Officer with British Transport Police, but she didn't stay long.'

'What about your children? Is anyone picking them up from school?'

'Yes,' she said, nodding. 'I take them there in the morning, and yesterday and for the next few days, Beth has offered to pick them up. She sometimes gives them their tea as well.'

'What did you do before having children?' he said, with a nod to the framed photographs in the bookcase.

'Oh, that was when my team were involved in a large chemical company divestiture.'

'What's that?'

'I used to be a Mergers and Acquisitions specialist at a large German bank. The particular job in the photograph involved a large conglomerate that wanted to sell parts of their business to shore up an ailing balance sheet. It all seems like another life now, lived by someone else.'

Walters walked in with the tea and handed the mug to Anita.

'Thanks.' She took a sip. 'Oh, I should have told you, I don't take sugar.'

'Just drink it this way for once,' Walters said. 'It should make you feel better.'

'Mrs Vincent,' Henderson said, 'the reason we came to see you today, apart from to offer our condolences, is to find out from you what Alex's state of mind was on the day he died.'

'Okay.'

'Perhaps you can talk me through the day, from, say, the time you were having breakfast.'

'I'll try.' She paused as if gathering herself. 'He'd got up earlier than me. I'm the one who's a crap sleeper; it's a mum thing, having one ear tuned to a sleeping child. I think with Alex, the murder of his colleague was getting to him.'

Henderson nodded.

'I expect you know more about the subject than anyone else. By the time I came downstairs, he had laid the table and filled the cereal bowls for the boys. He liked to have something different for breakfast every day, some days Weetabix, others a boiled egg. He was standing at the worktop, swishing up some eggs for scrambled eggs. He asked if I wanted any. I said yes.'

She was on the verge of tears, encouraging Henderson to jump in with a question.

'How would you characterise his state of mind?'

She wiped a tear away with her hand. 'Normal, I would say. He ruffled the boys' hair when they finally made an appearance, and was interested to hear what they would be doing at school that day.'

'He didn't seem worried or preoccupied?'

'The opposite, I would say. It gave me hope that he was at last putting Martin's death behind him.'

'Could he have been faking it? Putting on a good show to hide some inner turmoil?'

'No way, I would have been able to see through it, the boys too.'

'How can you be so confident?'

'Inspector, I told you, I was in Acquisitions and Mergers.'

'Yes?'

'I was bloody good at my job, and the main reason was that I was good at reading people. When you're in a room with a group of directors, eager to sell a company because they know there's a major corporate fraud case looming, or they're covering up a serious Health and Safety breach, it pays to know if they're hiding something. That morning, Alex gave me no indication he wanted to take his own life.'

'You're sure?'

'Yes, I'm sure. We've talked in the past about these things. You know the sort of thing, what would you do if you knew you had only three weeks to live or one of us had a terminal illness?'

He nodded.

'Poison would have been his preferred method of dispatch. He was a chemistry wiz at school, and the subject he studied at university.'

'I didn't realise, him being a lawyer.'

'When he finished at Imperial, he decided not to pursue a career in chemistry, and took a law conversion course instead. It was a hard route to choose, as he was competing against people who had studied law for three years at degree level, but being as smart as he was, he soon caught up.'

'If Alex didn't commit suicide, what do you think happened to him?'

'I can only think he slipped after being jostled by some other passengers nearby, and lost his footing. I'm telling you, Inspector, there's no way he committed suicide.'

TWENTY-SIX

Henderson walked down the road from his apartment and turned right onto the seafront. This Saturday evening he wasn't in running gear, but in the smart-casual clothes he had worn into work earlier in the day. It was already dark, and the working day over for most of the team, but for him there was one last thing he needed to do.

For once, on reaching the seafront, he didn't have his hair messed up or his jacket almost ripped from his shoulders. It had been a calm day in Brighton with little wind, and looking out to sea at the sky in the fading light, it looked as though it was going to be a tranquil evening too. The calm day wasn't the harbinger of good weather to come, merely a lull in proceedings; the months of early spring often brought wild storms and teeming rain to the south coast.

He crossed Kingsway and walked along the esplanade overlooking the Channel. The view of the grey sea and the twinkling lights of the pier in the distance weren't as interesting as glancing into the windows of the houses and apartments he would have passed if he had stayed on the other side. Going this way, however, had the advantage of not having to cross the numerous busy side streets that peppered this part of the city.

There were plenty of people about, but their numbers increased as he approached the entrance to the Palace Pier, a popular meeting spot. The crowds multiplied by yet another factor when he passed the Brighton Centre. An American singer-songwriter was playing there tonight and hundreds of her fans were queuing outside. In adjacent West Street, the pubs, clubs, and restaurants were thronging, including many youngsters fuelling up for the long night ahead.

He crossed the road and headed into the Grand Hotel. It was an oasis of calm in comparison to the buzz of activity going on all around it, making him feel as though his blood pressure had fallen a few notches. He made his way to The Consort Room and took a seat close by.

Inside the room, members of the Sussex Legal Society were enjoying their annual dinner with speeches from a former cabinet minister, and then from their president, Robert Haldane. They had been in there since five o' clock and, by Haldane's estimation, it would wrap up around eight-thirty, when they would all retire to the bar.

Ten minutes later, the door opened and those inside began to filter out, pour out more like, as several looked the worse for wear. Henderson hoped they had booked a room for the night and weren't intending to drive home. Haldane was one of the last to leave, and, befitting the president, he was accompanied by several hangers-on.

He said goodbye to those beside him and approached Henderson. They shook hands.

'Evening, Inspector.'

'Evening, Mr Haldane. Was it a good dinner?'

'No, not for me it wasn't. Thank you for coming here this evening. I know it's an imposition, as even officers of the law working on a high-profile murder investigation need a break now and again.'

'It's not a problem. I do understand why you wouldn't want to have this sort of discussion in the office.'

'Quite. I've found a room we can use. If you follow me.'

Haldane strode off, Henderson following behind, trying to keep pace. Passing a bank of lifts, the doors opened and four stunning women, decked out in magnificent dresses, bedecked in all manner of jewellery, and with their hair beautifully coiffured, stepped out. Henderson had seen most of the attendees at Haldane's bash and suspected these ladies weren't the other halves of those doughty lawyers, they were too young and the lawyers too old. Coming to places like this often made him reflect how this sort of thing went on while he was at work, and if not, while he was recovering after a hard day.

Haldane opened a door and led him into a small room with a long table, five chairs either side and a whiteboard at one end. During the week, it would probably be in use every day as a meeting room or a break-out room from a bigger gathering, so it was no surprise to find it empty. It would be a strange sort of business that forced their staff to come up with strategy and business improvement ideas on a Saturday night.

Haldane took a seat at one side of the table and Henderson the other.

'What's the verdict on Alex?' Haldane asked.

'So far, we have found no evidence to think he committed suicide. The CCTV doesn't tell us one way or the other, but everyone who knew him are adamant he wasn't a suicide risk.'

'I can only agree. He could be a miserable sod at times, if I can speak ill of the dead, but with a wicked sense of humour which made a sporadic appearance. He didn't give me any indication he was depressed or feeling down, and he hasn't socialised much with Martin these last few years, so I don't think he fell to pieces over his death.'

'Therefore, if we discount suicide, it leaves two possible scenarios; he slipped, or he was pushed.'

'What do you think?'

'Reviewing the CCTV pictures, Alex is standing on the platform when a man comes up and stands behind him. It's not an unusual thing to do, as this part of the platform was busy. We now have someone who is in a position to push him, but the man's body obscures our view of Alex so we can't ascertain if he did, or Alex slipped.'

'I see.'

'We are trying to find CCTV pictures from other angles, but it's not proving easy.'

'Talking about this is harder than I thought. I didn't drink much during the dinner, but I need one now. Would you like one?'

'If you don't mind, I'll have a whisky with ice.'

'I'll go and find a waiter.'

Haldane left the room. If Henderson had been interviewing a suspect or a witness, he would have stopped him leaving, not giving him time to concoct a better story or disappear entirely. In Haldane's case, his hands were shaking and he looked fraught. Henderson didn't think it had anything to do with how well, or otherwise, his speech had been received.

Haldane returned a few minutes later and sat down. 'When you asked if it was a good dinner, I forgot to mention Charles Smart, the PM's former foreign secretary. He was good value and told us some stories which he assured us weren't in the recently published memoir of his old boss.'

'I've never been to a dinner with a political speaker, but I've heard a few football managers and they have some stories to tell.'

'I'll bet.'

There was a soft knock on the door, and a white-jacketed waiter entered bearing two drinks on a tray held expertly in the palm of one hand. He placed them in front of the two men and disappeared as silently as he'd come in.

'Cheers,' Haldane said, lifting his glass; whisky, Henderson guessed.

'Cheers,' Henderson said, and took a drink. It wasn't his usual brand, but a good one nevertheless.

'Mr Haldane, it pains me to say it, but I think it's unlikely Alex would have slipped. It's possible to think he might have been accidentally bumped as there were groups of kids either side, but the one thing the CCTV pictures do confirm is they didn't make contact with him.'

'I see.'

'By a process of elimination, and although we have no clear evidence yet to support this, we think Alex may have been pushed.'

'This is what I feared. Do you know this person who was standing behind Alex? Have you got his picture?'

'Yes and no. We have a picture, but the quality is not good enough for a positive identification. I have tasked my staff with following this individual via town centre cameras to see if we can get a better view.'

'It sounds a sensible approach.'

'With two solicitors dead, I think we must entertain the notion that someone is targeting your firm.'

'Do you think so?'

'If Alex was killed by an assailant, and let's assume he also killed Martin, it provides two possibilities. Either Alex knew Martin's killer, and his death was to silence him, or it's a systematic attack on your firm. From the work we've done so far, we can see little connection between Martin Turner and Alex Vincent, other than in their professional lives, but now this is something I feel we cannot ignore.'

'I see where you are coming from, but why would someone be targeting us?'

'You tell me. It should be easier to think about after tonight of all nights. Mentally go round the tables at dinner and think about the men and women occupying each of the seats. Have any of them ever expressed envy or contempt at the success of your firm, or offered to buy it, or merge with it? You say, after all, on your website you are Sussex's premier legal practice.'

'We are.'

'A statement of this type could, I imagine, get someone's back up.'

'Let me think about this for a second,' Haldane said. He cradled his whisky and looked into the distance. 'For the dinner tonight, we only allow one partner from each firm, so in the room we had representatives from twelve of the largest legal outfits in Sussex. Edward Oswald from Chichester has always pestered me to poach Martin; Jeffrey Campbell too; and Stephen Baldry from Horsham, was jealous of the success of our Medical Negligence division.'

'It's a successful business?'

'Seeking compensation from health boards and doctors for botched operations? Yes, and growing. People now realise the chronic back pain they suffered after childbirth may not be natural, but perhaps the result of negligence, for example. And in cases of children with disabilities, where financial help can be invaluable, people are starting to realise they have options.'

Henderson nodded but said nothing. He knew many doctors and the pressure they were under. It wasn't just the time constraint of making a snap diagnosis and following through with treatment, but they often complained about faulty equipment, the lack of appropriate drugs, and the absence of adequate support staff, with some, including themselves, too tired to think straight.

If doctors could be sued for malpractice, how long would it be before the same thing happened to police officers? Already they appeared in court in a variety of circumstances: cases of wrongful arrest; the suspicious death of a suspect while in custody; perjury at a previous trial. Would they soon be prosecuted or sued for not catching a killer sooner, or for the anguish suffered by a woman raped by a serial rapist after being questioned about something else and set free?

To try and calm himself, and not say something he shouldn't, Henderson lifted his glass and took a long, slow sip.

When he put it down, he said, 'Going back to my original question, Mr Haldane, can you think of anyone in particular who might have a specific grudge against Jonas Baines?'

'I don't know, Inspector. Law isn't like a normal business with corporate raiders and aggressive cost cutters. We swim in much gentler waters, with the whiff of an old gentleman's club.'

Henderson stood. 'I wasn't expecting an answer tonight. I just wanted to raise the topic and give you something to think about. Let me know if anything comes up. Good night, Mr Haldane, and thanks again for the drink.'

TWENTY-SEVEN

He paced up and down the living room. He could hear his mother's voice in his head saying he would wear a hole in the carpet, which he tried to dismiss, but nevertheless, his tracks were clearly visible. Trevor Robinson had been shaken by the death of Martin Turner, and now with the death of Alex Vincent, his old teenage anxiety, which he had managed to control these last few years, had risen to the surface with the force of a humpbacked whale. There was only one conclusion to draw: he would be next.

He didn't believe in witches, voodoo, or karma, but in the laws of chance. What were the odds of him making it to the end of the month when his office companion was dead and so was the guy next door? It was as if he was wearing a target on his back – *Me Next*!

Yes, they were a big firm, and employed heads of Medical Malpractice, Property, International Law, and all the rest, but they were upstairs or in other parts of the building; some were even in offices in other parts of Sussex. He, for his sins, was stuck in the same part of the building where two of his closest colleagues had been killed.

He continued pacing. Luckily the guy living below was partially deaf and refused to wear a hearing aid;

he might mistake the rumble above his head for thunder or an aeroplane. Talking to other colleagues at the practice, they were also upset by Alex's death, but he could see the pity in their eyes. They all expected him to be next.

A strange trilling noise sounded, disturbing his thought processes. He was so startled it took him a few seconds to realise it wasn't his alarm clock or the building entry system, but his phone ringing. He picked it up.

'Trevor, it's me. I'm downstairs in the car. Are you ready?'

'Eh? Yeah, I'll be down...'

'Are you okay? Don't tell me you've just woken up?'

'Woken up? I've hardly slept.'

'Sorry. I'll find a place to park and wait. Try not to be too long.'

He trudged into the bathroom and splashed water on his face, but he didn't feel any more refreshed or less anxious. In the bedroom, he picked up his jacket and put it on. He slipped his wallet and phone into a pocket, and after taking one last look around his apartment, closed the door and headed downstairs.

Before opening the front door and stepping outside, he stopped, feeling as though he had forgotten something. On work days he carried a leather case containing paper and pens, anything he needed for a meeting, but rarely client stuff. He hated working from home and giving the firm free hours not on the clock. Today, he was visiting Miranda's parents. This being Sunday, and with both of them working the following day, it was only lunch. He opened the door and headed down the steps.

Climbing into Miranda's Mini Cooper, he leaned over to kiss her. Seconds later, the car shot off. He was forced back in the sports seat, trying to put on his seatbelt as Miranda made short work of Brighton's busy and narrow streets. He had forgotten how fast she drove, and it always came as a shock whenever he climbed into her car.

'How are you feeling?' she asked, looking over. The speed limit in the streets around Brighton and Hove was twenty miles per hour, but she either didn't notice, or care. She drove as fast as the conditions allowed. He just wished she would keep her eyes on the road and stop looking over at him.

'Not good, as you can imagine.'

'You don't look so hot. I wonder how people in our office would react if two of them were killed?'

'Maybe no one would notice. You've said to me they're a bunch of unfeeling slobs, more interested in their code than people.'

'They can be. I mean, it's mainly guys and most people would regard them as geeks.'

'I feel as if there's a *but* in there.'

'They're *sensitive* geeks. If one of them was murdered and another fell under a train, it would devastate everyone. No work would be done for weeks; in fact, few of them would come into the office and we'd all need months of counselling.'

'It's not a bloody therapist I need, it's a bodyguard. Some big bastard who thinks nothing of taking a bullet for me.'

'Where would we put him in this little car, and how would we stop my mother having a paw at his pecs?'

He looked at her and saw she was smiling. He had to admit, Miranda was good to look at. She had shoulder-length naturally blond hair, sparkling green eyes, and even, white teeth. If this sounded too much like a description of a horse, she was also intelligent, well-read and terrific company. So much so he often wondered why none of the guys in her office had ever asked her out. Maybe she was right, they were so entranced by their code they couldn't relate to the beautiful woman sitting beside them.

They were on the A23 heading north, the dangers to pedestrians, parked cars, and cyclists of Miranda's nip and tuck driving left far behind. However, he still couldn't relax. Miranda jetted down the outside lane doing ninety, making irritated gestures at lane hoggers, undertaking those who refused to move over, and braking sharply when some idiot misjudged the Mini's speed and pulled out in front of them.

They turned off the A23 at the Crawley junction.

'What sort of lunch can I expect?' he asked. 'Is your mum or dad a good cook?'

'They're traditionalists. Around midday, my dad will take the dog and they'll go down to the local pub for a pint while my mum cooks. When he comes back, they sit down to a roast with all the trimmings.'

'Just the two of them?'

She nodded. 'Sometimes, when they can't be bothered, they eat at the pub, but on Sunday, it's a roast without fail.'

'Good job we're not vegans.'

'Not any more, you might say, but I'll save that story for another time.'

Away from the roundabouts and traffic lights of Crawley, the country roads around the West Sussex/Surrey border put Miranda firmly in her element. It was like sitting beside a rally driver, the scenery passing by in a blur, like fast-forwarding through a movie. When they did slow down and he could see the view without it blurring, there were picturesque villages, wood-enclosed fields full of cows, sheep, and occasionally horses, and large country houses to lust after.

Miranda's parents lived in the village of Betchworth, in a quaint ivy-fronted cottage, with a large pub at the end of the road.

'This is lovely. Is it the house you grew up in?'

'No, we lived nearer Croydon back then. They bought this when I left home for good.'

They got out of the car and walked towards the front door. The door opened and an older version of Miranda stood there. She was no less beautiful, with a few more inches around the waist, several more wrinkles, and a few more grey hairs streaking her equally straw-coloured hair.

'Hello Mummy.'

'Darling, it's great to see you.'

Miranda and Julia hugged. Not the air-hug of the Oscar red carpet, but with genuine warmth and affection. They parted.

'So,' Julia said, 'who is this you've brought with you?'

'Mum, this is Trevor.'

Julia sized him up first, and, expecting a handshake, he was surprised when she leaned over and hugged him. For a moment his mind flipped. It was the hug his mother never gave him, the feeling of being enveloped, not for sexual pleasure, but for security and a sense of belonging. He wanted to stay there for ever and let the fear and concern he felt melt away into the distance, but observing social niceties, he stepped back. The sensation of longing persisted, and perhaps Julia had noticed it too as she gave him a look which lingered a second too long.

They walked inside the house and, unencumbered by bags, headed straight into the lounge. Miranda was in front of him and threw her arms around her father, who had risen from the settee where an open *Sunday Observer* was spread out behind him. Robinson knew, without being told, she was a daddy's girl.

Miranda did the introductions, but this time, thank goodness, he and her father, Michael, settled on a handshake.

'Something to drink, Trevor?' Miranda asked.

'A beer?'

'No problem. I don't need to ask what you want, Daddy.'

Miranda wandered off to the kitchen, leaving him with her father. He'd been told he was a school science teacher and, to Robinson, he looked like one. In fact, he looked as though he was about to deliver a lecture on the rudiments of particle physics. He was around fifty-five with a pleasant, clean-shaven face, a mop of salt-and-pepper-hair, and a bit of a beer belly, a problem Robinson would have too if he lived in a house with a decent pub at the end of the road.

'Miranda says you're a lawyer, Trevor.'

'Yes, I am. With Jonas Baines in Brighton.'

'I've heard of them. What sort are you?'

'Criminal.'

His eyebrows rose. 'You must meet some scumbags. Come to think about it, some of them are probably former pupils of mine.'

'We meet our fair share of rough characters I grant you, but everyone is entitled to a fair trial.'

There followed a discussion he had heard a hundred times, mainly from middle-class Little Englanders, about how street-wise punks played the system to their advantage, all to the detriment of the hard-pressed British taxpayer. Difference was, neither Michael nor Julia would have described themselves as such. He worked in a so-so comprehensive in South London, and she in the Probation Service.

'Jonas Baines is the place where I've been reading one lawyer was murdered and another fell under a train. Were they colleagues of yours?'

'Yes they were. The guy murdered worked in the same office as me, and the guy who fell under the train from the one next door.'

'Good Lord. You must have known them both well?'

He nodded, fighting back emotion.

'It's a terrible business. It must be very hard for you.'

'It was, and still is.'

'I've read quite a bit on the topic, knowing you were coming today. It's difficult to see what someone would gain by breaking into a lawyer's office. Lawyers are known for robbing people blind, but most money is moved across wires nowadays.'

'We can't fathom a reason for it either.'

'Perhaps the killer was searching for some incriminating documents, or doing the opposite, planting them.'

This sparked a thought. The last time he'd met Hassan Khouri in the casino, he'd been taken aback by the man's insatiable interest in Martin's murder, and his hostility towards Raymond Schofield. Despite Schofield being on the periphery of the murder investigation, Khouri had instantly managed to turn the conversation back to him. This had encouraged Robinson to see if there was a connection between the two men on the web.

About five years back, he'd read, when Ray and Rebecca were still a happy couple, she had gone to Khouri's surgery for a nose job and some lip enhancing. When the bruising and redness abated, Schofield claimed her features were worse than they were before. Khouri claimed he had followed Mrs Schofield's instructions to the letter, even suggesting she might have had the operation to spite her husband.

Schofield went bananas and took to social media with a vengeance. The story taken up by the tabloids, some publishing pictures of Rebecca and Khouri out on the town, suggesting an affair was behind the enmity. What if Khouri, or someone in his pay, had gone to Jonas Baines to plant some incriminating evidence in Mrs Schofield's divorce file, and Martin had disturbed him?

It was one thing to plant or steal documents, the actions of a petty thief or burglar, but another to stab a stranger, the actions of a killer. However, there was something dark and mysterious about Khouri he couldn't quite grasp. He had always put it down to cultural differences, believing Brits were more open and revealing about their private lives than those from the Middle East. Now, he wasn't so sure. Perhaps he needed to keep a closer eye on Brighton's famous celebrity cosmetic surgeon.

TWENTY-EIGHT

She turned and put her glass down on the small, cluttered table surrounding the pillar. Clare and Ray were standing in the bar of the Criterion Theatre during the interval of a dreary play which Ray wanted to see.

It was clear to her the heads of big companies were such driven men they had no time to appreciate culture. Yes, many of their businesses supported the arts. They sponsored exhibitions, plays, and pumped money into ballet and opera, but she would bet when they were sitting in their expensive box seat they were only thinking if sales would meet their targets, and if managers would come under their cost budgets. This wasn't because they were vacuous or thick, although some undoubtably were, just time poor.

'Hello Ray, how are you?' a man who suddenly appeared out of the melee around them asked. He stuck out his hand.

'I'm fine,' Ray said, returning his handshake.

'What are you up to these days?'

'Apart from getting divorced and giving away a large slice of my fortune?'

They both laughed.

'I've established a vehicle to invest in start-ups. Not so I can make another pile of money, but to solve some of society's more pressing problems.'

'In what sorts of areas are you thinking about investing?'

'In particular, I'll be looking at electric cars, battery development, household power generation, and Artificial Intelligence.'

On and on he droned. Clare noted the use of the word 'I'. It summed Ray up; he was a selfish bastard. Raybeck was founded on ideas generated by Rebecca, but according to their corporate literature, it was Ray's drive, determination, and his eye for the bottom line that brought them to fruition. Now, he was spouting ideas developed by Clare, ideas which stopped him becoming a lazy scumbag, heading down the pub the minute it opened. A huge self-centred streak permeated throughout Ray's life. If she'd thought she was the only woman in his life, as Ray frequently told her, it would have made her as naïve as any reality television contestant.

She had known for a long time about the other women ensconced in houses owned by him. At Raybeck, he would take trips out, ostensibly to visit coffee shops and health clubs, but she knew where he was going. His visits were somewhat curtailed at the moment, not because she was adept at satisfying his sexual desires, as she would only have sex with him if leaving it any longer would make him suspicious, but he had less reason to go out in the car. She didn't fear the women becoming frustrated or lonely; more likely, they were glad of the peace. They could thank her later.

The interval bell rang and Ray's visitor made his excuses and departed.

'That was an FT journalist I've dealt with before,' Ray said, taking her arm and walking back into the main body of the theatre.

'He could prove useful at some point in the future,' she said, 'if and when any of our companies decide to float.'

'I thought so too. How are you enjoying the play? I think the guy playing Jonathan Holbein is terrific, don't you think?'

'Yes, he is.'

The second half of the performance was worse than the first. Many of the red herrings and twists had been signalled as obvious as buses, but the main point of the story, about a ghost and the disappearance of a woman, failed to provide a satisfactory conclusion. She couldn't relate to the missing woman's plight and the poor acting of her distraught partner did little to convince.

'I thought it was brilliant,' Ray said as they walked out of the theatre. 'I loved it and could watch it again. Did you enjoy it, Clare?'

'Yes, I thought it was great.' If she said what she really thought, that it was dreary and ill conceived, Ray would sulk for the rest of the night and their late supper at Ernie's Bistro would turn into a damp squib.

Ernie's was packed when they entered, but she had expected it to be and had previously booked a table. It was just as well a member of staff led them to a vacant one, as Ray wouldn't stand any excuses about overbooking or losing their reservation. He would demand to see the manager right away, and if not available, he would cause a fuss until he was given their mobile number.

She wasn't big on eating generally, and after eight at night especially, despite feeling hungry. She'd had little to eat since a salad lunch around two, and didn't participate with Ray when his housekeeper, Lyn, made him a cheese sandwich a few hours before they left the house.

'What are you having?' he asked.

'I think I'll go for the fish.'

'I fancy a juicy big steak and a big meaty Barolo to go with it. I don't suppose you want to join me?'

'With the steak, or the wine?'

'The wine.'

'I don't think it will go well with sea bream.'

'Oh.'

'It's something I can't cook myself.'

'You cook fish. You do it for me.'

'I know, but I hate the smell that lingers for days. I like fish, but I don't like cooking it at home.'

'Can I get you something to drink?' The waiter who was now standing beside them asked, his pen poised.

'Indeed you can,' Ray said. 'I fancy a Barolo.'

'The Barolo we offer is this one,' the waiter said showing Ray the wine list, 'but it only comes by the bottle.'

'Not by the glass or half-bottle?'

'No sir, I am afraid not.'

'I can't interest you in the steak?' he asked Clare.

She rarely ate meat and never in the form of a steak. Ray knew this. She shook her head. 'No, thank you.'

'I'll just have the bottle, then,' he said to the waiter.

'Yes sir. And for you, madame?'

'A glass of Chablis.'

'We're ready to order food as well,' Ray said.

'No problem, sir.'

They ordered and sat back. It never ceased to amaze Clare how places like this could be busy serving food at ten o'clock on a Sunday night, and with new patrons arriving with monotonous regularity.

'Are you prepped for tomorrow's meeting?' he asked.

'As much as I'll ever be.'

'Tell me what you think. I haven't had a chance to look over the material yet.'

She gave him a look. What else had he been doing? His failure to read couldn't be due to time constraints as it had been at Raybeck, perhaps it was a lack of interest.

'They operate in the field of Artificial Intelligence.'

'I gathered as much.'

'The system they're developing is to streamline market research. Companies spend millions every year researching trends, either to improve existing products or launch new ones.'

'I'm listening but it's not grabbing me.'

'AI takes their research, adds in other analysis done elsewhere, such as industry data, and then extracts social media data.'

'Your Barolo, sir.'

Clare waited while Ray examined the label, took a sip, approved it, and invited the waiter to pour a large glass. Ray wasn't so discerning when it came to wine, it could be Pinot Noir or Cabernet Sauvignon for all he knew. The drinks served, she waited to see if Ray picked up the AI cudgel again or, bored with the topic, moved on to talk about something else. If so, she would visit the company in question alone.

'So,' he said, putting his glass down after taking a large slurp, 'this system takes all this information from those various places and does what with it?'

'It crunches the numbers, which allows the company to target markets more precisely. For example, a manufacturer of trainers will now be able to determine which areas within counties or states are the best places to spend their marketing budget. It can add to this the state of the weather, local trends, local terrain, and socio-economic data.'

'I like the social media angle. From what they know about us, they can extract age, gender, interests, political affiliations, the works; it's better and more accurate than is available from almost anywhere else.'

'What really sells this system is its precision, the speed of results, and the low operating cost, way cheaper than conventional market research.'

An hour later, they stepped outside and into a taxi. If she'd just chewed her way through a large sirloin and downed the best part of a bottle of wine, she would have walked back to the flat in Bayswater to burn some of it off. In Ray's case, he was so pissed, as he had not only drunk the wine, he'd also downed a couple of G&Ts at home, plus a few more in the theatre, he was in danger of heading in the wrong direction and wouldn't get home until the following morning.

The taxi dropped them outside the apartment in Queensborough Terrace, and like a couple of drunks, she staggered towards the door with Ray on her arm. They made it without mishap to the first floor. This was Ray's pied-à-terre in London, a place he had owned for over ten years. He would stay there after attending a late-night meeting or an after-work dinner, but always without Rebecca. She hated London and couldn't wait to return to Sussex, no matter the hour.

The apartment had been remodelled at great expense two years before, and still looked and smelled as if the decorators had recently departed. With Ray no longer working in central London, there wasn't much chance to use it, which only added to the not-so-lived-in feel.

'I'm knackered,' he said as she closed the front door and walked inside the apartment. 'I'm off to bed.'

'Don't you want to watch the programme on Netflix we talked about?'

'No, you watch it if you like. I'll catch it tomorrow. 'Night.'

'Goodnight.'

She headed into the lounge and turned on the television. Before sitting down, she went into the kitchen and filled a glass with water. The programme they had agreed to watch was a drama centred around Artificial Intelligence. She suspected it wouldn't contain much to help with the meeting tomorrow, but it would have succeeded in getting both of them into the right frame of mind.

It was far from certain if Ray would be in the right state of mind at all, as he could be a bear with a sore head when suffering with a hangover. When he was still chief executive, he didn't drink much. The responsibility of the top job weighed heavily and the chance that something could go wrong at any time of the day or night kept him on his toes. He seemed to be making up for it now, but the lack of practice had put him into the lightweight category.

Ten minutes in, she was getting bored. She got up and walked to the window and parted the curtains. It was a quiet street; on a Sunday night close to midnight, many lights were off and few people were walking the pavements. In London, on many streets like this, offices jostled cheek-by-jowl with residents, but she'd seen the buildings nearby in daylight and knew people lived there.

She closed the curtains and began mooching around the large bookcase and display unit which dominated one wall of the room. If she was intending having a long-term relationship with Ray, she would have put her stamp on this place long ago. Despite the recent redecoration, it still felt like a luxury man cave.

She knelt on the floor and opened a few cupboards, but most were empty, reflecting the London flat's position in Ray's scale of residences. She was looking for a safe, the last one on her list. She knew one was located here, as Ray had referred to it many years ago, but the problem was, she didn't know where it might be. She pulled open the large middle door, believing it to be bare, but lo and behold, a safe had been inserted into the wall at the back.

In common with some hotel safes she'd come across, this one was awkward to access. She was forced to lie on the floor with hands outstretched. She knew the combination, it was the same for all of Ray's safes, but given its position in an apartment he didn't often visit, its limited accessibility, and with Ray not being the nimblest of individuals, she wasn't hopeful.

She opened it and pulled out everything from inside. There was nothing obvious to suggest if the documents had been accessed, or added to lately, but at least she wasn't shrouded in dust.

Much of it related to Raybeck's takeover of Blake's Health Clubs, the place where she used to work. She sifted through the documents one at a time. A minute or so later, she came across what seemed like a flurry of correspondence between Ray and Allan Blake's wife, Tracey.

What she saw stopped her in her tracks. Many of the emails were dated months before Allan's death.

TWENTY-NINE

Henderson arrived in the office early, a large cup of coffee in his hand. On Sunday night, he and Kelly Jackson had gone out to a small restaurant, close to where she lived in East Hoathly. He had intended taking it easy on the alcohol so he could drive home, but they didn't leave the restaurant until late. They finished off a litre of the house's red wine, plus a couple of whiskies afterwards. Rather than call a taxi and have the problem of retrieving his car in the morning, he stayed over at her house.

Kelly had been through one divorce, same as himself, in her case to a banker five years before. It wasn't always helpful or healthy to talk about exes with a new partner, but Kelly's ex, Rob, would have made a good perpetrator in a psychological crime novel. He was a reluctant party in the divorce and resisted all the way. When the inevitable happened, he bombarded Kelly with texts, emails, and messages on social media. When this failed to work, she started receiving food deliveries, flowers, and Amazon parcels, none of which she'd ordered. At times, on a weekend, she would open the door to a delivery driver six times a day.

A court order and a stern police warning had kept him at bay, but Kelly had a lurking suspicion he could be making a comeback. Stalking was a major topic in the new book she was writing, but for a victim with first-hand experience, she was late in getting it to her publishers as she was finding the subject difficult to put into words.

Henderson managed to take a couple of sips from his cup before Steve Houghton breezed in.

'Morning, Angus. How are you?'

'Morning Steve, fine thanks. How's yourself?'

'I'm looking forward to the International at the weekend. Do you think your lot are in with a chance?'

'Are you going?'

'Yep. I received the tickets a couple of days ago.'

'Put it this way, I think we're better at rugby than we are at football.'

'I can't agree with you more, although with the match being played at Twickenham, I don't think Scotland have got a good record there.'

'You might be right. The forecast suggests it won't be cold or wet enough.'

'What's the latest on Martin Turner?'

'We've gone through all his criminal clients, as you know, and at the moment we're wading through Alex Vincent's.'

'The divorces?'

'Yes.'

'This is because Turner's body was found in his office?'

'Aye, but also because Vincent had reported the absence of some files, believed stolen by the intruder.'

'I remember you mentioned it. Why would the intruder do that?'

'There's nothing we can see to connect the missing files. Divorce files have disappeared, also Medical Negligence, and Business and Commercial.'

'It sounds like he was trying to cover his tracks, deflect us from the real reason for the break-in. Talking of Vincent, what's the latest?'

'I'm about to review all the CCTV evidence we have, see if we can determine for certain what happened to him.'

'Angus, I'm concerned about the cost and time being taken on this. Martin Turner, I accept, as it was a brutal murder, but the death of Alex Vincent is a clear suicide, everyone says so. We are wasting time and money confirming the blindingly obvious.'

'If we only had the Vincent death to deal with, I would be forced to agree with you. I probably wouldn't even have gone to see the incident and viewed the CCTV and written it off as yet another jumper, but I cannot ignore the fact that he's the second lawyer to die at Jonas Baines in suspicious circumstances. Their deaths must be related.'

'They're related all right. After hearing his mate was killed, Vincent topped himself out of remorse, or guilt.'

'There's no evidence to suggest Vincent was the least bit suicidal, nor was there a deep emotional connection between the two men. In many ways, they were simply colleagues working for the same firm.'

'Really?'

'Yes, no relationship beyond a working one. It wasn't from guilt either. His alibi that he was playing badminton in Henfield the night Turner was killed, checks out.'

'Hmmn.' He paused. 'Okay, take a look at the CCTV today, but if the verdict is still inconclusive or, as I suspect, it confirms suicide, I want this case closed. If, as you say, the perp removed a number of files, this is what the team needs to be concentrating on now. Right?'

'Yes, sir.'

Henderson woke up his pc while drinking his cooling coffee. He clicked on *The Argus* website to see what the press were saying about the death of Alex Vincent. It was hard to find the story beyond the day it had happened; just another suicide to add to the grim statistic: the greatest killer of men under the age of forty-five in the UK.

It was no different with the other local newspaper sites he looked at, and the story didn't appear at all in any of the nationals'. He'd bought a couple of Sunday papers the day before to see if one of the feature writers had done a piece. He could envision a series of intriguing-sounding articles: *Legally Dangerous*; *Is the Legal World too Stressful*; *Lawyers on the Brink*, or a statistical analysis comparing the death rate of lawyers to other professions. Having spent the majority of the afternoon and evening with Kelly, he hadn't yet had a chance to look through them.

He had told Steve Houghton about the list of Alex Vincent's clients and the law firm's attempts at identifying the missing files, believed stolen by the intruder. What he didn't go on to say was they had compared Vincent's list to that of Martin Turner, and the name of Raymond Schofield tumbled out. He was the only one to hit the bullseye three times in a row: he was a criminal client of Turner, his wife had engaged Vincent to represent her in their forthcoming divorce, and her file was missing.

Trevor Robinson had told them it was not uncommon for the wife of a serious criminal, facing years in prison, to issue divorce proceedings. They didn't want to spend such a long period on their own, and some were ashamed of the crime which their partner had committed, others to be associated with such a cruel or corrupt person. The DI wasn't sure what the appearance of Schofield's name meant, as he could see no reason why he would murder Martin Turner, but he would store it at the back of his mind for future reference, as he believed it to be significant.

Walters appeared in the doorway, bearing files and looking business-like. 'Ready, gov?'

'Aye, as I'll ever be.'

He picked up his own papers and they headed out. They walked downstairs, out of their building and across the car park to the CCTV control room.

'How are they getting on with Alex Vincent's clients?' he asked.

'The team are concentrating on those who've ticked two boxes: they're a client of Alex Vincent and Martin Turner, or if they're a client of Vincent or Turner with files missing.'

'How's it going?'

'Once we've got a few names, we'll talk to the folks at Jonas Baines and try to determine if the missing documents would have had a material effect on the defendants' cases. Would it be enough to impact the financial settlement in a divorce case, for example, or to reduce the impact of a criminal defendant's evidence, forcing their lawyer to present a weaker defence?'

'All this is ongoing?'

'As we speak.'

They walked into a room with multiple CCTV screens, and operators monitoring a live feed from county-wide cameras. They were led to a bank of four screens where the tapes from Brighton Station, and those from a variety of town centre cameras, had been loaded. With luck, the footage would contain the last known moments of Alex Vincent, and a clear illustration of the movement of the man standing behind him.

The operator instructed them on how to use the controls and left them to it. On Screen 1, the pictures they had already seen from the camera looking across the platform. On Screen 2, pictures from another camera located close to the buffers and facing down the tracks. On Screens 3 and 4, the movements of passengers as they exited Brighton Station.

They ran the pictures on the first two screens. The detectives were familiar with the content of Screen 1 and used it as a reference to view Screen 2. This time it wasn't a platform-centric camera, set up to monitor passengers as they joined and alighted from trains, but a ticket office-based camera looking across all platforms.

They could zoom in and out, but their view was obscured by the gaggle of girls to Vincent's left. When the train arrived, they were standing so close to the platform edge, one of them could easily have fallen on the tracks.

They called the CCTV operator over and asked him to change the video to another based on the platform opposite. Henderson reckoned it would be more useful, as its field of vision might not be obstructed by a stationary train.

With this camera loaded, they saw Vincent take up his position facing the camera. The girls to his left were messing around, causing him to look over, and he did the same with the boys on his other side who were equally animated, and looked capable of accidentally knocking him onto the tracks. Moments later, the man with the coat draped on his shoulders moved in behind Vincent.

It was more obvious now how close behind Vincent the mystery man stood. It begged the question, if his presence was innocent, why was he there? He could have moved further up the platform where there were less people. However, even Henderson, not a regular train passenger, knew that some people would only travel in specific train carriages; some had to face the same direction as the train was moving, and others liked to sit in the same seat every day.

The train arrived and Vincent fell. They turned it back, and this time had the option of slow motion. Focussing on his face, they could see Vincent didn't have his teeth gritted, or the determined expression of a jumper, but the shocked expression of the unforeseen.

'We still can't see from this angle if he was pushed,' Henderson said, 'as there's little discernible movement from the guy behind. What I would say is the look on Vincent's face is unequivocal.'

'He didn't mean to jump.'

'Question is, did he slip or was he pushed?'

'I'm sure he didn't slip.'

'What if he edged too far forward because he thought the guy behind was invading his personal space?'

'Let's look at his feet.'

They ran the sequence again, focussing only on Vincent's feet.

'Nope,' Walters said, after it finished, 'he didn't shuffle forward, and his feet were well back from the edge.'

'If he did slip, his movement would have been different. It would have been one leg in front of the other and with his arms flailing all over the place. Both legs would not slip at the same time.'

'I agree.'

'I'm confident the guy behind pushed him, but with so little body movement it didn't even register.'

'The key thing is we need to find this guy. He's the only person who can tell us what really happened.'

'If he pushed him or pressurised him in some way,' Henderson said, 'he's not about to give himself up voluntarily.'

'This is why we need to find a good picture of him.'

They started up the video on Screen 3, watching the man walk out of Brighton Station towards Queen's

Road. He was keeping his head down, the trilby-style hat he wore set low over his eyes.

'He looks tall, trim and muscled, and judging by the smart clothes, which I would say sit easily on him, this isn't a bricklayer or a shop assistant dressed up. We're looking for a dapper gent.'

'If he's done what we think he's done, no way can he be called a gentleman.'

THIRTY

Henderson woke but he hadn't slept well. He'd been dreaming about a man in a trilby hat coming into his apartment and attacking him. It had forced him awake two or three times, the last time, leaving him bathed in sweat. He was sleeping alone, as he and Kelly were taking it slowly, mindful of her experience with her ex. In any case, she had a publishing deadline to meet and needed to spend much of her time writing.

There was nothing else for it; he got up, showered, dressed, drank a cup of tea and then drove into the office. He was so early, many of the night shift were still working.

On his desk in front of him he placed two sets of photographs. On one side, pictures of the man who had broken into the offices of Jonas Baines taken from their security camera, on the other, the man in the trilby hat walking through town. For the deaths of Turner and Vincent to be connected, as he believed they were, both victims had to be killed by the same man. He knew of killers working in tandem, or paid assassins who carried out one murder while their paymaster performed the other, but in his mind, statistics were against it.

The key thing he was looking at was body shape. The man in the trilby looked slim, with a strong upper body, but he wasn't fat, or conversely, with the defined physique of a weightlifter. It was hard to be too sure as the coat he wore had been kept draped over his shoulders and it did a good job of hiding the complete picture.

The intruder at Jonas Baines was wearing tighter clothes and yes, he did look equally tall and slim with broad shoulders. Henderson found an image of his face, a partial with his head down and woolly hat covering his head, but it was the nose he was looking at. It was noticeable, not because it was prominent, but elegant and styled. He believed it was called a Roman nose, straight down with no bone bump, and thin.

Next, he did the same with the man in the trilby hat. They had a fairly decent picture of him before he disappeared from view at the bottom of Queens Road, close to the Clocktower. He had looked up towards the camera when he almost collided with another pedestrian. Not a full facial, as much was hidden by the hat. Henderson was no expert, but the noses looked the same. He needed someone else to look at it, in case he was seeing what he wanted to see, so it would be parked for later.

A rumbling stomach reminded him he hadn't eaten breakfast, and he decided to remedy this now. He left his office, descended the stairs and walked across the car park. It was no surprise to see a lot of movement, mainly cars driving in. As well as police officers working shifts, admin staff were employed to ensure the 999 service operated 24/7, and IT staff were doing the same with the computer systems.

The restaurant was quiet; he was in that little window before the next upsurge, those coming in for breakfast at eight. He chose a bacon and egg roll with a large mug of tea, a dish he didn't have time to make for himself in the morning. It was too early for any of his team, so instead of looking for a familiar face to sit beside, he took a newspaper that he found lying on another table, and his breakfast, to a table near a window.

The first bite was delicious, even more so as he had been eating less meat since meeting Kelly. She was vegetarian, had been since her early teens, and was forever encouraging him to try meat-free options in restaurants and teasing him about the contents of his fridge and cupboards.

He flicked through the newspaper, seeing if any article caught his eye. He wasn't expecting to find anything about Alex Vincent's death, if his troll of internet news sites the day before was anything to go by. He was about to turn to the sport and see how the Albion were doing, when he decided to flick through the business section.

He often found, when wrestling with a major investigation, reading articles about business and sport, subjects completely unrelated to police work, put his own issues and problems into some sort of perspective. It wasn't to belittle what he did, but reading about businesses struggling under mountains of debt, or a football team plagued with injuries, ensured he didn't forget that other people had many big issues to overcome as well.

A short article about Raymond Schofield caught his eye. It was a puff piece, written probably following no more than a five-minute phone call between a journalist and their subject. It was enough for any self-respecting journalist to generate a five-hundred-word article, which many achieved by repeating the same points several times over.

In essence, it was designed to keep Schofield's name in the public consciousness by informing us what he was up to now, following the process of divesting himself of his former business empire. It sounded a laudable ambition for him to be investing in new businesses aimed at social improvement.

Henderson had viewed him as an aggressive businessman, of which he'd met hundreds, and no matter how they dressed up their praiseworthy aims, their focus was all too often on the bottom line and the size of their bonuses. Perhaps this time he had misjudged the man, but as his name had checked three boxes on his checklist, he imagined he would be talking to him again soon.

Henderson left the staff restaurant and while walking across one of the smaller car parks, spotted Steve Houghton heading his way. Often, if they met like this, Henderson would give him a quick update on the current case, and he would do the same from his perspective. This time, he would want to know the result of their CCTV analysis.

Yet again, it was hard to draw any other conclusion than to believe he was pushed, based on Vincent's movement and facial expression, but there was no firm evidence to back it up. This would encourage Houghton to tell Henderson to drop the investigation and mark Alex Vincent's death as suicide. He ducked behind a high-sided 4x4, tying his shoelaces until the CI passed.

Henderson walked past his office and into the Detectives' Room. It was beginning to fill now. He headed over to the three whiteboards in the corner, now covered in pictures, notes, and with lines joining connections, all related to the murder of Martin Turner. His phone rang. Expecting it to be Houghton, because he'd surely seen his less-than-subtle swerving routine, he was surprised to find it wasn't.

'DI Henderson.'

'Hello sir, it's Sam on Reception. I've got a Ms Clare Mitchell to see you.'

'Did she say what she wanted?'

'She said she had some information that you might find useful.'

'Okay Sam, I'll be there in a few minutes.'

He left the Detectives' Room and walked downstairs into Reception. It was human nature, in situations like this, for the interviewer to glance across the line of those waiting to guess who their subject might be, but also to suss out those who they hoped it wouldn't be. It wasn't the guy with tats around his neck, the young girl with the lank hair who looked like a drug user, or the nervous businessperson in a suit who was clearly wondering how he had ended up here. It had to be the gorgeous lady at the end.

When Sam on the desk had dealt with his enquirer, he looked over. 'Ah, DI Henderson.'

'Yes.'

'The lady sitting there,' he said nodding, 'the one on the end.' His eyebrows rose in appreciation. 'I'm putting you in Interview Room 4.'

'Thanks.'

He turned and walked towards his visitor, who seemed to be unfazed by the flotsam of society around her, the institutional furniture, and the grim posters warning about aids, dirty needles, and stalkers. She looked up when she heard his approach.

'Clare Mitchell?'

'Yes,' she said.

'I'm Detective Inspector Angus Henderson.'

She stood and they shook hands.

'I understand you'd like to speak to me.'

'I do. Is there somewhere we can talk privately?'

'Yes, if you will just follow me, we can use an interview room.'

'Fine.'

She was tall, a few centimetres above his shoulder height, and while walking, he noticed how she carried herself well, like a catwalk model, aware of her posture.

They took up positions either side of the table. 'Despite this being an interview room,' he said, 'none of the recording equipment is operating.'

'Suits me fine.'

She spoke with little trace of an accent and if he was guessing, and judging by the smart business clothes, the neat makeup, and the styled hair, he'd imagine her to be the head of a London-based PR agency or television company. He knew her by name, at least, after viewing pictures of Ray Schofield with her on his arm. The photographs didn't do her justice.

'I've come to see you this morning as I have information which implicates Raymond Schofield in several serious crimes, including murder.'

THIRTY-ONE

Henderson looked at Clare Mitchell, the words she had said filling him with concern and confusion in equal measure. He was beginning to think Ray Schofield was grease-coated, with his name appearing in many parts of this investigation but with no incriminating evidence sticking. Was this about to change? Even if it was, he realised he had to tread carefully, otherwise he would have Houghton to answer to.

'What's your relationship to Mr Schofield?'

'I'm, to all intents and purposes, his girlfriend. Nowadays, I'm also his business partner, although sometimes I do wonder.'

'Are you referring to the investment vehicle you and Mr Schofield are starting up, the one recently featured in *The Financial Times*?'

'You saw it?'

He nodded. 'It was reprinted in *The Times*.'

'I'm impressed, not many policemen, I suspect, read the business pages.'

'You could be right.'

'You might not have noticed, but it goes to prove the point I just made, no mention of me is made in there.'

'Why would you want to pass incriminating information to me about your partner and business colleague? Some might suggest you have an ulterior motive. Is this it?'

'I said I'm ostensibly Ray's girlfriend, but I know he has many others. Several are installed in houses owned by him. Putting them to one side, before I joined Raybeck, Ray's company which he recently sold, I was Financial Director of Blake's Health Clubs, an operator of twelve large gyms, based in Kent. It was owned by a man called Allan Blake, a person I highly respected.'

'I know some of this story. He was the man who drowned when Schofield's yacht was hit by a bad storm.'

Her eyebrows rose. 'Is your interest in this personal or professional?'

'His name has turned up in another investigation.'

'Interesting. I have information to prove Ray Schofield killed Allan Blake.'

Henderson's confusion returned. He could see a way forward with Houghton if this meant new charges, but not with something Schofield had already been acquitted on. Plus, he was sceptical there could be any new evidence about a yacht drowning.

She removed from her case a sheaf of papers and placed them on the table. She pushed them over to the DI: email printouts, bank statements, and hand-written notes.

He intended to speed-read them, but soon realised Schofield and his correspondent, Tracey Blake, didn't believe in wasting words. In fact, in the space of ten minutes he'd read every one, twice.

He paused for a minute, thinking. 'If I'm reading these correctly, Mr Schofield was in negotiation to buy Blake's Health Clubs from Tracey Blake, months before Allan's death, on the proviso that he didn't return from his sailing trip.'

'Macabre, isn't it? Tracey had taken no interest in the business in all the time I've known her, but she was planning to divorce him. She had a new boyfriend and wanted the whole fifty-million that Ray was willing to pay for the company all to herself.'

'Why take the risk? Why not wait for the business to be sold, then divorce him? Twenty-five million's a lot in anybody's book.'

'She'd signed a prenup. She wouldn't get a penny from the sale of the business. Why should she, when she had never been interested or involved? Plus, Allan had been rebuffing Ray for years; he didn't want to sell. Only with him out of the way was Ray able to buy it.'

'Does Mr Schofield still have the laptop those emails were sent from?'

She thought for a moment. 'He's got a new one, but I'm sure the old one is sitting in a cupboard at the house in Warninglid. Why?'

'A smart lawyer could try and discredit these as fakes or forgeries. If we have the laptop they were sent from, it provides a more compelling argument.'

'I'll get it for you.'

'There's no need for you to take any unnecessary risks. With this information, I could get a court order to search the place.'

'You said 'could', does that mean you have some reservations?'

'I do, I wouldn't embark on this course of action without giving it a lot of consideration first. This is a serious accusation, Ms Mitchell, against a well-respected public figure.'

This new accusation presented him with two problems. One, the difficulty going after such a high-profile individual as Raymond Schofield. Two, landing another, unrelated murder on his plate.

'Why would Mr Schofield keep such incriminating information? If he deleted the emails, we would all be none the wiser.' As Henderson asked the question, he realised the answer.

'Ray is a conniving sod and trusts no one,' she explained. 'Fearing that Tracey would double-cross him if he was implicated in Allan's death, he kept them hidden in his London flat, ready for his lawyer to retrieve. This way, if he goes down, she would go down with him.'

'Conniving, right enough.'

'If that doesn't convince you about Ray, this might.'

She handed over another piece of paper, this time looking more like the output from banking software. He noticed the total figure, a few thousand short of five hundred million pounds.

'Those are amounts Ray has hidden away in Caribbean banks, not to be included in his divorce declaration.'

'His divorce from...Rebecca, isn't it?'

'When I mentioned to her that I had the schedule, she told me she had previously supplied it to her divorce lawyer.'

'Just to be clear,' Henderson said, '*The Times* article we talked about earlier stated he pocketed around eight hundred million from the sale of his businesses. He squirreled five-hundred-million away in those Caribbean banks, and he's saying he's only worth three-fifty, of which Rebecca is entitled to half.'

'Newspapers always publish rounded figures, it makes it easier for readers to understand, but you're more or less correct. As Raybeck's former FD, I assure you, the sums do add up.'

'How does he account for the missing money? The eight hundred million number is being used by all the newspapers I've seen.'

'He's produced dummy documents from friendly banks and financial institutions saying he spent it on consultant fees, bank charges, and repaying loans.'

'If this is what he did, and I've no reason to doubt you, it's morally reprehensible, but it's not illegal. Divorce is a civil matter, not criminal. I believe Russian oligarchs salt money away all the time.'

'I know it's a civil matter, but I'm not just talking about divorce. I'm talking about a motive for the murder of Martin Turner at Jonas Baines, and possibly Alex Vincent as well.'

'Go on.'

'The schedule you have in front of you was removed from a safe at Ray Schofield's Bayswater apartment in London.'

'By you?'

'Yes. It had only been in the safe a matter of weeks as before then, it was in a file in Alex Vincent's office at Jonas Baines.'

Henderson could immediately see the implications of this. 'You think it was removed the night of the murder by the killer?'

'I'm sure of it. You see, it was originally taken from Ray's office by Rebecca and handed to Alex Vincent to form part of the divorce settlement.'

'But it disappeared following the break-in?'

'Yes.'

'How do you know this is the same schedule and isn't a copy?'

'I've talked to Rebecca and she assures me it is. If you don't believe me, turn it over.'

He did so.

'That's Rebecca's handwriting,' she said pointing. 'When she first got hold of it, she made a series of notes to remind her of some of the abbreviations used by banks.'

'How do you think Ray managed to retrieve this document? We have CCTV of the intruder and from memory, Mr Schofield isn't as tall or as well-built as the person in the pictures.'

'I don't think he would have done it personally, he never does the dirty stuff himself, but he knows a great number of people, some of whom work with Pete Hammond.'

'Who?'

'He's Ray's odd-job man, but he's more than that. Yes, he can fix washing machines and mends fences, but when Ray was at Raybeck, Pete was responsible for dealing with protestors, problematic tenants, and for silencing a journalist who was engaged in a long-running hate campaign against Ray.'

'I wouldn't think a leisure business attracts much aggro.'

'You'd be surprised. With the coffee shops, people would object to a big chain putting local coffee shops out of business, while on the hotel side, we were often accused of desecrating local icons. Most of the time, they were referring to unsightly water towers or crumbling windmills, but some people will protest at anything.'

'Pete's role in this was what?'

'He was in charge of organising a group of guys to break-up protests, eject problem tenants from properties owned by Ray, all manner of things.'

'So, you think Hammond, or someone else, broke into Jonas Baines and retrieved the financial schedule?'

'I'm sure of it. It's not beyond Hammond's range of skills. He's a former soldier with several convictions for violence.'

Henderson had already noted Hammond's name. He put the words PNC - Police National Computer – check, beside it.

'I can see how this gives Pete Hammond or someone else, a motive for being in the offices of Jonas Baines at night, and I thank you for that, but you also said you had reason to believe Ray was also behind Alex Vincent's death.'

'Yes, when I was in St Lucia with Ray a week ago, I heard him talking to Pete Hammond, yelling at him, in fact, to get rid of someone. Days later Alex Vincent was dead.'

'Why would he want to kill Alex Vincent?'

'Rebecca told me she was creating such a stink about losing this financial schedule, Alex had decided to talk to forensic accountants who would go over Ray's financials with a fine tooth-comb. He killed him to stop it happening.'

THIRTY-TWO

'I wish I'd been there,' Walters said to Henderson, as they walked between buildings towards the Custody Suite.

'Why?'

'To see your reaction. Me and Phil looked her up on the web, and when he saw her pictures he went gaga. I have to admit, even cynical me was impressed.'

'Well, you can tell him and anyone else who's interested, she's a very attractive woman, but no way did I go gaga. She's also principled. Don't forget, it must have taken a mountain of courage for her to walk in here. At the end of the day, she's biting the hand that feeds her.'

'She won't starve. According to the papers, Schofield gave her ten mill when he sold Raybeck.'

'He might decide to take it back if, or when, we charge him.'

'What's the verdict? Do you think we will?'

'You've seen the emails, what do you think?'

'It's pretty damning stuff.'

'You said it.'

They walked into the Custody Suite. They found Raymond Schofield in Room Three, sitting at the table with the celebrated Brighton lawyer, Jeffrey Campbell. Henderson expected nothing less from the millionaire businessman. Aside from Martin Turner's defence team at Jonas Baines, Campbell was the best in the business. He just hoped the brief hadn't instructed his client to keep schtum.

Housekeeping complete, Henderson looked over at Schofield. He looked tanned, relaxed and confident. The DI imagined he had faced many situations like this: negotiating to buy a business they didn't want to sell, trying to raise capital to finance a new venture, being grilled by rapacious journalists with a hidden agenda. To him, it would simply appear as an intractable problem, requiring the deployment of skilful negotiation and tact to overcome.

'Mr Schofield, thank you for coming in here today.'

'I'm always happy to help the police.'

The last time they'd met, he had been dressed in casual clothes, and not his more familiar sharp business attire. It was the same again now, a black jacket and white shirt, but he still looked elegant. His combed back, thick brown and grey hair must have been cut regularly, or it didn't grow much, as it looked the same as the hundreds of pictures of him that were on the web.

'I'd like to talk to you about your purchase of Blake's Health Clubs.'

He didn't know what Schofield expected to be questioned about, but clearly it wasn't this. He looked suitably taken aback.

'Erm, I'd wanted to expand into the health clubs market for some time. I owned hotels, coffee shops, and marinas, so stock market analysts considered us a leisure business, and talked about us in the same sentence as Center Parcs or Thorpe Park, which was crap. The addition of health clubs would move us into the lifestyle and fitness sectors, places where I wanted the company to go. You see, I'd also planned to buy a chain of sports shops and start a sports clothing brand, but this all got superseded by the decision I made to sell-up.'

'What made you do it?'

'I'm sure it was reported at the time, but I saw the light after the death of my beloved mother, rapidly followed by a health scare; a dodgy ticker requiring the fitting of a pacemaker.'

'I see. I understand the owner of Blake's Health Clubs, Allan Blake, was reluctant to sell.'

'I hope,' Campbell said, 'you are not trying to drag up that old murder charge again. My client was exonerated with a clear conscience, thanks to all the good work done by Martin Turner and his team at Jonas Baines, God rest his soul.'

My goodness. Jeffrey Campbell never ceased to amaze him. Here he was not only expressing empathy, but religion too, principles he imagined the man was devoid of.

'I'm not dragging up anything, merely trying to establish the background to the takeover.'

'I'd approached Allan over the years, but each time he refused to sell. On my last approach, he told me he'd had testicular cancer. An op had got rid of it, as they'd spotted it early, but it gave him a scare. I thought a cruise on my boat would do him good, and before you get out the violins, I also thought he might be more willing to cash in his chips.'

'You bought the business from his widow?'

'She was reluctant to sell at the start, she wanted to preserve Allan's legacy and all that, but when I told her about his change of heart on the boat, and she realised the business would only be a burden she didn't need, she relented.'

'Allan Blake changed his mind?'

'Yes, on the boat and over a few whiskies he told me of his intention to retire.'

'He wasn't old. Mid-fifties I believe.'

'Same age as me, but a health scare changes a man. I think he'd had enough and wanted to focus on his well-being.'

'So, you returned from your trip, you were acquitted at trial, and when the dust settled over Allan Blake's disappearance, Tracey decided to sell.'

'That's about the sum of it. We settled on a fair price and she went away happy.'

'That isn't quite true, though, is it?'

'Are you calling me a liar?'

He fixed Henderson with a steely stare, an intimidating look, part-malice, part-probing, honed to perfection, no doubt, in update meetings, budget discussions, and financing negotiations. The DI had to admit, it made him feel unnerved.

'Did you speak to Tracey before your ill-fated yacht trip, trying to persuade her to sell, and for her to work on Allan, to encourage him?'

'We'd met a couple of times for dinner: me, Rebecca, him and Tracey, so it wasn't true that I hadn't spoken to her before. What we didn't speak about was the business; why would we? She took no interest in the health clubs at all. If she did, I might have tried to get her to talk to Allan about it, but the way things were, he wouldn't listen to her. She had no credibility on that front in his eyes.'

'What then, Mr Schofield, do you make of this?'

Henderson opened the folder in front of him and passed over three of the most incriminating emails. They were now encased in protective clear folders. At the moment, it was the only evidence they had and he couldn't risk them being scrunched or torn to bits by an angry Schofield.

His reaction took Henderson by surprise. His face took on a furious look and his lightly tanned hue turned bright red, a Scandinavian after two days in the Spanish sun.

'Where the fuck did you get these?' he shouted, waving one of the emails around. Henderson was glad of their plastic protection.

He sprang to his feet and began pacing the floor, the email gripped tightly in his hand. If he made a beeline for the door, Henderson would stop him, if need be, by arresting him. The meeting today was only an exploratory interview, but if he could not provide a satisfactory explanation to dismiss the evidence, the ramifications were serious.

'This is outrageous,' Campbell said, 'springing this on my client.'

'Before you go on accusing me, Mr Campbell, remember this is not a formal interview, I can do what I like. However, I suggest you do not encourage your client to leave.'

'Or what?'

'You know what. Mr Schofield, please sit down.'

'This is unbelievable. Where did you get these?' He spun around, threw the email on the table, and put his hands down, glaring at Henderson. 'Did that bitch give them to you? I should never have trusted her.'

'Which bitch are you referring to? I understand there are several.'

'Hmph'.

'Sit down!'

He pulled out the seat and sat, his face thunderous.

'Now,' Henderson said, 'what those emails make clear is that you were in negotiation to buy the business from Mrs Blake in the weeks and months before her husband's death. This contradicts what you told me earlier, and indeed, what was said at your trial.'

'Ray, don't answer that,' Campbell boomed. 'You'll perjure yourself.'

'I'm not as sharp as I used to be,' Schofield said. 'I must have got the dates mixed up.'

Henderson gave him a sceptical look. There was nothing wrong with Schofield's brain, or indeed his ability to try and brazen this out.

'The dates are only one part of it. What explanation can you give me for the content of those emails? They are not conversational in the least. They are short and snappy, more like a business negotiation. Wouldn't you agree?'

Schofield was lost for words, maybe for the first time in his career.

'I draw your attention to the phrase, *If Allan doesn't come back, the business is yours*. This sounds like an invitation for Allan Blake to have a nice little accident.'

'I didn't kill him, he fell over the side of the boat. It's a coincidence.'

'I must protest, Detective Inspector. My client has already been exonerated on this charge. You cannot accuse him of it again without new evidence. These emails don't prove anything.'

Henderson ignored him. 'Raymond Schofield, you are under arrest on suspicion of murdering Allan Blake. You do not have to say anything, but it may harm your defence if you do not mention when questioned something which you later rely on in court. Anything you do say may be given in evidence. Do you understand?'

THIRTY-THREE

It was some hours after Ray Schofield had been charged that he calmed down. Henderson and Walters made their way again to the interview room.

While he was being booked in, a search warrant had been issued and a team were now sifting through the contents of his Warninglid property. Clare Mitchell had told Henderson about the house Schofield owned in London, one in Portugal, and another in St Lucia. Henderson would wait until the Warninglid search was concluded, his main residence, before he would decide what to do about the others.

This time, Schofield was being interviewed under caution, meaning anything he said now could be used in court. All the lights were illuminated on the recording equipment

'Mr Schofield, I'm not here to talk to you about the death of Allan Blake.'

'No? What is it this time? An old cold case you found in your files this morning? Are you keeping me here just to improve your stats or something?'

'I will speak to you about Allan Blake's death in due course, but for the moment I want to talk to you about your divorce from Rebecca.'

'Why? What's that got to do with you people?'

'Bear with me and all will be revealed.'

'I can't wait.'

Henderson didn't say anything: he had raised the subject and it was up to Schofield to respond.

'What can I say?' he said with an exaggerated shrug. 'We were married for twenty seven years and fell out of love. The spark evaporated, for want of a better metaphor. It happens to even the best marriages; one day I decided I'd had enough and wanted a divorce.'

'The way she tells it, based on the various newspaper articles I've read, it was more to do with your affairs with various women. The straw that broke the camel's back, to use another metaphor, was your dalliance with her best friend, Sylvie Goss.'

'She says this, and I say that. I don't care. It will all come out in court and be pored over endlessly by the tabloids in any case.'

'Rebecca is being represented by lawyers at Jonas Baines. Alex Vincent, to be precise.'

'Poor guy, such a gruesome way to die, under the wheels of a train.'

'Hear, hear,' his lawyer, Jeffrey Campbell said.

'Following a break-in at Jonas Baines in the early hours of 8th February, four weeks ago, when one of their lawyers was stabbed to death, a number of documents were discovered to be missing. This includes one I have since supplied to Mr Campbell and I'm showing the defendant now. It lists a series of Caribbean bank accounts all in your name, Mr Schofield, with the balance of all the accounts displayed. In total, it amounts to around five hundred million pounds.'

Schofield's anger showed once again, but as this indiscretion wouldn't award him any more jail time, it didn't reach the volcanic heights of the earlier interview.

Schofield was about to say something, when Campbell laid a hand on his arm, a sign for him to shut up.

'This is money,' Henderson continued, 'which I believe you moved off-shore to stop your wife's lawyers including it within your declaration of assets.'

'This is conjecture, Inspector,' Campbell said.

'It's not conjecture, Mr Campbell. I've seen the recreated divorce files at Jonas Baines. I assure you, none of those accounts and amounts are listed there.'

'Listen, Henderson, this is a shit-load of money that was earned through long hours and bloody hard work. Why wouldn't I try to hide it? I'll tell you the reason, I didn't want that scheming bitch to get her steely claws into it.'

There it was, the condescending 'B' word once again. Was this how Schofield regarded women, even those close to him?

'I know it's a lot of money, Mr Schofield. It's an amount most people would do anything to lay their hands on.'

'What are you trying to imply?'

'The schedule you have in front of you was lodged with Alex Vincent at Jonas Baines, but around the night of the break-in resulting in the death of Martin Turner, it went missing. The schedule was supplied by your wife, Rebecca, which she said she found in your office.'

'The conniving cow.'

'Where did your copy come from, Inspector?' Campbell asked.

'I'm not at liberty to say, but as it's covered in Mr Schofield's fingerprints, it's safe to say he's seen it before.'

Schofield's demeanour darkened and his face took on the expression of a cornered cat. 'I know where she bloody well got it,' he growled.

Henderson had warned Clare Mitchell to be on her guard once he had questioned Schofield. There would be enough clues bandied about in an interview for him to know exactly who had done the dirty on him.

'If this document has been obtained by illegal means,' Campbell intoned, 'you, of all people, should know it cannot be used in a court of law.'

'It hasn't been obtained illegally,' Henderson said.

'Yeah,' Schofield said, 'it's out of my bloody safe in London.'

Schofield wasn't the slow, half-wit he claimed to be earlier. It did indeed come out of the safe in London, but what Henderson wanted to know was how it got there.

'It's not the divorce itself that concerns me, Mr Schofield. Did you, or did you not, send someone into Jonas Baines to recover this document?'

'Inspector, you're fishing with no bait. My client doesn't need to answer.'

'I'm not accusing you of doing it personally, Mr Schofield. It's not your profile that appears on CCTV pictures we have of the perpetrator, nor does your name appear in the visitor log.'

'I've haven't been anywhere near their offices since the trial.'

Henderson said nothing, waiting for him to continue.

'I know they had an intruder there.'

'If you remember, we came to your house in Warninglid to talk to you about it.'

'What are you fucking implying,' he exploded, his face red and angry. 'I told you, Martin Turner did a great job for me, why the hell would I kill him?'

'Sit down, Mr Schofield.'

'I'm warning you,' he said leaning on the desk and pointing a finger at Henderson's face, 'if you're trying to fit me up because you didn't get me first time round, I'll have you. That break-in and the murder of Martin Turner had nothing to do with me, or Pete.'

'Pete?'

'What? Did I say Pete? I meant just me.' Schofield looking confused, returned to his seat.

'I take it you're referring to Pete Hammond?'

'How do you...? I suppose with your lot raking through my stuff, his name must have appeared somewhere.'

'From the financials, he looks like an employee. If he is, what does he do?'

'He sorts problems out for me.'

'What sorts of problems?'

'In addition to the Antigua and Portugal houses, I own a number of properties in the Sussex area with sitting tenants. It was,' he said with a dismissive wave of the hand, 'an abortive move into the retail property market that eventually ran out of steam. If anything goes wrong, the likes of burst pipes or loose roof tiles, Pete goes over and fixes it.'

'So, he's a handyman?'

'In a manner of speaking.'

'Did you ask Pete Hammond to go to Jonas Baines and retrieve the schedule of secreted money for you?'

'I must object,' Campbell intoned. 'Say nothing Ray, you will only implicate yourself.'

'Keep your hair on, Jeffrey,' Schofield said, 'it's nothing. Pete had been involved in a fracas at his local pub, and on my recommendation, made an appointment to talk to Trevor Robinson about representing him on the assault charge. Knowing he was going there, I asked him to see if he could find the document in Vincent's office, nothing more.'

'It doesn't sound like a very well-thought-out plan. Alex Vincent might have been in his office, or if he wasn't, he could have come back at any moment.'

'Pete's a resourceful guy. He'd got a friend to call Vincent pretending to be housebound. He spun a story about a disabled woman, disappointed with the help she received from her lazy husband, and saying she wanted to divorce him. When Vincent went to see her, and Robinson went to the loo, Pete nipped into his office and picked up the document.'

'Consider this, Mr Schofield. Say Pete Hammond failed to find the document the first time, maybe he was disturbed or somebody else was using Vincent's office. Using his own initiative, and I'm not suggesting you asked him to, he went back there at night and took another look.'

The surprised look on Schofield's face told Henderson everything.

'You've never considered that, have you?'

'Well no, and he's never mentioned anything to me. You see, Inspector, Pete's a practical guy, ex-army, but I know he wouldn't kill anybody, I'm sure of it. When I say he does stuff for me, I don't mean anything strong-arm. He picks up my car from the garage and argues for a reduction if they don't complete all the work they claim. He negotiates with builders who double their prices when they see the size of the house, or if they know it's for me. He's good at doing those sorts of things.'

'Maybe you didn't set the parameters too clearly, and this time he went beyond the call of duty.'

'If he did, and I don't think he did, as he never said anything about it to me, then it's fuck all to do with me. You can't hang another bloody murder on me, Henderson, no way.'

THIRTY-FOUR

Clare Mitchell poured a glass of orange juice and sat down at the kitchen table. She covered her Weetabix and blueberries with chilled oat milk and tucked in. She felt relaxed. No longer did she have to feel the tension in her gut whenever Ray walked into the room, his head throbbing with a hangover, or his face simmering with resentment because of an appointment she had scheduled for him that day.

Her top-floor apartment in a small, modern block in Hove was all she needed. She didn't hanker after a smart villa in St Lucia or a larger, grander one in the Algarve. She hadn't gone out with Ray for the money, fame, or the adornments he showered upon her. At the start, she genuinely liked him, respected him for his achievements, and perhaps there was also an element of flattery that such a prominent businessman would listen to her advice.

In time, she had seen him for what he was: a serial philanderer, obsessed with his own definition of self-worth. Despite all the gifts and compliments whispered in her ear, when it came down to it, he didn't give a damn about her. She had wanted to leave him a while back, but that was before she overheard a phone call between him and Tracey Blake many months after Ray's acquittal.

Their familiarity struck a chord as it was more than business, it was intimate, coy, sexual; another notch to add to his heavily marked bedpost. If Clare needed it, this was another reason for leaving him, but when she got over the effect of the call and reflected on its substance, doubts began to grow in her mind.

It encouraged her to delve into Tracey's relationship with Allan, and the more she looked, the more she realised she wasn't the stoic cheerleader of her husband's achievements she latterly purported to be. According to friends and family, she hated him with a passion, resenting the fact he had refused all entreaties to sell the business, denying her the pampered lifestyle she craved. All Clare needed was proof of her complicity in Allan's disappearance. It had taken many months but she had finally found it in the safe at the Bayswater apartment.

After breakfast she tidied the kitchen, made a cup of coffee, then took a seat at the table. She hadn't given any thought to what she would do after Ray and Tracey were arrested. Her eyes had been focussed on the big prize, and like an Olympic athlete, she didn't have a clue what she should do now that her race had been run.

Money wasn't a problem as Ray had given her ten million as a bonus when the business was sold. If he could somehow rescind it, although she didn't know how as it was now spread across various bank accounts, it wouldn't leave her in penury. She had been earning a six-figure salary as FD of Raybeck Leisure for a number of years. She also had a substantial sum invested in unit trusts and shares in companies that Ray had encouraged her to take an interest in.

Back then, they would scour the financial pages looking for companies with good ideas, and she would run the numbers to see if they were worth a punt. It was fun while it lasted, but it was his passion, not hers, and the reason behind their decision to establish a high-tech investment vehicle.

She knew the details of their partnership contract, and the only thing left to do now to finally sever the business link between her and Ray, was to dissolve it. She had a substantial sum invested, and she would make sure she received it, but not a penny more. She didn't want Ray or his legal representatives accusing her of stealing from him.

She needed to get into the Warninglid house to do this, but nothing more. She didn't know if Ray had noticed, but she had not been in the habit of leaving much of her stuff there, other than a change of clothes and a few items of toiletries. If Ray hadn't, his housekeeper certainly would have, but Lyn was a circumspect individual and Clare doubted she would ever have brought it to her employer's attention.

She had decided to go on holiday with her boyfriend, Jamie, and if he couldn't get the time off, she would go alone. It had to be somewhere warm. There, she would go for long walks in the morning and spend every afternoon on the beach. She would use the first week to think about nothing but walking, listening to music, and relaxing, in order to clear her head of all that had gone on before. The second week would be used to plan out her future.

She stood and stretched. Before devoting a few hours to her laptop, deciding where they should go, she needed to buy some food. Her cupboards were almost empty as the last few months had been hectic, spending much of her time travelling, staying in hotels, and eating and sleeping over at Warninglid.

She put on a jacket and left her building. She walked down Eaton Gardens and turned into Eaton Road heading west. When she reached George Street, the pedestrianised area which she regarded as the centre of Hove, she turned into it. Several cafés were dotted on both sides of the street, and with it being a sunny but cold day, many people were seated on the pavement drinking tea and coffee, wrapped in big jackets and wearing woolly hats, cupping their mugs with their hands.

While working for Raybeck, she often shopped on the run, between meetings or on the way home after a long day at the office. Today, in the large Tesco supermarket in Church Road, she took her time, and enjoyed the novel experience. She didn't need much, only enough for the next few days, due to her plans to go on holiday.

Stepping outside with two bags of shopping, one in each hand, she decided not to hail a taxi. It was a Ray-like response to any mobility difficulty, and they weren't too heavy. She walked along Church Road, a bustling thoroughfare with loads of interesting shops on either side of the road, but two lanes of busy traffic in between.

She wasn't used to walking around Hove at any time, and for sure, not in the middle of a working day, and was surprised to see it a hive of activity. Buses thundered by, young mothers walking or sitting outside cafes drinking coffee while rocking a pram, and casually dressed young men and women, carrying takeaway drinks and pastries, heading back to their offices, or apartments to continue home working.

She walked past the home of the former Town Council, Hove Town Hall, unused as a council chamber since Brighton and Hove became a unitary council in 1997. The sixties building was constructed of concrete and glass in the Brutalist style so derided by modern architects, but at least the designers had tried to make it interesting by ribbing the exterior slabs, allowing it to age with some grace. She noticed the owners were still looking for a suitable tenant or purpose which could make full use of the large space inside.

Walking across the small piazza bordering the building, she heard someone call her name.

She was surprised, as she didn't know many people in the area. She turned to see someone lounging against a doorway of the Town Hall building, the emergency exit for the building's inhabitants in the event of a fire. It was Pete Hammond.

She walked over.

'I knew you lived in Hove,' he said, 'but I didn't know where.'

'You struck lucky.'

'I did that.'

Hammond had the marked and worn face of a pugilist, and the stern look of a man who had been dealt some of life's harsher cards. He was Ray's 'fixer', a man who did the dirty jobs Ray didn't want to soil his hands on or be associated with.

Hammond had lived in Sussex for about ten years, but still spoke with a strong Newcastle accent. In prosperous Hove, where many well-dressed and stylish people could be seen, Hammond looked out-of-place and scruffy in his worn leather jacket and ill-fitting work jeans.

'I was over at the Warninglid house this morning to see Ray. It's crawling with cops.'

'Haven't you heard?'

'Heard what?'

'Ray's been arrested.'

'What for? It wasn't for the murder of that fucking lawyer in Brighton, was it? They questioned him about it at the time, but they've got nothing. Couldn't hang a fucking cat on his jacket, never mind murder charges.'

'No, it's not about the lawyer. It's for the murder of Allan Blake.'

'What? He was cleared of killing him. Hang on, what about double jeopardy laws? You can't be tried for the same crime twice.'

'I'm no expert,' she lied, 'but I think you can be tried again if there's compelling new evidence.'

She had researched it. What was the point of her looking for evidence against Ray if he couldn't be tried for murdering Allan a second time? It would be akin to poking a dampened fire with a newspaper. Once freed, Ray would set his rottweiler, the man in front of her, on his accuser: namely her.

'Is there new evidence? Although, in my book, it would be hard to find. Who could say if someone falling off a boat in the middle of a storm was an accident or not?'

'I don't know, but I assume there is. Why would they re-arrest him if there isn't?'

'So,' he said, narrowing his piggy eyes, 'where did they get this new information?'

'How would I know?'

'You sure? See, I think you had something to do with it.'

'What? Why me?'

'Everybody knows you held a candle for the Allan Blake fella, even I knew about it. I wouldn't put it past you to stiff Ray to get your own back.'

'Why would I do that? We set up a new business together. I was about to move in with him.'

'So you say, but he told me he thought you were holding something back; like you were going through the motions but your heart wasn't in it. I spotted it too, the way you looked at him sometimes. It was as if you'd scraped something off your shoes.'

'I'm not standing here to be insulted by you.'

She made to move, but an iron grip on her arm pulled her back into his shady corner.

'Hey, stop it! You're hurting my arm.'

'I'm not finished with you yet.'

'Let go of me!' she said, struggling, not easy as she was still holding two shopping bags.

'Shut the fuck up or I'll give you some of this,' he said pushing a fist into her face.

He leaned in, smelling of coffee and tobacco. It was too early for beer. 'What's in it for you if Ray's put away?'

'Absolutely nothing. The house is his, the villas are his, same with the money in the bank. It will still be his when he gets out.'

'Don't fucking lie to me. What about the investment thingy you two are doing together? He told me he's stuck a couple of million into it. What happens to that?'

'I put money in too. If I wanted my money out, I would only take what belongs to me.'

'Why am I not convinced? I think you set him up so you could bag the lot.'

He reached into his pocket and pulled something out. She couldn't see what. He then punched her twice in the stomach. They weren't hard punches, but when she tried to pull away again, she felt something warm trickle down her belly. She knew. The tension in her hands released and she dropped her shopping bags. When he let go of her arm and backed away, the strength in her legs vanished and she slumped down on the hard paving like a rag doll.

THIRTY-FIVE

'This is Pete Hammond,' Henderson said, tapping the picture behind him on the whiteboard. 'He works for Raymond Schofield as some sort of fixer. Not an odd-job man in the conventional sense, but a man who makes Schofield's problems disappear. Schofield has admitted instructing him to go to the offices of Jonas Baines to remove a schedule his wife had given to Alex Vincent. This schedule is a list of bank accounts in the Caribbean where he had secreted five hundred million pounds.'

It was the morning briefing and Henderson hoped the team would be just as invigorated by this new lead as he was.

'It's a lot of money,' Sally Graham said.

'Enough to kill for,' Phil Bentley suggested.

'Hammond obviously succeeded in his quest to steal the document as Clare Mitchell found it in Schofield's safe at his London apartment. The scenario we're investigating at the moment is whether Hammond failed in his mission to steal the document at his staged appointment. Then, either because he didn't want to disappoint Schofield, or he was still under his instructions, he went back at night and disturbed the sleeping Martin Turner. According to Schofield, Hammond booked an appointment to see

Trevor Robinson a few days prior to the murder. A quick call, Phil,' he said, with a nod at Phil Bentley, 'to Robinson should be enough to confirm that part of his story.'

'I'll sort it.'

'We need to find Pete Hammond. I won't be issuing a warrant for his arrest, as it's all conjecture at this stage, but we do need to talk to him all the same. Vicky, I'm tasking you with finding out what you can about him: his background and where we can locate him. If the usual databases don't provide, try calling the search team at Schofield's house in Warninglid. You would think Schofield would have his details in his phone, little black book, or a laptop.'

'No problem. I'll get onto it.'

'Talking of Schofield, you should all be aware he's now been charged with the murder of Allan Blake. His co-conspirator, Blake's wife Tracey, has also been arrested. A team headed by DS Vicky Neal, overseen by myself, will take charge of the Blake case.'

For the next ten minutes they discussed the analysis being done on the list of Alex Vincent's divorce clients. It had been cross-referenced to the list of Martin Turner's criminal clients, but Henderson was reluctant to interview anyone yet.

They had also examined interviews conducted with Alex Vincent's family and friends. He had a more conventional background than Martin Turner, having gone to a state school. He was the first member of his family to attend university, and indeed, to work as a lawyer. Despite coming from a rougher part of town, his family and relatives were equally as devastated by his death as Martin Turner's were, and like Turner, no one had a bad word to say about him.

At the end of the meeting, Henderson returned to his office. He didn't sit, but scanned through the notes left on his desk and the emails received. He was about to head over to the staff restaurant when his phone rang.

'Henderson.'

'Hello sir, Gerry Thomas here at the Warninglid house.'

'Hi, Gerry, how's it going?'

'Not bad. Despite it being a big house, most of the rooms don't contain much furniture. It's easy to spot any hiding places.'

'It's very minimalist, at least the rooms I saw, but I take your point, there's nothing worse than having to search through a house full of junk.'

'Too true. The reason I called is the housekeeper just received a call from the Royal Sussex Hospital. They were looking for relatives of a woman brought in yesterday found with stab wounds in Hove. The call came here as they'd found Raymond Schofield's business card in her bag.'

'Do you know the woman's name?'

'Clare Mitchell.'

'What!'

'You know her?'

'I was talking to her on Tuesday. She's Ray Schofield's girlfriend.'

'Is she? So, can you handle this, sir?'

'Yes, I will. Leave it with me, Gerry.'

Henderson put the phone down. He felt stunned. It seemed bad things happened to anyone who had any connections to Raymond Schofield: Martin Turner, Alex Vincent, now Clare Mitchell.

'You all right, gov?'

He looked up to see Carol Walters standing at the door.

'Clare Mitchell is in hospital with stab wounds.'

'Good grief. Is she alive?'

'I believe so.'

'Is this Schofield going down and taking everyone he knows with him? It was the reason, after all, he kept those incriminating emails between him and Tracey Blake.'

'You're right, but he was locked up at the time of her stabbing.'

'Maybe he got someone else to do it.'

'Who, Pete Hammond?'

'It's what he does, sorts out problems that Schofield can't.'

'We need to find him and ask him.'

'No problem,' she said, holding up the piece of paper she held in her hand. 'I have his address.'

**

They were driving along the A27 towards Worthing, the town where Pete Hammond lived. The DI didn't have an arrest warrant as Hammond wasn't being accused of anything, yet, so if he wasn't at home when they arrived, they didn't have due cause to break down the door. By the same token, and despite Hammond's reputation, it was only himself and Walters. No big cops to back them up if Schofield's bully-boy turned violent.

Vicky had checked him out on PNC, The Police National Computer and on the web, and he had a chequered past. A former Marine, he had been drummed out of the service for being drunk and emptying the magazine of his SA80 rifle into the water tower at the army barracks where he was stationed. He had served time in a couple of prisons, for stealing cars and the selling of stolen goods, the most audacious, a container-sized consignment of Samsung laptops.

He hadn't been in trouble for about eight years. This mirrored the time when he had become an employee of Schofield. The way Schofield talked about Hammond, they only got together when there was a problem to solve. There must have been plenty for him to do, as Hammond had no other income or employment that his officers could find.

'I'm thinking out loud here,' Walters said, 'but is it possible Clare Mitchell was trying to play a smart double-cross game, and lost?'

'How do you mean?'

'She digs up this damning information about Schofield, and don't forget, she might have been sitting on the information for months, as none of the emails between him and Tracey Blake are recent.'

'Why would she do that?'

'She might have been waiting for the right time, say, when he'd left Raybeck and had sold all his businesses. She brings it to us, we arrest him, and she gets, I don't know, the house, money, the villa in Portugal. Schofield finds out what she's done and sends someone after her.'

'I don't see it, plus there's the divorce to add to the mix. I'm sure Schofield's wife, Rebecca, would have something to say about it if Clare started laying claim to portions of Schofield's estate. Plus, Schofield's no fool. The house, villas, and all the rest won't be easy for anyone to take. They're all owned by off-shore companies that I'm sure only he knows anything about. No, I think her stabbing is in revenge for him landing up in jail. What other reason could there be for someone to stab a businesswoman in a suburban street, in the middle of the day. It doesn't make sense.'

'It doesn't feel like a random stabbing. Hove doesn't have a gang problem, and most of the drug use is between professional types.'

'The drug issue might be an area worth exploring.'

'Might be. You hear of these high-powered people snorting cocaine in the toilets before going into big meetings. Could be Clare had an argument with her supplier.'

Brooklyn Avenue in Worthing had a nice ring to it, almost sounding posh. Pete Hammond lived in a squat block of flats, about half-way along. Despite the obvious limited dimensions of his apartment, it wasn't such a bad place to be. At the end of the road was a sizable parade of shops, and when they got out of the car, he could smell and hear the sea, always a plus point in his book.

Henderson pressed the bell to Hammond's flat and waited. No response. He pressed again, and once again, no answer.

He was about to press the bell of a neighbour when he heard someone walking towards them, an elderly lady carrying two Co-op shopping bags.

'Looking for someone?' she asked.

She had wispy white hair, skin drawn tight across her face, and stooped as if she had a back problem, or her shopping bags were heavy.

'I am Detective Inspector Henderson and this is Sergeant Walters. We're from Sussex Police. We were hoping to have a word with Mr Hammond, but I don't think he's at home.'

'Oh, the police,' she said, setting her bags down on the ground. She stared at him intently. 'Is he in trouble? Has he done something wrong?'

'No, we only want to ask him a few questions.'

'Oh, I know when you say that it's just before you drag him off to jail. I saw it on *EastEnders* the other day.'

So it must be true, he wanted to say. 'No, I assure you, madam, we're here to talk to him, nothing more. Do you know where he is?'

'Mr Hammond you say?'

'Yes, Pete Hammond.'

'Peter is a nice man, although I must admit, he sounds a bit gruffer than he really is, on account of his regional accent. He's from Newcastle, you know.'

'Yes, we did.'

'He came back here last night in a bit of a hurry.'

'Did he? Around what time was this?'

'Ten-thirty-five.'

'You sound very sure.'

'I have a seat near the window and if I see anything unusual, I write it down in my notebook. My son told me if I need to remember something, I should write it down.'

Henderson imagined this helpful guidance didn't stretch to spying on her neighbours. 'Good advice.'

'Peter came out twenty minutes later, carrying a holdall. He threw it into the back of his car and drove off very fast, like a cat with its tail on fire.'

'Do you know anything about the car he drives, the colour maybe?'

'I can do better than that. In my book I have all the cars of everyone who parks around here, so I know if a stranger is using one of our parking places. Come up with me to my flat and I'll show you.'

'Okay.'

'If you wouldn't mind, could you bring my shopping bags? I must be getting old, the walk from the shops has worn me out.'

THIRTY-SIX

Saturday morning, and for once Henderson wasn't going into the office today. He needed a break and until they had located Pete Hammond there wasn't much that couldn't wait until Monday. There was also something else he needed to do. He left his apartment and walked towards St George's Road.

In one of the shops he passed, the DI bought flowers, a newspaper, and a bottle of sparkling water infused with lime. He carried on walking up the slope of College Place until he reached Eastern Road. He crossed it, quiet at this time of the morning, and headed towards the entrance of the Royal Sussex Hospital.

The search for Pete Hammond was ongoing. Daisy Hardcastle, the elderly lady who lived in the same block of flats as he did, had not only supplied them with the make of his car, but also the colour and registration number. Henderson wouldn't be surprised to hear, if she was more able, that she had snuck out in the middle of the night and noted down the vehicle's VIN number.

For all the sniggering and the tut-tutting this story generated in the office, the world would be a much poorer place without the action of its nosey parkers and interfering busybodies. Where would Crimestoppers, Neighbourhood Watch, and a host of abused women and children's charities be without the information they provided? He had lost count of the number of crimes he had investigated, which had been uncovered as a result of a phone call from a concerned neighbour, a passer-by crossing the road to see what was going on, or someone concerned because they hadn't heard from their friend for a while.

The details of Hammond's car were now up on ANPR, but he stressed to all the patrol crews, that the object of the exercise wasn't to arrest him. He was a bit higher up the scale than a person they wanted to question, as the DI had intimated to Ms Hardcastle, but the answers he gave to their questions, along with any evidence they could produce, would determine if he faced any charges or not.

Henderson had been in the Royal Sussex so many times he knew the direction board off by heart. He made his way to Surgical 2 with some trepidation as to what he would find. He had called ahead and received agreement from the staff nurse that he could visit Clare Mitchell. However, he was instructed not to go in, or to come out if already in, if it was during a meal-time, she was being given a bed bath, or the doctor was doing the rounds.

He was aiming to arrive after breakfast had been served, but as anyone who had stayed overnight in a hospital could testify, this could stretch over a two-hour window. What he couldn't plan for was the presence of the doctor; in fact, not only him, but eight medical students in tow. He heard the youngsters being asked a question about suturing, and the benefits and drawbacks of dissolving stitches, before he backed out and took a seat outside.

He pulled out his newspaper and waited. From the information he had gleaned about Clare's injuries. and his limited clinical knowledge, he imagined her case was an archetypical stab wound, not much different from the numerous knife injuries the surgical team faced on a typical Friday or Saturday night. In order for a doctor to stop at her bed, there had to be something more interesting about her condition, or was it purely because she was extremely attractive? Either way, the students would learn something.

Ten minutes later he put the newspaper away and, with a nod to the nurse behind the desk, walked into the ward. At first glance, Clare looked better than he expected. Someone had clearly applied a little make-up, and she was propped up on pillows, the swelling of a bulky dressing noticeable under the sheets.

'Hello Clare.'

'Morning, Inspector,' she said in a slow, deliberate voice. 'I didn't expect a detective to be my first visitor.'

'I get special privileges, I suspect as I've been here so often.'

'I apologise if I don't seem too compos mentis. I've been given so much medication lately, I'm not sure what day of the week it is.'

Henderson placed his purchases on the side table. She didn't look to see what he was up to, either because she couldn't easily turn around due to the strapping, or the drugs were slowing her reactions.

'What are you doing?'

'I'm putting a couple of things I brought for you on the table.'

'What things?'

'Some flavoured water, and flowers.'

'Thank you.' Suddenly, her face melted and she burst into tears.

Like most men, Henderson was pretty hopeless when it came to situations like this, made especially awkward as he didn't know her well. Where was Walters when he needed her? He found a box of tissues, pulled one out and handed it to her.

'Thank you,' she said, dabbing her eyes and then blowing her nose. 'I don't normally cry. I suspect it's something to do with the medication, but thanks for bringing the flowers; I love receiving flowers.'

Henderson lifted over a spare seat, sat down, and left her a minute or so to compose herself.

'How are you feeling? I assume the operation was successful.'

'No complications, according to the surgeon. Luckily, it was a small knife, and both wounds are in my stomach. They've stitched it up, hence the lump here,' she said indicating her abdomen. 'Barring any setbacks, I should be back to normal in about three weeks.'

'I'm glad to hear it, although I imagine eating might be a problem for a while.'

'True, but as I'm not a big foodie, it won't bother me much. Grabbing snacks in between meetings has been my style for so many years, it will take some time before I can eat like a normal person.'

'Can you tell me what happened?'

'There's not much to tell. I was walking back to my apartment in Hove after shopping in Tesco when Pete Hammond called me over. This was beside the old Hove Town Hall. Do you know it?'

'I do. Pete Hammond, you're sure?'

'Yes, without doubt. He's been to the house in Warninglid many times. He works for Ray.'

'Okay, go on.'

'He'd just found out about Ray's arrest, and accused me of setting him up.'

'I was afraid something like that would happen.'

'How did he know I was behind it? Is there a leak in your department?'

'Did he say anything to suggest he had inside information?'

'No, he made it sound like, if Ray had been arrested, then I had to be behind it, as neither he nor Ray trusted me. He seemed so sure of his facts, but he's not a bright guy, and asking him to make his own assumptions would break him out in hives.'

'Are you suggesting Schofield's behind it.'

'Without doubt.'

'We issued a press statement following Mr Schofield's arrest. This isn't unusual, but we felt it was imperative in this case due to Schofield's high profile in the community. In it, we said new information had come to light and we would be petitioning the CPS for a retrial. At no point did we hint or imply who had supplied it.'

'Well, someone did, and I ended up in here. I suggest you find the leak and plug it, Inspector, before someone gets killed.'

**

Radio 4 was playing in the car as Henderson drove to East Hoathly, but he wasn't listening. All members of the murder team knew the origins of the email traffic which had resulted in Ray Schofield being charged with the same murder he had been acquitted of three years before. Clare's assertion that her stabbing had to be the result of a leak in the murder team didn't hold water. No newspaper had published Clare's name, and even if one of his team was in the pay of a journalist, it was clear they hadn't sold the story. No, it had to be as Hammond had said to Clare before stabbing her; he didn't trust her, and it was because of her that Schofield was now in jail.

The Caribbean banking schedule, and the emails between Schofield and Tracey Blake used to snare him, came from Schofield's safe and office. Only Clare had access to both, and Henderson had warned her at the time that Schofield could easily work it out and she needed to be careful.

The only explanation he could think of was Schofield had either used his lawyer, or had called Hammond from a prison phone; he wasn't convinced Hammond would have acted off his own bat. The only way to resolve it would be to ask Hammond himself, but as yet, he hadn't surfaced. They were now in with a better chance of catching him, as Henderson had called the office and told them to apply for a warrant; he was now wanted for serious assault, and perhaps, dependent on his motive, attempted murder.

All thoughts of accusations, leaks, and charges were driven from his head as he drove down the road towards Kelly's house. She lived in an old place, not far from a thinly-populated rural road. It would be considered remote by most people's standards, especially at night, where in the surrounding forest the hooting of owls, screeching of foxes, and the rooting of other nocturnal animals could echo for hours. Lessening its remoteness, Kelly's house was one of three, built in a semicircle, their neat, green front gardens in contrast to the kaleidoscope of greens, browns, and blacks of the forest and its haphazard display.

It was a four-bedroom place, now too big for a single woman living alone. Given the aggressive behaviour of her ex before, during, and after their divorce, it surprised him when he heard her former husband didn't want the house, or even his share of it. He was, according to Kelly, ambivalent when it came to money and material possessions; one of those rare beasts, a banker circumspect at looking after other people's money, but crap at taking care of his own.

The wind was bitter as he stepped from the car and stopped for a moment to chat with her neighbour cutting her front lawn. When Henderson walked into Kelly's house, he was glad to find it warm. She wasn't one of those starving authors who had to resort to burning chairs and chopping up the table to keep a meagre fire going.

They kissed and hugged, and with his foot he pushed the door closed. The chances of being overlooked were low to non-existent, but old habits and his memories of previous bruising encounters with the paparazzi died hard.

'Your timing's good, Angus, lunch is about ready.'

'I'll just go and tidy myself up.'

He walked into the downstairs toilet and after filling the basin with hot water, washed his hands and face. Despite visiting Clare in a post-operative ward which was sterile clean, hospitals had a way of leaving residues on the skin and odours in the nostrils. Some he could wash away, others he couldn't.

'How was your morning?' he asked as he walked into the kitchen. Whatever Kelly was cooking, it smelled delicious. This was in part because she was a very good cook, but also because food tended to smell better when someone else was cooking it.

'In a word, marking. My lot were involved in exams last week and I've a pile of scripts to go through.'

'Don't you have time to do it during the working day?'

'I do most of the time, but the last week has been manic. I'd brought in a couple of guest lecturers to give them a change from my boring voice—'

'Hassling, lecturing, counselling maybe; never boring.'

'I think there's a compliment lurking in there somewhere, but it's not obvious. I also wanted them to have a different take on a module I'm teaching about the Criminal Justice System.'

'Interesting.'

'Yes, I thought so too. The upshot was, I spent a lot of time hand-holding, not the students, the visiting lecturers: briefing them about the course, taking them to lunch, organising taxis to take them back to the station. All in all, I didn't get a minute. Hence, I had to bring this work home, but don't you worry Angus,' she said walking over and wrapping her arms around his neck, 'there'll be plenty of time for us.'

THIRTY-SEVEN

It had been a week since Trevor Robinson visited Miranda's parents. Michael, her father, turned out to be a much nicer man than the leftie trade unionist Miranda had painted him to be. Her mother, on the other hand, had enough politics in her system to start a new political party. No matter the topic, she could turn it into a failure by the government, or, if they had done something, it was another example of their profligate use of public resources.

During the week, he had gone back to the Belgravia Casino in Hove. This time he went with two purposes in mind. One was to satisfy the gambling urge, gnawing away at his brain, which only calmed when he was holding a set of playing cards. He also wanted to see Hassan Khouri again. He'd achieved both aims. On the gambling front, he'd won, and he'd seen Hassan, who'd dressed up a casual drink as another interrogation about Martin and Alex's deaths, and how he believed Raymond Schofield was the person responsible.

The surgeon was pleased, no, better than pleased, ecstatic, when he heard about Schofield's arrest, but his joy was tainted when he realised it was for the murder of Allan Blake. When were the police going to realise, he was also the killer of Martin Turner and

Alex Vincent, he asked. On and on he ranted about Schofield's guilt, showing little sensitivity for the person he was speaking to. Vincent had been a close colleague of Robinson, and yet Khouri was talking about the dead lawyer as if he was nothing more than a blunt instrument to bash Schofield with. It only succeeded in reinforcing his suspicions about the man.

Robinson laced up his running shoes and headed outside. After labouring up to the top of Lansdowne Place, he turned the corner and, out of sight of any nosey neighbours in his street, he stopped. With hands on his knees, he bent over, panting hard. The tracksuit, orange top, running shoes and all the rest he'd bought one January a couple of years back, when he decided he needed to get into better shape if he was to make a decent fist of online dating.

The fitness kick had lasted no more than a fortnight, culminating in an errant dog running across his path and forcing him into a hedge, where he'd twisted an ankle. Upon recovering, several weeks later, what remained of the running 'bug' had evaporated like steam on a bathroom mirror after opening a window. He realised he hated running, and the only reason he didn't see the dog, was because he was concentrating on repeating a motivational mantra heard on a podcast, developed to help listeners succeed in doing anything they didn't like.

To the average runner, the two-point-five kilometres from his apartment to Khouri's house in Mallory Road was a breeze, a warm-up before they embarked on something more challenging. To him, now walking, it was a slog. Most of the journey seemed to be uphill, and this was borne out by the views he saw as he walked along Shirley Drive, out to the Palace Pier and the tall buildings lining the seafront.

He stopped and pulled out his phone. He set it to block the caller ID, then called 999. When put through to the police, he said, 'I live in a flat opposite Cavendish Body Sculptures in West Hove. I've just seen a dark figure running around the back of the building and a few moments later, I heard breaking glass. I think there's a burglary in progress.'

He declined to give his name, and when the operator said she would send a car round to check, he terminated the call. When the patrol car arrived, they would indeed find a smashed window around the back; the one he'd broken the previous night. They would also find the name and number of the building's keyholder on an *In The Event of Fire* notice visible on the front door.

He continued walking. He could now see the benefit of venturing out early on a Saturday or Sunday morning. He enjoyed the fresh air on his face and being awake before almost everybody else. If he didn't have something else to do, he would pick up a newspaper and breakfast rolls before they sold out, but not running. It was better to walk and not feeling hot, out of breath, and have a line of sweat trickling down his face.

Khouri lived in a newly built modern house. A number of these houses had sprung up in Hove in recent years, replacing the dilapidated homes of elderly residents who had lived in the same area for many decades. Houses in this area were much sought after, and a vacated property or a building plot didn't stay in its undeveloped state for very long.

He stood a distance down the road with a view of Khouri's house. In many ways, it resembled the man himself. It was clean and tidy, the patio garden, recently swept and not sullied by so much as an errant leaf or a discarded piece of paper. Glass dominated the structure, more prominent than the white-painted brick, and every pane looked spotless.

He waited. In time, the door of the integral garage opened and the Porsche 911 belonging to Khouri raced out. The surgeon didn't wait for it to close, and Trevor would also bet he didn't have time to set the house's alarm system. He jogged across the road and, after glancing around for non-existent traffic, in effect making sure he wasn't being watched, he ducked under the open garage door before it automatically closed, trying to look like Khouri's jogging companion returning home.

The one thing he couldn't be sure about, and it was a realistic possibility, was if anyone had been staying with Khouri the previous night. He was a well-known ladies man and, if Robinson believed everything Schofield had written about him, he was not averse to using some of his charms on his own clients. By all accounts Schofield's ex-wife, Rebecca, was a stunning woman in her day, and her continued visits to Khouri's clinic, ostensibly to prolong her beauty, but also to receive some of the celebrated surgeon's other treatments.

He opened the door between the garage and the kitchen and heaved a sigh of relief: the silent air wasn't spoiled with the *cheep-cheep* of an alarm system, before it could take a deep gulp and bellow its concern to all and sundry in the neighbourhood. In addition, only one place was set at the breakfast table, a part-eaten slice of toast with some strange brown spread on top, beside it a half-full mug of coffee.

In common with what he'd seen outside, the inside of the house had all the warmth and feel of a building site show home. The kitchen looked stunning, all black marble and matching appliances, but the shiny equipment didn't look much used, and the minimalist furniture in the lounge didn't look like it had ever been sat upon. The pictures on the wall were strange, not bad in what they depicted, but they failed to evoke any emotion, as if purchased from a set designer warehouse.

One by one, he searched each room. In truth, he wasn't sure what he was looking for, but if Khouri was engaged in a vendetta against Schofield, he imagined it would leave some evidence. It could be in the form of a scrapbook or a folder of newspaper cuttings, anything to confirm his suspicions: that Khouri's hatred of Schofield was deeper and more venomous than he'd conveyed to Robinson.

He climbed the stairs. Unlike staircases in older houses, where carpeted steps would hide all manner of squeaks and creaks, these were open and unadorned. The only sound he made was the dull tap of his trainers while the whole staircase swayed gently under his weight.

He checked the first three bedrooms, his heart was in his mouth as he pushed open each of the doors. He was half-expecting to see a sleeping woman, or one with her knees up and a questioning look on her face, not expecting her lover to return so soon.

He entered the main bedroom, occupying one end of the house, and gasped at its size and opulence. Through huge sheets of floor-to-ceiling glass, there were stunning views over the back garden, the rooftops of his neighbours, and the sea in the distance. At the opposite end of the room, no spectacular views but a sumptuous en-suite bathroom. He hesitated, not sure if the acres of glass would make it easy for someone to see him from outside, but he needn't have worried. The house wasn't overlooked at the rear, and large trees masked his presence at the front.

He opened a door at the end of a long line of fitted wardrobes. It was similar in colour and shape to the others, but around the handle there were more marks, suggesting it had been used more often. It led to a small anteroom, perhaps a dressing room, and what he saw inside made him gasp. Moments later, he heard the sound of a car approaching.

With his heart racing, he ran to a window and looked out. It wasn't Khouri returning, or the police investigating, but a neighbour, back from the shops with morning rolls and a newspaper. He returned to the 'den', pulled out his phone and photographed its contents, paying particular attention to a section on the rear wall.

He put his phone away and headed for the stairs. Reaching the bottom, he heard the unmistakable sound, even to a non-car nut, of a high-performance engine as it decelerated. Robinson stood in the hallway and listened, waiting for the garage door to open. He felt trapped. He had all the evidence he needed to snare this monster, but he couldn't think of a way of getting out of the house.

He then spotted the key sitting in the front door lock. He waited until he heard Khouri open the driver's door of the Porsche, before turning the key and pulling open the front door. He closed it quietly behind him, took a deep breath, and started running the opposite way he'd come, as it wouldn't be a good idea to run past the open garage. To neighbours, perhaps more vigilant than in other areas as people around here had more to steal, he hoped he looked like Khouri's house guest heading out for a run.

He kept the illusion going for as long as he could, despite his lungs, legs and brain screaming for him to stop. He ran along Mallory Road and turned left onto Woodruff Avenue. By the time he reached the halfway mark along Shirley Drive, he stopped and remembered why he hated running. His breath was coming in short gasps, and his legs felt like jelly, as if they couldn't support his body. The shoes were chafing his toes, and his chest ached, making him fearful he was about to have a heart attack.

He vowed when he reached home he would put all the gear he was wearing in the bin. If his flat had been equipped with an open fire he would light it and take pleasure at adding each item to the flames, so that if he ever felt the notion to take up running again, the idea would be strangled at birth.

There were numerous routes he could take to go home, just as well, as he didn't want to go back the way he had come. He was walking along Wilbury Gardens when he heard a car behind him slow down. He looked ahead, but couldn't see any obstructions or traffic lights. He turned and was shocked to see the blue Porsche 911 belonging to Hassan Khouri.

It stopped in front of him and the passenger door swung open.

'Get in, Trevor.'

'No. Why should I?'

He was about to run off when he saw the gun aimed at his midriff.

'I said, get in.'

THIRTY-EIGHT

Henderson drove into work listening to a politics debate on Radio 4's *Today* programme. He often wondered if this surfeit of political debate which dominated the discussions most mornings reflected the interests of the common man, or was something more commercial at work? The news desks of radio, television, and newspapers were all located in London, close to the House of Commons and most of the main offices of state. Wasn't it simply too cheap and easy to send a radio car a few streets away and talk to a government minister, than to cover a more interesting story in far-flung Barnsley or Hull?

After visiting Clare Mitchell in hospital on Saturday morning, he had spent the rest of the weekend with Kelly Jackson. They'd enjoyed long meals and lengthy walks, punctuated with quieter times as she marked student exam papers and he watched football on television. It was the perfect antidote to a murder investigation, leaving his mind clearer and brimming with optimism, and his body full of energy.

Before heading to his office, he walked over to the staff restaurant for coffee and something to eat for later on. Coming out after a few minutes, carrying his purchases, he saw his boss, Steve Houghton. With nowhere to hide this time, Henderson walked over in his direction.

'Morning Angus.'

'Morning Steve.'

'I'm getting a lot of heat about the arrest of Raymond Schofield. I'm sure you're aware he's a pillar of the community.'

'I remember you telling me, but you've seen the evidence.'

'I know, I know, but it doesn't mean I'm comfortable with it. Plus, he's beaten the charge before, who's to say he won't beat it again? If he does, he will make us look foolish and, with some justification, probably sue us for harassment.'

Henderson shook his head. 'He won't beat it this time. Not a chance of it. The CPS are happy with the evidence.'

'What about our dead lawyers? Does any of it land on Schofield?'

'It may or may not. We're still trying to track down his man, Pete Hammond. We know he entered the offices of Jonas Baines to steal documents, what we don't know is if he did it during the day or night.'

'Well, keep me posted,' Houghton said, his face stern.

Henderson walked back to his office in thoughtful mood. Houghton was the boss and he had to respect his opinion, but it seemed to him the Chief Inspector was more concerned with the public edifice created around Schofield than any dirty dealings he had enacted to get there. The 'jewel in the crown' of his empire, according to the financial press, was the health clubs, but this was built in part with the business he bought from Allan Blake's widow, after murdering its owner, following his refusal to sell.

He took a seat in his office and opened the top of his coffee cup. One sip in and Walters appeared.

'Morning gov. How are you? Had a good weekend?'

Henderson gave her a potted account of his weekend, starting with his visit to see Clare Mitchell, which he had already phoned the DS about, and then his trip to Kelly's bolthole in East Hoathly.

'I had a date with a new man on Saturday night, and we went out for a pub meal on Sunday afternoon. Near you in East Hoathly, as a matter of fact.'

'Have you come into my office just to be sociable, or was there something else?'

'Oh yeah. I came to tell you we've tracked down Pete Hammond.'

'Where is he?'

'At a house in Northgate, Crawley.'

'Good. I would normally say collar a couple of detectives and instruct them to pick him up, but after the conversation I had with Clare Mitchell on Saturday, I think we might need to be a bit more cautious. Call Crawley, ask them for a car with at least two officers, and we'll take a couple from here. We'll head out in about half an hour. That should give you enough time to get it organised.'

'Yeah, I should think so.'

'Good. It'll allow me to finish this coffee and check what's been happening overnight.'

**

The house in Northgate where Pete Hammond was holed-up looked unremarkable, nestled as it was in a sea of similar-looking semidetached houses. At the front, a small garden laid to grass and bordered with rose bushes, a single garage, and with about three compact bedrooms upstairs.

It was the home of Sonia Leonard, an agent with an insurance broker in the town. Neighbours reported she lived quietly, having moved there about eighteen months back following a divorce. Recently, they had started seeing a man about the place. Their description of him – less than average height, stocky in appearance, with an aggressive, unpleasant resting face – sounded like the man they were looking for.

In common with many planned estates in 'new towns', the area exuded an open feel, something he couldn't say for the tight, narrow streets of Brighton. As such, it was difficult to move a police car, or any car for that matter, along roads without being spotted. With this in mind, Henderson decided they would have to do this 'smash and grab' style. He briefed the Crawley officers and they set off.

The three cars raced along the road before braking hard, coming to a halt outside the target house. The Crawley officers ran to the rear of the property, while Henderson, Walters, and the other two uniformed cops headed to the front door.

Henderson rang the doorbell. For this house call he refrained from pounding the door with his fist, or bellowing 'Police!' through the letterbox. There was a chance, albeit a slim one, Hammond would still be in bed, unaware it was the police outside and thinking it was the postie with an oversized letter.

Upon receiving no reply, he rang again. This time he heard the sound of footsteps on the stairs. The door opened and the craggy face of Pete Hammond appeared. He was dressed in working clothes and looked dusty, as if he had been undertaking some DIY work upstairs.

In a millisecond, he clocked the two uniforms and slammed the door hard. The edge of a copper's foot was stopping it closing, nevertheless he still managed to engage the security chain. Henderson stood back as one of the burly cops put his shoulder to the door. The sturdy chain didn't budge. The cop stepped back and shouldered it again, this time with more effort. It was successful and Henderson had to reach forward to catch the material of his uniform to stop him falling as the door sprang open.

'Search the downstairs!' he called to the two cops as he, followed by Walters, headed upstairs.

They pushed open all the doors in the upper floor until they reached the bedroom at the end. A window was lying wide open, and unless Hammond and his girlfriend were fresh-air-freaks, he had to be out there. Henderson ran over. Below the window was the flat roof of the porch, and tearing across the road was the ungainly, portly frame of Pete Hammond.

'He's out there, running across the road!' Henderson shouted, as he sprinted for the stairs. No way was he tempted to jump on a fragile porch roof, already weakened by Hammond's considerable bulk.

Henderson ran outside, and hoped Walters and the cops were on his tail. He also trusted the Crawley boys would have the sense to jump back into their car, because they had lost sight of Hammond, and in the warren of streets around the area he could be anywhere. Henderson approached a road junction, the one they'd travelled down earlier. It was a main one leading into town, and across from there was a small patch of overgrown land filled with trees and brambles.

He directed the cops to look in the streets to the right, and when the Crawley police car appeared, he instructed them to go left. Henderson and Walters walked straight ahead into the dim light of the trees. The undergrowth looked as though it hadn't been cut for months, as it was filled with metre-high nettles and thick brambles, some lying across the path and capable of being a trip hazard.

He indicated for Walters to move to the right and he veered to the left. It was only a small patch of ground and if they didn't spot anyone hiding the first time round, for sure they would when they walked back. When his eyes became better accustomed to the gloom, he decided to investigate a dark bundle over to the right. A phone started ringing.

He silently cursed Walters for being so stupid, before remembering he had watched her put her phone on airplane mode at the same time he did, minutes before they entered Hammond's house. Instead, the glow from an activated phone was being emitted from the dark bundle.

'Get up Hammond. We see you.'

The bundle moved and Pete Hammond emerged from the gloom of the undergrowth, twigs and leaves falling from his frame. He held a knife in his hand. 'You lot can't leave it alone, can you? If you want me, you'll have to take me, won't you?'

Henderson had been half-expecting this and had been keeping his eye open for weapons. Moments earlier he had spotted a stout branch. He reached behind him to retrieve it. The branch was about the length of a baseball bat and just as thick. A whack against a tree verified it didn't have a rotten core.

He said nothing and approached their target. By keeping to the left, he had forced Hammond to turn his back on the advancing Walters, who, having spotted the danger, Henderson hoped she would go off and alert the other officers.

Hammond waggled the knife casually in Henderson's direction, giving the impression he was a street punk. The DI knew this was a deception, trying to make him think he was unskilled and careless. He was a former soldier and, apart from knowing how to dismantle and assemble a SA80 rifle in the dark, he knew how to handle a blade. For a few moments, they sized one another up; Henderson waiting for him to make a move, Hammond doing the same.

Without warning, Walters rushed forward and whacked Hammond over the head with a weapon of her own. The branch she used wasn't as thick as Henderson's and it didn't drop the man. Instead, it only enraged him. He turned to deal with Walters, now unarmed and rooted to the spot. Henderson had only seconds to strike. A two-handed blow hit

Hammond on the side of his head, and he dropped like a stone, the knife falling without sound into the undergrowth.

Henderson moved forward and cuffed him while Walters searched for the knife. He hauled Hammond to his feet and read him his rights. His face was streaked in blood and gave the appearance of being drunk.

'Fuck,' Hammond said, as he was being led away, 'if it wasn't for my bloody woman reminding me about an Amazon delivery, you lot would have walked right past me.'

THIRTY-NINE

Henderson and Walters walked over to the Interview Suite. He was confident the forthcoming interview would give them the attacker of Clare Mitchell, and perhaps information about the murderer or murderers of Martin Turner and Alex Vincent. On the other hand, would it take them off on another tangent completely, much like it had when they'd questioned Raymond Schofield?

'Did you hear?' Walters said. 'Detectives in Derby have now interviewed Allan Blake's widow, Tracey. When they suggested to her, a bit cheekily in my opinion, that Schofield was spilling his guts down here in Sussex, she confessed to the lot.'

'Did she?'

She nodded.

'Has she implicated Schofield?'

'Hook, line, and sinker. She verified the reliability of the emails between him and her, and talked about Schofield concocting a plan to get rid of her husband.'

'It's Schofield's plan now, is it?'

'She says she knew about it, how could she deny it, but it was Schofield's decision to kill him. She didn't ask or tell him to.'

'That's not what some of the emails suggest, but we can argue it out later with Derby. At last, some good news. I think Houghton is still harbouring a hope Schofield will beat the charges like he did last time. A confession from her puts a big boot into that.'

'It certainly does, and she can deny that she had no part in Allan's death all she wants, because as soon as Schofield hears about what she's done, the sparks will start to fly.'

'You can bet they will.'

Henderson pushed open the door to Interview Room 2 and walked inside. Two people were sitting on the other side of the interview table, Hammond and his brief, David Lomax. It was a toss-up to decide who looked the more uncomfortable in their chairs. Hammond was big, part fat, part muscle, and seemed to dwarf it, while Lomax, he knew, had a fondness for Mars Bars and yum yums, and the suit he was wearing was straining to contain him, never mind the chair.

Henderson went over the housekeeping while Walters started up the recording equipment.

'This interview is being conducted under caution, Mr Hammond. You are accused of stabbing Ms Clare Mitchell.'

'No comment.'

Walters opened a file and spread out a series of CCTV pictures in front of Hammond and his brief.

'I am showing the suspect,' Walters said, 'CCTV pictures taken from a camera sited close to Hove Town Hall.'

'You might have picked a more secretive place to attack someone, Pete. Here's you walking along Church Road, and again in Tisbury Road, and stopping at what used to be Hove Town Hall. The crossroads where you were standing has two commercial banks at opposite corners, and if there's one business paranoid enough about security to install plenty of cameras, it's a bank.'

'Yeah, so I went for a walk in Hove and stopped for a smoke, so what?'

'Is this the best you can do?' Henderson said. 'Stopped for a smoke? We've got witnesses who saw you, and we've got the knife you used, the one you pulled out on me.'

'This is conjecture, Inspector,' Lomax said.

'I'm surprised to hear you say that, Mr Lomax, as the witnesses and the knife are fact. You've seen, and I assume have read, the witness statements yourself. We have one lady who saw the whole incident. She was the one who made the 999 call. No way would I call her evidence conjecture.'

Hammond shrugged as if the six to eight years he might receive in prison didn't bother him.

'I know you stabbed Clare Mitchell, this isn't in question. What I want to know is, why did you do it?'

'No comment.'

'She was going to expose you, wasn't she?'

'Fuck off.'

'Or, maybe she had something on Schofield?'

Hammond leaned over the table, his face a twisted expression of menace and anger, and pointed a finger at Henderson. 'She's got fuck all on him, and it's Mr Schofield to you, copper.'

'So, is this what it's all about? Raymond Schofield?'

'She fucking set him up, didn't she?'

'This is why you accosted her in Hove?'

'Do not answer that question,' Lomax said.

'Mr Schofield wouldn't be in jail if it wasn't for her.'

'How do you make that out? Did Schofield pass you a message from jail.'

'Did he fuck and stop calling him that. I bloody told you, it's disrespectful.'

'So, she put him in jail, and you stabbed her in revenge?'

'Bloody right I did. No way was she getting away with it.'

'How did she set him up? It's not as if your boss is facing these charges for the first time. He's been through it all before.'

'I don't know, I just know he wouldn't be where he is if it wasn't for her.'

'How do you know this?'

'Whenever she was with him, it was like she was holding something back, something she didn't want Mr Schofield to see.'

'Take it from me, Pete, a lot of women are like that, reluctant to commit.'

'Whatever, but it's what I think.'

'No, I don't think so, it's what you've been told. You've talked to Mr Schofield since he's been in prison, haven't you?'

Henderson had asked someone to check, but Lewes Prison hadn't as yet come back to them; still, there was no harm in fishing.

'What if I have? It's not a crime the last time I looked. I needed to know what was happening with a few things he'd asked me to do.'

'Like what?'

'Nothing to interest you lot.'

'Try me.'

Hammond sighed. 'Now and again, he'd visit a couple of women who are like caretakers at some of the houses he owns. He usually calls me if there's something needing doing, like plumbing or electrical work.'

'Or to sort out any men who are hanging around.'

Hammond gave him a quizzical look. Clare Mitchell had told him, but he wouldn't be saying this to Hammond.

'Believe what you like.'

'When you talked to Mr Schofield, did he ask you to kill Clare Mitchell?'

'You've no need to–' Lomax said.

'No fucking way!' Hammond exploded. 'If I'd wanted to kill her, she would be dead and no mistake.'

'So, stabbing her was, what? A warning, some form of retribution?'

'To tell her to keep her fucking nose out of it.'

Henderson didn't want to go around in circles with this one. He believed Schofield's hand was behind Clare's stabbing, but unless Hammond said it out loud, he couldn't prove it. Why Hammond was willing to do Schofield's dirty work and take the fall for it, was beyond him.

'Tell me about the time Mr Schofield asked you to retrieve a document from the offices of Jonas Baines.'

'There is no mention of this on the charge sheet,' Lomax said.

'You're right, Mr Lomax. I'm not accusing Mr Hammond of doing anything illegal, merely trying to fill in a few blanks.'

The client looked at his lawyer, who nodded.

'Rebecca, Mr Schofield's wife, had taken a schedule out of Ray's office,' Hammond said, 'which he didn't want her lawyers to have. He wanted it back.'

'Was it this schedule?' he asked, placing a printout in front of Hammond.

He pulled it towards him. 'Nah, that's not it.'

Henderson reached into a file and pulled out the real one. If he had produced it first, Hammond might have denied all knowledge of it, but this way, Henderson wanted him to acknowledge that he knew what it looked like.

'My mistake,' Henderson said. 'Is this it?'

'Yeah, it looked something like that. Accounts and amounts.'

It was good enough for Henderson. It didn't prove much, only that he had gone into Jonas Baines to retrieve it. The big question was, when?

'You took this from Alex Vincent's files?'

'Yeah.'

'When were you there?'

'I was up on an assault charge. I went too far with one of the men taking too close an interest in one of Mr Schofield's women.'

'Okay.'

'I'd arranged to see Trevor Robinson, one of the criminal lawyers at Jonas Baines. Ray suggested it and offered to pay and it's true what they say, you get what you pay for. This guy did the business for me. He was heaps better than the guy I used before.' He turned to Lomax, 'No offence, mate,'

'What happened when you were there?'

'Before I went, I put a call through to Alex Vincent, Rebecca's divorce lawyer, and got him off the premises. When Robinson went to the loo, I sneaked into Vincent's office and picked up the document.'

'How could you do this in the middle of the day? I've been there, it's a busy office.'

'When lawyers are out for the day, they lower the blinds in their offices, I suppose to tell everyone they're away. All I had to do was go in there and find the file.'

'Which you did.'

'Like I said.'

'You didn't come up with a blank, go back at night and break in to retrieve it?'

'What are you trying to say?'

'It's a fair question. Did you pick it up first time, or did you go back later and try again?'

'No, I fucking didn't go back again. I picked it up that afternoon. Breaking and entering is not my style.'

FORTY

Henderson drove into the car park at Jonas Baines with a heavy heart. He had hoped the next time he came here he would be the bearer of good news. Unfortunately, this wasn't it.

He climbed the stairs to the second floor. It had been two weeks since the death of Alex Vincent, but his death, and the murder of Martin Turner five weeks before, had left its mark. To an outsider, it might look like a fully functioning office, but the mood was subdued and voices were hushed.

Pete Hammond had now been charged with stabbing Clare Mitchell, resisting arrest, and being in possession of a knife. No deals were on the table as Henderson was confident Hammond had nothing more to tell him, other than that Schofield had instructed him to do it, and this he would never say. The only thing he was interested in finding out was who killed Turner and Vincent, and even if Hammond knew, which he suspected he didn't, no deal he could offer would ever encourage him to admit to that.

Hammond, for all his thuggish attributes and mentality, was not, in Henderson's opinion, a good fit for the man they were looking for. Hammond was short and stocky, and waddled like a heavyweight boxer. The man who appeared on the CCTV pictures the night Martin Turner was murdered, and the person who had stood behind Alex Vincent at Brighton Station, was tall and slim.

At some later stage, he would question Schofield about the stabbing of Clare Mitchell. Henderson suspected it was his hand behind it, but no way would he expect the man to admit to it and have another charge added to his sheet. Henderson's aim was to try to understand the connection between Schofield and Hammond, and Schofield's relationship with Clare Mitchell. A few weeks back, she would have been described as the closest woman to Ray Schofield, not to mention his business partner. Why then did he turn on her with such violence, treating her like a chattel, to be disposed of when he was finished with her? Was this the measured, anticipated reaction of someone betrayed, or the actions of a psychopath?

What was behind Henderson's interest was that, contrary to Hammond's statement that he could have killed Clare Mitchell if he'd wanted to, the DI believed Hammond had been instructed to kill her, and had botched the job. He had stabbed her twice and if it wasn't for the quick-thinking of a woman nearby, who knew basic first-aid and had called an ambulance, she would have bled out. It was true what Clare had said, Schofield was a vindictive sod. If he was going down, he was making sure everyone around him suffered as well.

Henderson was shown into Robert Haldane's office and took a seat. By any standards it was impressive; not large, but appointed with tasteful furniture, wall coverings, and paintings, and missing the mounds of paper so common in other offices around the building.

He was handed a cup of coffee by Haldane's secretary and by the time he was halfway through drinking it, the man himself appeared. They shook hands.

'I'm sorry I wasn't here when you arrived, Detective Inspector. I was in a meeting with staff who, I expect you realise, are beside themselves with worry.'

'I'm sure they are. If we can make a start, I'd like you to tell me everything you know about Trevor's disappearance.'

'Yesterday, Monday, was a normal working day. With Martin no longer here, Trevor has a large workload. So, no way would he slope off or pull a sickie.'

'I understand. When he didn't turn up at his usual time, you did what?'

'He was scheduled to attend an important client meeting at eleven, and we felt sure, even if he had a prior engagement like a dental appointment, he would make an appearance for this. When he didn't, and the said client went into a hissy fit calling us all the names under the sun at the top of his voice I started to worry. I sent someone around to his apartment. They gained access to the building and stood outside Trevor's door, but there was no movement inside. He's not answering his phone or responding to emails. They didn't hear his phone ringing inside his apartment to suggest he was still in there. We are at a loss what to do, and what with the murder of Martin and the death of Alex, I...'

Haldane's normal solid edifice was crumbling; not a good sign.

'Is he prone to taking unexpected periods of time off?'

'No, not that I'm aware.'

'He doesn't have childcare issues, an elderly relative, a drink or drugs issue, something to make him take off without warning?'

'I know he likes to gamble, but I don't see how...'

'I've heard he's a serious gambler.'

'Is he? Clearly you know more about it than I do. Do you think this had something to do with his disappearance?'

'I don't think so, although we shouldn't rule anything out at this stage.'

Henderson was tempted to hand the search for the missing lawyer over to the uniform branch, who were the experts at finding missing persons, way better than members of his team. They would check all the likely places he might be, such as responding to a family emergency, stuck on a country road beside a crashed car, or lying behind the door of his apartment. On the other hand, it would be remiss of him not to investigate the disappearance of a lawyer from the offices where two other lawyers had died in mysterious circumstances.

'It would help if you can tell me something about Trevor. Where does he live?'

Haldane opened a folder on his desk. Upside down, Henderson saw a photograph of Trevor Robinson's face. It looked like the firm's personnel file.

Haldane handed a sheet of paper to him, a copy of the front page from Robinson's file, with his picture, date of birth, address, phone number and so on.

'Excellent,' Henderson said. 'Now, does he socialise with anyone in this office?'

'No, not much.'

'Is he dating anyone from here?'

'No, but one of the girls in Medical Litigation is a friend of the girl he's seeing at the moment. She doesn't know where she lives, but she can tell you the place where she works.'

'I'm sure that address would prove useful.'

'Good. I'll just go and get the details.'

Haldane left his office with a touch more spring in his step than before. What they were doing at the moment, information gathering, clearly made him feel as though they were involved in doing something constructive.

Henderson was resigned to undertaking some of the duties he'd carried out when first in uniform: dealing with the obvious so he could get on with investigating what wasn't. The first part he was clear about, but the second was a dark hole. He had no idea why anyone would kidnap, harm, or kill, Trevor Robinson.

It could be a gambling debt, heavies giving him the once-over in a deserted warehouse, but this tended to happen to those less well paid, up to their necks in debt with a variety of lenders, not smart lawyers earning eye-watering salaries and generous bonuses. He felt it had to be connected to the other two deaths, although he couldn't see how. If he didn't find out soon, who was to say something wouldn't happen to the whole senior legal team at Jonas Baines? Perhaps another five or six lawyers?

Haldane returned bearing the name of Robinson's girlfriend, and the phone number and address of her employer. Henderson wished Haldane goodbye and was pleased to say he looked a tad happier than when the DI first arrived. The presence of the police didn't often have this effect on people, so he enjoyed it while it lasted.

Henderson drove to Lansdowne Place and parked. He tried ringing the bell to Robinson's apartment, but as expected, received no reply. He rang the doorbells of the three remaining apartments, and it wasn't until he reached the one at the bottom, that he heard the electronic crackle of someone answering.

An officious looking woman aged around mid-fifties opened the door. He showed her his warrant card which appeared to mellow her stern features, perhaps preferring his presence to a council official, complaining about her overflowing bins or an unpaid Council Tax bill.

'I'm here to see the man who lives on the top floor, Trevor Robinson, but he isn't answering. He also hasn't appeared at his place of work and his colleagues are worried. Have you seen him lately?'

'Trevor on the top floor, you say?'

'Yes.'

'Let me think. Yes, he went out for a run early on Sunday morning. I don't sleep well, you see, never have, and I like to read a book while sitting at the window, for the light, you understand. I therefore see all the comings and goings in this building.'

'Did he often go out running? Was he keen?'

If so, Henderson could see him handing at least part of the search over to the uniform branch. An injured runner lying in a ditch would be easier for them to find than anything his team could do.

'I would say not. I'm not an expert myself, I've had a bad knee for several years, but I'd never seen him do it before. By the way he staggered up the hill, I would say it wasn't something he did regularly.'

'What time did he get back?'

'Here's the funny thing, He didn't. When someone goes outside, you see, it sort of knocks over a flag in my head. It doesn't pop back up into position until they return.'

'I see, but what if you were in the bathroom or cooking lunch, you wouldn't know, would you?'

'Oh, but I do. No one closes the front door quietly but me, and everyone thumps upstairs, as if they are wearing Army boots. Trevor was the only one to go out on Sunday morning and I'm quite sure he didn't come back.'

'You haven't seen him since?'

'No, I haven't.'

'If I may, I'd like to come in and see if he's in his flat.'

'Oh yes, of course. Do come in,' she said holding the door wide.

Henderson walked to the stairs, glancing down at the letters on the hall table and spotted one addressed to Robinson with yesterday's postmark.

'I would come with you, but not with this knee. I might make it up, but I would never make it down.'

'I understand, but thank you. You've been most helpful.'

Henderson left his assistant standing at the bottom of the stairs and began ascending. Judging by the décor, the hall carpets and the marks on the wall, this wasn't a palatial block, but it wasn't a dump either; it landed somewhere in the middle. It smacked of residents too busy or unconcerned to tack down the edges of the curling carpet or touch-up the scores and scratches on the walls.

Standing outside Robinson's apartment on the top floor he was pleased to see it was secured only with a Yale-type night latch. This, in his opinion, was poor security, although the building's dwellers had the added reassurance, perhaps misplaced, of a locked front door downstairs, not to mention the eyes and ears of a watchful ground-floor neighbour.

He looked around before pulling out his wallet. His caution was perhaps unnecessary, as he had rung the doorbells of all Robinson's neighbours and none were at home. He removed something that from a distance looked like a credit card. The card was about the same size as an ordinary credit card, but made of metal and a few millimetres thicker to give it added strength. He pushed the door gently with his shoulder to expose the latch, slid the card against, it and pushed. Slowly, the lock retracted and the door opened.

He closed the door behind him and stood for a moment taking in the view from the hallway. No one had responded to the noise of the door opening and closing, and he still couldn't hear anything except the quiet rumble from the fridge in the kitchen.

He pushed open the door to each room in turn and looked inside. This activity always created an anxious knot in his stomach. It was possible Trevor could be lying with his head caved in with an iron bar, on the living room floor with the pale face of a heart attack victim, or in the bathroom with a heroin needle sticking out of his lifeless arm. Yes, he was a middle-class lawyer, but as Martin Turner had proved, even those sorts of people had demons of their own to deal with.

A quick search in the wardrobe and the chest of drawers reinforced Robinson's neighbour's view: the lawyer wasn't a regular runner. If he was, Henderson would have expected to see a selection of spare running tops and shorts, and maybe even a change of shoes, one pair for the road and a different pair for forest trails.

He walked into the lounge and took a seat on the settee trying to think. Robinson was last seen heading out for a run, but as far as was known, he didn't come back. This was borne out by the contents of the apartment. There were no signs of any recent food intake, no indication of a hastily-packed suitcase, and no obvious gap in the clothes in the wardrobe or the toiletries in the bathroom.

Henderson knew about running and no way would a novice like Robinson have the confidence or stamina to venture out much beyond the streets of his locality. The main advice given to all novices in books and magazines was to travel no further than the distance you knew you were capable of running back.

Something untoward had happened to Trevor Robinson, and he knew he had to find out what.

FORTY-ONE

He woke, his head groggy. Had he drunk too much the previous night? If so, it was unusual, as he wasn't a big drinker. Then he remembered, and his spirits sagged. When Trevor Robinson had climbed in Hassan Khouri's Porsche two days ago, they didn't go back to Khouri's house in Hove as expected. Instead, they drove into the country. The last road sign Robinson saw before the car headed down a track between a line of trees was Plumpton.

At the bottom of the track, he saw a dilapidated cottage. It still had a roof and windows, but the garden was overgrown, render was missing from the walls, and the peeling paint on the door suggested it hadn't been inhabited for a number of years.

He was led into the building at gunpoint and shown into the bedroom. For a moment he panicked, thinking he was about be murdered or raped, but instead, he was tied to a bed. It was an old-fashioned cast iron thing with a musty and dusty bedspread on top. His hands were tied together and then to the frame, but there was about two metres of rope between him and the bed, allowing him to lie on the bed and to move around the room a bit. A portable toilet was also within easy reach.

Khouri had left a pile of books and magazines on a chair, the out-of-date ones from his surgery, no doubt. With nothing better to do all day, Robinson would have spent every minute plotting how best to get out of this place. Instead, he had spent the last two days reading.

For the first time since he'd known him, Khouri had looked flustered. The normally self-assured and in control cosmetic surgeon was pacing the room after the first time tying him up, muttering, 'I don't know what to do with you.' No bloody wonder. Losing three lawyers from the same legal practice would not only ring alarm bells inside the offices of Sussex Police, soon it would create panic in Scotland Yard, the Law Society, and the Bar Council.

Robinson wasn't sure if an indecisive Hassan Khouri was a good or a bad thing. On the one hand, him recognising that his actions would only exacerbate the on-going crisis at Jonas Baines might save him, while on the other, an impulsive act by an irrational man could do the opposite. An overriding consideration had to be he'd seen enough to believe it was Khouri who had broken into the offices of Jonas Baines and murdered poor Martin. If true, he had killed before, so what was stopping him from doing it again?

When his head cleared from the fug of his fitful sleep, he went over his plan once again. His indolence over the last few days had served a purpose: he now could see a pattern to Khouri's movements. At around seven o'clock in the evening he would arrive and untie his prisoner, allowing him to use the toilet, a normal one for a change. It was as run-down as the rest of the place with a large and rust-streaked cistern, but at least it worked.

He would then tie him up again. Before leaving, some food and water would be removed from Khouri's rucksack. It was mainly dried fruit, nuts, and cereal bars, and while it wasn't gourmet cooking, or even a heavily discounted value meal past its use-by date, he wouldn't starve.

He had been exploring the bed frame as best he could with both hands tied, looking for a sharp or ragged edge. He had found one, and after having something to eat and drink for breakfast, he walked to the bottom of the bed and lifted one corner of the mattress.

He dipped his shoulder under the mattress and instead of supporting it as he had done the day before, he tried moving it away from him. It was a big heavy thing, and he knew it wouldn't be a good idea to drop it if he didn't want to be showered in a cloud of dust and grime.

He managed to move it about a metre, but the effort had left him breathless and sweating. The breathlessness he didn't mind, but sweating in this cold environment left him feeling clammy, his clothes sticking to his body. He sat on the edge of the bed frame and when he had cooled down and his heart felt normal, started to move his bindings back and forth along the ragged edge of the bed frame.

He was sawing at the small space between his wrists, not an easy prospect as they were tied close together and, unlike the cottage and its furnishings, the rope looked new. He didn't know for sure, but thought it was a ship's rope. Khouri owned a speedboat which was kept at Brighton Marina. He didn't strike Robinson as a dedicated sailor, more a white-suited show-off, one hand on the tiller and the other around a pretty girl, as he gunned the big engines and pounded over the waves.

Robinson knew a little about old ropes as he would play with them as a boy and knew how some frayed one strand at a time. With ropes made from nylon and polypropylene he imagined nothing would happen for a while, but when it finally succumbed, it would only be a matter of minutes before the whole thing fell apart.

He had been sawing for about half an hour and felt weary. When he looked at his progress, he was disappointed to find the rope looked untouched, while the edge of his hand was red and tender. He took a drink and decided there was nothing else for it. A more ragged part of the frame lay further over. He hadn't selected it at the start, as the edge was wider than the one he'd been using. This time, he would need to put his hand closer to the bed frame, effectively sawing the edge of his hand as well as the rope.

He took a deep breath and started sawing. He gritted his teeth as the rusty edge was serrating the soft flesh at the edge of his hand. He kept on sawing, the pain intense, sweat dripping into his eyes, as blood dripped on the floor, while repeating to himself the choice was either a sore hand or a bullet in the brain.

Five minutes later, he felt a space opening between his hands, signalling a weakening of the rope. He sawed on, trying to ignore the pain in his hand and the sweat on his head dripping into his eyes.

A minute or two later, although it felt much longer, pieces of the rope started to separate. When they finally parted, he sat back, exhausted, as if he'd run a marathon. He looked down at his hands, a ragged, bloody mess.

The blood had soaked through the rope changing it from white to red. He walked to the door, intending to head into the bathroom to bathe his hand before wrapping it up in a towel, but when he tried the handle, found it was locked. The only thing he could use to stem the bleeding in the bedroom was his pillowcase. Before going to sleep the first night, he had shaken and punched the bedcovers and pillow, trying to get rid of the dust.

He pulled the cover off the pillow and it was so old, he easily tore it into strips. He wrapped a long thin piece around his hand several times and knotted it as best he could using one hand. He stuffed a few of the remaining strips into the pockets of his tracksuit bottoms, thinking they might come in handy later. He looked at his makeshift dressing; it wasn't leaking blood. With one problem out of the way, he turned to tackle the door.

It was a sturdy looking thing equipped with what looked to him like a standard bedroom lock. It wasn't the latest in high security, but enough to stop kids interrupting their parents enjoying a Sunday morning love-making session. He lifted a foot and stamped on the door, but it made no impression and only succeeded in hurting his foot. No wonder, as he was wearing running shoes not steel toe-capped building boots.

He stood looking at it for a few seconds trying to find a weakness. He soon realised it was staring him in the face. The design of the door consisted of a sturdy frame with three rectangular panels running up the centre. He tapped each of the panels in turn with his knuckle, and realised they were constructed from a thinner piece of wood than the frame. He decided to tackle the one at the bottom. If he managed to create a crawling space, it would be easier to do this close to the floor than higher up.

He sat down on the floor and propped his back against the bed frame. Lifting a leg, he stamped at the panel. To his delight, it started to give way almost at once, but despite repeated stamps it didn't pop out as a single piece as he expected. His foot had damaged a corner and by bashing it with both feet he managed to make a ragged space big enough for him to squeeze through.

He got down on all fours and took one look at the freedom beyond before pushing his arms through. Soon it became obvious he hadn't made the hole big enough as shards of wood stabbed and slashed at his chest and arms. When at last he managed to pull his legs through, he realised it had ripped his running top in a couple of places and torn the flesh underneath. The wounds were stinging and when he looked at his hand, blood was seeping through, but he decided his freedom meant more than any pain he had to endure.

He was about to walk to the front door, which in this old place he would no doubt have trouble opening, when he heard the sound of a car approaching. He dashed to a window and in the distance and through the grubby glass, he saw the Porsche 911 belonging to Khouri, and being driven quickly. The only reason he could think why he would be coming here at this hour of the morning, and in such a rush, was because he had decided what to do with him: kill him.

He ran from the window and into the kitchen. He was pleased to find the cottage had a back door, as he didn't fancy jumping out of a window. The key was on the windowsill. When he inserted it into the lock, it refused to turn.

The car had come to a halt and moments later, he heard the sound of one of its door's opening and closing. He turned the key in the lock one way, then the other, repeating the twisting action again and again. Finally, the key engaged and the lock turned. He hauled the door open, stepped out, closed it and started running.

He hoped the sound of him opening and closing the door would be masked by Khouri's own noise and the squeaks and creaks as he opened the front door. Robinson reached a stone wall at the end of the garden and ran through a gap where the stones had fallen. Instead of carrying on into a copse and on towards the hill in the distance, he ducked behind the wall, ran for a bit in a crouched position, before stopping and hunkering down.

He had stopped there not only to give him a chance to rest and stretch previously unused muscles, but to keep him out of sight. If Khouri had spotted a retreating figure running through the woods beyond the wall, he would know exactly which way he had gone. By stopping, and in the time it took Khouri to notice he was no longer tied to the bed, he would be in several minds about which direction he had gone.

He heard a screech and despite knowing little about birds reckoned it wasn't caused by anything covered in feathers. He heard the back door being flung open and slamming against a worktop. Khouri came stomping into the garden with all the subtlety of a water buffalo. A flurry of resting crows in the woods in front of him flew into the air in panic.

'Trevor, where are you?' he shouted. 'I didn't mean you any harm. I'm sorry I locked you up, but I was desperate, you see. It's all sorted out now. I came here early to let you out and take you back to Brighton.'

Was this true? His hand was throbbing like a big bass drum and his chest and stomach were stinging as if he was sitting on a hornets' nest. If he wasn't so frightened, he would move from his position to check. He wanted to stand and say, *Here I am. Take me to a doctor,* but something stopped him. He remembered the cold look on Khouri's face when he told him to get into his Porsche, and the determined look when he tied him to the bed at night, pulling the knots so tight it caused him to cry out.

He pushed his body as close to the wall as he could, hoping this section was sturdier than the piece further up, so it wouldn't collapse under his pushing.

Moments later, he saw the studied, intense face of Khouri standing at the wall scanning the copse and the grassy slopes of the South Downs in the distance, his eyes searching for the movement of a retreating figure through the trees. Robinson's decision not to stand and reveal his position was vindicated seconds later when he saw what was poking out in front of his seeker. It was a gun.

FORTY-TWO

It was the third day of Trevor Robinson's disappearance. They had published his picture in all the local papers with the caption: Have You Seen This Man? They didn't mention he was last seen dressed in running kit, a piece of information that would be used to separate real witnesses from time wasters. So far, it had not yielded a result. It was just as well they hadn't mentioned his attire as some Sunday mornings hundreds of runners could be seen, particularly around the seafront.

Day three of any missing person enquiry and doubts would start to creep in. Most missing persons, or mispers for short, were located within the first day or two of them going missing, when the anger had abated or when the hungry and cold runaway had decided to approach a police officer. The DI didn't believe Robinson's running had got him into trouble, as he didn't consider him a serious runner. If so, they would be forced to look within a ten- or fifteen-kilometre radius of Brighton, a distance that would encompass streets, parks, and hundreds of rural roads, a huge undertaking.

The only other explanations he could think of were that he had become involved in an accident, which hospital enquiries had so far failed to corroborate, or more likely, was being held against his will.

With the deaths of two other people in his office, it didn't take the logic of a genius, or a mighty leap of faith, to believe the same person who killed Turner and Vincent was also responsible for the kidnapping of Robinson. It was all conjecture, of course, as he had no evidence to back any of it up. It was perfectly feasible for Robinson to be enjoying a week's holiday in Ibiza, a break he'd forgotten to tell colleagues about because of all the turmoil at Jonas Baines, or having a nervous breakdown at the house of a friend. Henderson picked up his car keys and headed outside.

It was a typical spring day as he walked through the lines of cars in the Malling House car park. Big fluffy clouds were racing across the sky as if they had somewhere better to go, and now and again a stiff wind would gust, rattling the branches of nearby trees.

Henderson's drive into Brighton was challenging. On open stretches of the A27, the wind shook the car as if it wanted to remove it from the road, and in its wake, pieces of debris: branches of trees, bits of newspaper, and noisy beer cans, came careering across his path.

He decided to park along the seafront, a more open area than in the side streets where he could return to find the car's roof caved-in by falling masonry, or the back window speared by a rogue scaffolding pole. The offices of the Lightning Software Group were located above a row of shops in Black Lion Street. For staff, it was a brilliant location for shopping at lunchtime or heading out in the evening with colleagues for a drink at the end of the day, but an expensive undertaking for those using town centre car parks.

He was shown into a meeting room and waited. Unlike many of the US tech giants, the offices here were not equipped with bean bags, snooze rooms, or vending machines filled with computer accessories, although he did see a water dispenser crammed with all manner of fruit pieces. From what he knew about the company's business, they weren't at the 'sexy' end of software engineering, designing beautiful systems and devices for tech-savvy consumers, but in the arcane world of telecoms, making mobile networks work better and faster, in the words of their founder.

The door opened and Miranda Moss entered. He knew Trevor Robinson well enough to imagine the sort of woman he would go out with, and it looked as though he was punching above his weight. She was fair-haired, attractive, with nice teeth and eyes, and an open, pleasant face without blemishes.

They shook hands and sat down.

'I take it you haven't found him?'

'No, we haven't, but we're still looking.'

'There's still hope, isn't there? I mean, with two deaths already in his office...' She bent over and started sobbing.

'Miranda, there is nothing to suggest Trevor's disappearance has anything to do with what happened at Jonas Baines.'

'You're not just saying that for my benefit?'

'No. It's true.'

In a strange way, it was turning a negative into a positive. Not being able to link the deaths of Turner and Vincent was hampering the investigation. However, not being able to connect Robinson to the deaths of the other two victims was a relief for Miranda.

'Trevor was last seen going out for a run by his neighbour on Sunday morning.'

She sniffed and wiped her nose with a handkerchief.

'A run?'

'Yes.'

'That's odd.'

'Why do you say that?'

'In all the time I've known him, about six months, Trevor has never gone out running, talked about running, or taken me into an athletics store to look at the kit. In addition, he's never raised the topic with friends of mine who are keen runners, and whenever there's a race going on in Brighton, I have to cajole him to watch it, and even then he would be bored stiff.'

'I get the same impression. So, why do we have him setting out early on a Sunday morning as if he was going for a run?'

'I really don't know.'

'Has he recently received a health scare, or expressed concern about his weight, for example?'

She shook her head. 'When you first mentioned it, I thought it might be connected to the deaths in his office, his way of living life, improving his chances, or just getting it out of his system. The more I think about it, the more I realise he wouldn't do such a thing. What he would do instead is more drinking, gambling, and partying.'

Henderson was surprised by her answers and their vehemence. He supposed he had harboured a hope that Robinson might have mentioned something to her about a need to improve his fitness, and then this would turn into a case of looking for a missing runner. He had another thought.

'This might sound a little odd, Miranda, but bear with me. If we assume he left his house on Sunday morning *disguised as* a runner, why would he be doing that?'

She paused for a moment. 'Now you mention it, I imagine a runner is a bit like a road repairer or telecoms engineer; once they put on a yellow jacket you see them, but you don't really notice them. If you ask someone to describe a guy digging a hole in the road, or a runner that passed a few minutes before, they probably couldn't.'

'This is what I was thinking; the question is, why? Was it related to one of his clients? Perhaps, someone wanted to meet him to discuss confidential information?'

'If so, do you think this person might have kidnapped him?'

'I wouldn't go as far as to say that at this stage. I'm trying to establish if there is something going on in his private or business life making him go out in a form of disguise.'

'I can think of someone.'

'Who?'

'I'm not sure you're going to like it.'

'Try me.'

'Trevor was sort of investigating the deaths of his two colleagues.'

'You're right, I don't like it. How do you mean, sort of?'

'He told me about this rich Middle Eastern-looking man he meets in the casino now and again. Did you know he's a bit of a gambler?'

Henderson nodded.

'I've been trying to persuade him to get help, join Gamblers Anonymous, but it's a long slog as you can imagine.'

'I can, from personal experience.'

'He thinks this person is involved, but he isn't sure how.'

'What's the man's name?'

'He wouldn't tell me. It was for my own protection, he said, making it sound like it was some sort of a joke, but events are proving otherwise.'

'So, you think this had something to do with him leaving his flat early on Sunday morning?'

'It's the only thing I can think of. It's the only thing I can say with any certainty that was bothering him. Trevor had talked to this man on several occasions and it was his repeated interest in the murder at Jonas Baines, and Raymond Schofield in particular, that made Trevor suspicious.'

He probed the issue a little longer with Miranda and by the time he left the offices of the Lightning Group he was confident she had told him everything. It wasn't a lot, in truth: a Middle Eastern-looking man he met in a casino. To his knowledge, many men from the Middle East were keen gamblers, and in the high-rolling casinos in London, the only ones with enough money to be regular visitors.

He supposed he could send a couple of officers into the casino near Brighton Station, and the one in Hove, places Trevor frequented at least once a week. On reflection, it was worse than a long shot. First, there was a problem with what constituted the definition of someone from the Middle East. Basing this only on facial features and dress, they could look no different from other people around them, despite being born in Saudi Arabia or Dubai. The second issue was the potential number of suspects they would come across per night and what to do with them. Approach them, follow them, or call them in for questioning?

No, he would file Miranda's information for the moment, and perhaps when they did have a reasonable suspect, use it for corroboration.

FORTY-THREE

The sight of a gun barrel poking over the crumbling boundary wall galvanised Trevor Robinson. Not into taking offensive action, how could he, but into pressing himself further against the wall and making his profile as small as possible. The weapon was in sight for no more than five or six seconds, but it felt like several minutes. All it would take was a glance to the right, and his almost-dayglo orange sports top would be spotted.

Instead, Khouri was concentrating on the woods in front of him and the fields ahead, leading up the hill to the South Downs in the distance. He was expecting, no doubt, to see the bedraggled figure of Trevor Robinson struggling up there, making it an easy shot for him.

Robinson stayed where he was until the gun disappeared and he heard the engine of the Porsche start. He didn't know much about cars but enough to understand it was a low-slung sports car. No way was Khouri getting behind the wheel so he could drive through the back garden and continue his search. He reckoned instead, judging by the current slow movement of the car, Khouri was now searching along the track that led from the cottage to the road. With some trepidation and his heart racing, Robinson pushed away from the wall and ran down the slope, into the small copse.

A vague plan was forming. On the other side of the trees, he would climb the hill. From an elevated position, he would look for a road and then head towards it. The copse consisted in the main of young silver birch trees looking bare in their post-winter dressing, providing little in the way of cover.

Away from the trees he was now tramping across an empty field. While walking, he couldn't help but glance back every ten seconds or so, feeling as though he was being stalked. His hands were shaking and his legs felt wobbly; the thought of Khouri's voice suddenly whispering in his ear, or a bullet thudding into his back, filled his head with a dark, sombre fog.

The South Downs were a bit further away than he thought, so he changed tack and veered to the right, the copse now blocking his view of the dilapidated, cold cottage. Through fields, he kept to the borders, not because he feared tramping over crops, as nothing much was growing, but the hedgerows and the occasional line of trees offered additional cover.

It was early spring and the ground underneath was not solid with the leaves crinkly as they were in summer, but muddy, thawed from an earlier frost, the leaves slimy and treacherous, especially when heading down an incline. He soon realised his running shoes weren't waterproof as he imagined all running shoes to be, and his feet were soaked through. However, in the scheme of things, any inconvenience or pain he felt from wet feet, a damaged hand, and scarred chest, were a small price to pay for not being roped to a bed in a skanky old cottage and having a bullet pumped into his brain.

He would have liked to use this trek to analyse Khouri's motivation for kidnapping him, like the criminal lawyer he was, and what he did in his day job with clients. He wasn't so interested whether they had done the deed or not, but why they found themselves in such a position, and what decisions they took while they were there. He wanted to know what Khouri was trying to achieve, but he couldn't think about it. He felt as soon as his mind wandered and focussed on something else, he would be unable to spot some obvious danger signal ahead. Before he knew it, he would be back in the Porsche.

From a slightly elevated position, he spotted a road and headed towards it. In fact, he couldn't see the road itself, but the wavy shape of the hedgerow bordering it. His plan was to walk on the field side of the hedgerow, and jump out if a car or van came along. If this wasn't possible, because he couldn't push through, he would adopt his least preferred option and walk beside the road itself.

He made his way across a ploughed field. It was tricky stepping between the raised rows, making him feel he was doing some strange leg exercise from a Joe Wicks video, but preferable to walking down the rows and adopting a gait like a Western-movie cowboy. Before reaching the hedgerow, he stopped to look and listen. It was a small country road with little regular movement. He continued walking. Moments later, his spirits rose when he heard a car approach.

Something about it tempered his initial enthusiasm. He wasn't sure if it was the tone, the deep gurgle of a big engine, and not the tinny rattle of a family saloon, or the sound of it being driven much slower than the road conditions allowed. He ducked down on his haunches before throwing himself flat on the ground when he saw a quick swatch of its blue body colour.

It was Khouri, driving at a slow pace as if he was experiencing car trouble, but in reality, looking for him. He felt sure a flash of his orange running top, most of it zipped inside his tracksuit top, would look incongruous against the brown and green of the ploughed field, but the tone of the engine didn't change. Khouri was either a cool customer and, having spotted him, would now wait out of sight around the next bend, or he didn't notice he was there.

Robinson decided not to take any chances. He abandoned his plan of reaching the road and flagging down a motorist, and instead ran across the field in the opposite direction from the way Khouri was heading, towards a collection of buildings. At the edge of the field, he vaulted a fence, forced his way through a hedgerow, ran across a small road and headed down a track. He was running on adrenalin and fear now, not caring if he was heading into kennels with dozens of dogs on the loose, or a farm with large machinery being operated.

He passed a large sign, which he ignored, so desperate was he to meet a friendly face and speak to someone in authority. The surrounding vegetation disappeared and he walked into a clearing where he stopped for a minute to try and breathe. It was the furthest he had ever run but he didn't think he could run another step.

It took him several seconds to realise a group of people in front of him were holding chainsaws, like extras in a horror film. It took a while longer to make sense of what they were doing. He walked towards the group, and a bloke in a yellow jacket with 'Instructor' printed on the back put his chainsaw down and turned to face him.

'Can I help you? This is a dangerous area for you to be in. This is a woodcutting class using chainsaws.'

'Where...am...I?' he gasped, finding it hard to breathe properly after his non-stop dash to get here.

'You're in the grounds of Plumpton College. What are you doing here? Are you lost? You look as though you've fallen out of a tree.'

He realised he must have looked a sorry sight, streaks of blood and mud, ripped clothes, hand bandaged as if done by a child, panting with exhaustion, looking like he's just run a marathon.

'I was... I was being held against my will... I escaped.'

'Hang on, I recognise you. You're the guy in the paper. What happened to your hand?'

'I had to... damage it to escape. Can I use a telephone?'

'C'mon, let me take you to the nurse and she'll take a look at your hand. Afterwards, you can use the telephone.'

He nodded, too exhausted both physically and mentally to resist. He said, 'Lead on.'

The nurse was a woman aged around forty, with a plain face and slim to a fault, with a busy, can't-keep-still demeanour. She removed the makeshift bandage from his hand and didn't wince when she saw the mess. He did, but tried his best not to show it.

She cleaned it up with some stinging fluid before spraying his hand with a freezing agent. She then picked up what looked like a glorified sewing kit, and began stitching the two parts of his hand together. As long as he didn't look, it didn't seem to hurt.

'The cut is ragged and might leave a scar. It's not like the knife and saw accidents I have to deal with around here, which are often more linear. In your favour is your age, which means it shouldn't take long to heal. You did it on an old iron bed frame, you say?'

'Yes, at a rough bit on the frame.'

'What caused the roughness?'

'Rust, I suppose. The place where I was being held didn't have any heating. It felt like it had never been heated for years.'

'You poor thing. In that case, you're going to need a tetanus jab.'

He nodded. 'I thought I might. Where do I get it?'

'I can do it. I will as soon as I've done this. Hold still.'

When she had finished stitching and headed to the fridge to find the vaccine, he inspected her handiwork. She'd done an amazing job and after the swelling and bruising went down, he was confident it wouldn't leave much of a scar.

After the injection, which hurt more than he expected, she took a look at the injuries to his chest and stomach. She cleaned the wounds, but none of the cuts were deep enough to concern her or require the use of her sewing kit. Instead, she stuck a bandage over the worst of them.

They chatted as she tidied up the surgery. He found out she ran an amateur dramatics society in the village where she lived, but she clammed up when he told her he was a criminal lawyer. It wasn't an unusual reaction when he told people, particularly if they had been a victim of crime, perhaps believing the criminals apprehended received a more lenient sentence than they deserved.

He thanked her for all her help, and meant it. He was fortunate to stumble into Plumpton College. He imagined the nurse was more experienced at dealing with this type of wound than a general hospital, what with students falling out of trees, being cut by a chainsaw, or having their hand sliced by a bandsaw.

'Can I make a phone call? I'd like to get back to Brighton.'

'No need, your transport awaits.'

'What?'

'Take a look outside.'

His trepidation returned like a big wave smacking the side of a boat. Had Khouri found out where he was, and was now parked outside waiting for him? Had he duped these nice people with charm and fine promises to look after him?

He looked out of the window and scanned the area, but he couldn't see the Porsche, only a police patrol vehicle.

'The police?'

'Yes, Geoff, the instructor, the guy you met when you first walked in, called them to tell them you were here. Big search parties have been out looking for you, in case you didn't know. Don't worry, Trevor, you're safe now.'

FORTY-FOUR

Henderson parked the car with an oblique view of the house owned by Hassan Khouri in Hove. It was early afternoon, not the time he would normally choose to start a surveillance operation, but he had no option in the matter. It looked a quiet residential street and no doubt the presence of a police car would vex some of the inhabitants. If so, there would be high anxiety and indignant letters to *The Argus* if they realised the innocuous blue van contained five officers, each armed with Heckler and Koch carbines and handguns.

A savvy copper from John Street, Celia Warren, had brought Trevor Robinson straight to the DI's office this morning. Warren's boss would probably give her a dressing down for this unauthorised use of her initiative. It didn't give him his place in the sun in front of the nation's cameras, his arm around the shoulders of the missing man. This was a minor consideration if half of what Robinson had told him was true.

The kidnapping of Trevor Robinson was sufficient grounds for mounting today's surveillance operation, but if the rest of what Robinson said survived close scrutiny, Khouri was also involved in the murder of Martin Turner and Alex Vincent. A little research had helped to fill in some blanks. Over the last year, Raymond Schofield had been orchestrating a hate

344

campaign against Hassan Khouri on social media, which on occasion leaked over into the tabloids.

This, as Schofield saw it, was for Khouri botching up a nose operation on his former wife, and embarking on an affair with her. This wasn't a salacious rumour dreamt up by a bored tabloid editor or trolls on social media, as pictures of Khouri with Rebecca Schofield on his arm, had appeared in the gossip pages of magazines, and were now on the web. Henderson didn't know what Schofield was on about as there looked to be nothing wrong with her nose, or anything else for that matter.

In addition, a serious allegation of negligence had been brought against Khouri; this time it wouldn't be played out in the press or social media, but in court. The case, brought by a fashion model, was being handled by the Medical Litigation team at Jonas Baines, and according to Robinson it wasn't only the divorce team that lost client data on the night of the intruder break-in, they did too.

Putting two and two together and perhaps making five, Robinson believed Khouri broke into Jonas Baines to remove incriminating evidence contained in the Medical Litigation file, which included original documents that couldn't be replicated. While he was there, he did the same to the divorce file of Rebecca Schofield. Robinson believed this was either to put a spanner in the works by delaying their divorce, or perhaps Khouri got wind of the schedule detailing the 'missing' millions from Rebecca. With this in his possession, he could publish details on social media and expose Schofield as a liar and a cheat.

However, if Khouri did break into Jonas Baines, he wouldn't be aware that Schofield's fixer, Pete Hammond, had been there a few days before and removed the incriminating schedule. A re-examination of the CCTV pictures of Martin Turner and Alex Vincent's killers weren't conclusive, but now with Khouri's profile to add to the mix, Henderson believed he was a much better fit, down to the neat Roman nose. He was certainly a better fit than either Schofield or Hammond.

All things considered, it now made Khouri his number one suspect, and a man with plenty of serious questions to answer.

'I don't think he'll be coming back,' Walters said beside him.

'Why not? He went to the cottage in Plumpton with the express aim of killing Robinson. Once he'd finished the job, he would return to Brighton and carry on with his life as he did before. He wouldn't have taken anything extra with him to help him escape: no clothes, laptop, food, phone charger. Sure, you can go far with only a credit card in your pocket, but if you're on the run and you don't want anyone knowing where you are, it's the last thing you want to be using.'

'I agree.'

'Also, consider what he knows about this situation. Robinson escaped, but with no money or phone as Khouri had taken them. In addition, as Robinson said himself, he didn't have a clue where he was, and even if someone told him, he doesn't know that part of Sussex well. It was only through good fortune he managed to stagger into Plumpton College. He could have fallen into a ditch and broken his ankle, or ended up walking around in circles for hours. It's possible Khouri still thinks he's out there.'

'Even if Robinson made it back to civilisation, there was no guarantee he would come straight to us.'

'That was another stroke of luck,' Henderson said. 'If he hadn't reached Plumpton College and instead, he'd been picked up by some upstanding citizen and, given his condition, would have been taken to the Royal Sussex or the Princess Royal in Haywards Heath. If they'd put him under sedation, we wouldn't have had any inkling about his story for at least 24 hours.'

'By which time Khouri would have had time to pack, and in all probability, jetted back to the Middle East. If so, it would have been the last time we would hear about him.'

'It's a smart house,' he said. 'There's obviously money in cosmetic surgery.'

'Big money, I think. I reckon he's knocked down the traditional house that once stood there; I assume it looked like the one next door. What he's replaced it with looks like something from *Grand Designs*.'

'All that glass. I would be frightened I would forget to close the curtains and expose myself to all and sundry, like that scene from *Life of Brian*.'

The radio crackled. 'Blue Porsche heading in your direction.'

'Roger and out,' Walters replied. She turned to Henderson, 'We're on,'

They sat in silence, their eyes focussed on the top of Mallory Road. The Porsche didn't just appear, it roared into sight. It raced along the road, braked hard and swung into the driveway at the front of his house. A man Henderson assumed to be Khouri, left the car in the driveway and sprinted towards the front door.

Henderson allowed him to enter the house before he called the ARU van. The driver gunned the van's engine and it sprinted up the road, stopping directly at the back of the Porsche, blocking its exit. As the officers decanted from the van, Henderson and Walters exited their car and ran over to join them.

'Armed Police!' the lead officer shouted as they entered the house, the two detectives right behind them. They didn't have to bash the door down, as Khouri had been in such a rush he hadn't bothered to shut it.

The house was large, too big for one man, open-plan, with glass all around. The downstairs area contained all manner of rooms appropriate for a single man: large lounge with sophisticated television and sound system, cinema room, modern-looking study with large Apple desktop, easy-to-use kitchen, and games room including a classic *Space Invaders* cabinet console.

Upstairs, it was more conventional. All bedrooms were spacious and every one had an en-suite bathroom. None of the doors were closed, and they peered into each before reaching the last one. This was the master bedroom and occupied a space across the width of the house with floor-to-ceiling glass overlooking the rear garden. A half-packed leather bag lay on the bed, with some clothes and toiletry items beside it.

Henderson grabbed it and looked inside. It contained clothes, and underneath, a laptop, some cables and a wad of cash. 'It looks like he was packing up when we spooked him.'

'Must have heard the movement of the van,' Walters said.

Henderson turned to the ARU officers. 'He's around here somewhere. Find him.'

The officers headed off to search inside wardrobes and to look under beds. Henderson looked around the main bedroom before spotting a small balcony outside, overlooking the garden. He searched for a way out. He found a handle, turned the already inserted key, pulled the handle and the patio door glided effortlessly on well-lubricated bearings.

Henderson headed outside. It took him only a few seconds to realise where Khouri had gone. He had climbed the wall at the end of the balcony and walked across the garage roof. He would have dropped a metre or so on to a low wall at the side of the garage. He then had the choice of jumping into the garden next door or running to the end of his own and climbing over a low wall at its border.

It was impossible for him to escape through the front of the house, as fences blocked access to the rear on both sides, and two cops were stationed there. In reverse, Khouri's escape route looked to be a good access route for a burglar, but then the balcony door would be locked, the house alarmed, and the CCTV camera above the balcony would be operating.

Henderson left the balcony and dashed downstairs, taking the steps and the movement of the open staircase as fast as he dared. He opened the door at the back of the lounge with the key in the lock, and dashed out to the rear patio with Walters hot on his tail. He ran to the end of the garden and stood scanning the trees, trying to spot the fleeing man. He stood there for a couple of minutes, but he saw no movement. No sign of Hassan Khouri.

'I can't see him,' Walters said.

'I think he's gone,' Henderson said. 'Our slippery plastic surgeon has flown.'

FORTY-FIVE

'You lost him? How the hell did you lose him?' Chief Inspector Houghton yelled. They were both standing in Henderson's office. Henderson had explained the situation, but nothing he said seemed to have any effect on his anger.

'What have you done to find him?'

'We searched the area and found evidence he escaped through a neighbour's garden. We've put out an appeal which will appear in this afternoon's *Argus* and on social media. I've issued an all-ports alert, and patrol crews have been briefed and they have his picture. On the plus side, he's out there with only the clothes on his back, he doesn't have a car, he can't go back to his business as it's being watched, and if he uses his phone or credit card, we'll find him.'

'I hope so, for your sake.'

Houghton stormed out. Henderson didn't know what was eating him. Yes, they had lost a suspect, one with a clear escape route in mind which he didn't hesitate to use. His escape route was confirmed, as a neighbour reported seeing him dashing through her garden. Henderson was more phlegmatic about the failed operation than his boss, as the only thing Khouri was being accused of at the moment was the kidnapping of Trevor Robinson. This wasn't in doubt, as they had found the house where Robinson had been held and there was plenty of forensic evidence to back up the charge. What was in doubt was Robinson's claim that Khouri had also murdered Martin Turner and Alex Vincent.

Henderson made himself a coffee in the Detectives' brew room and returned to his office. Feeling calmer, he loaded Google and spent the next half-hour researching the background of Hassan Khouri. In essence, he had received a similar number of complaints as any typical doctor or cosmetic surgeon working with rich and demanding clients; no more, no less. It was just unfortunate that one of his clients happened to be the wife of Raymond Schofield.

Schofield had gone to town on the man, resorting to using Facebook and Twitter when newspapers had got tired of publishing his accusations. He not only accused Khouri of being a terrible surgeon, he cast doubt on the legitimacy of the man's qualifications, alleged he'd abused Rebecca during their affair, and paid some of the surgeon's ex-girlfriends to blacken his name.

Khouri didn't hold back but responded in kind, and in many ways he was a nastier son of a bitch than Schofield. He dragged up anything he could find about him: his string of girlfriends while still married to Rebecca, bullying and sexual impropriety accusations made by Raybeck staff, suggestions that he had misappropriated company money, and of course, hints that he had indeed murdered Allan Blake.

With a number of different pictures of Khouri now at his disposal, he pulled up the CCTV pictures of the intruder at Jonas Baines. He believed there was a resemblance when he looked at it before, but now he felt sure it was him. It wasn't so definite he would testify in court, but good enough to put in front of Khouri when they caught up with him. With this thought in mind, he headed into the Detectives' Room to see how the hunt was progressing.

He walked over to see Walters.

'What was wrong with Houghton?' she asked when he approached.

'You heard him?'

'I was walking past your office but I suspect everyone in the place heard him.'

'Probably still pissed we're pressing ahead with the case against Schofield, but your guess is as good as mine. How's the hunt for the missing man?'

'His phone and credit cards, which it's safe to assume were still in his jacket when he skipped out, are being monitored, but he won't get far once his picture is out there.'

'I'm worried he makes a move before it happens.'

'I think he would need to know a lot about how we operate for him to have the confidence to do that. Imagine the risk he would feel he was taking by just walking into Brighton Station or Gatwick. He would think everyone was looking at him.'

'Yes, you're right. He's more likely holed up somewhere out of sight, but where?'

'According to Trevor, he had a string of girlfriends. Perhaps one who didn't get so annoyed by his womanising behaviour has put him up.'

'Hold that thought,' he said pulling out his ringing phone.

After the call, he looked at Walters. 'Grab your coat, Carol, the SOCOs have found something.'

**

Henderson guided the car down Mallory Road and eased it into a space in the driveway of Khouri's house beside the SOCO van. Taking more interest in his surroundings than he did earlier in the day when he was more focussed on capturing Khouri, he wondered how a house like this was ever approved by the Planning Department. The street was comprised of 1930s traditional houses: all red brick, sloping roofs, and multi-paned windows, and this one stuck out like a gold tooth in a mouth filled with white. It was more suited to the hills above Los Angeles than a street in strait-laced Hove.

They walked inside and looked around for one of the SOCO crew.

'We're up here, Angus,' he heard someone call.

They climbed the stairs.

'I hate stairs like this.'

'Why? No carpets, or because of the open style?'

'I don't like tread with no risers and the way it sways like a boat. I always feel I'll miss my footing and fall, and then there's the obvious problem when wearing a skirt.'

'Hi, Angus.' Jim Urquhart of the SOCO team was standing at the top. 'Come and I'll show you what we've found.'

They walked into the main bedroom and into what looked like a wardrobe at the end of a long line of fitted units. Upon closer inspection, it was a walk-in area, more like a dressing room, but it didn't contain anything connected to clothes.

Instead, pictures of Raymond Schofield adorned many of the walls. There were images cut from newspapers, photographs taken with a camera fitted with a telephoto lens, and other pictures and articles clipped from industry journals. It wasn't just clippings; someone, presumably Khouri, had annotated many with spidery handwriting: 'S in Brighton', 'S at Theatre', 'S walking the Dog'. Others contained more descriptive messages: 'Smug bastard', 'The tosser', 'What a woman', the latter in reference to Clare Mitchell, Schofield's former partner.

The back wall was a little different: the pictures were of Martin Turner and Alex Vincent. Scrawled across Turner's picture were the words Collateral Damage, and on Vincent's, Kill Him, Knows too much.

'My god, this is amazing,' Walters said. 'It must be the evidence Robinson was alluding to.'

'Then he went all coy, saying he had the evidence but it was on his phone, which, by the way, SOCOs picked up at the house where he was being held. I reckon Robinson's been here, either as a guest of Khouri or because he broke in. Maybe he's friendlier with the guy than we first thought. Either way, I suspect we won't hear the whole story until Khouri is caught.'

'By which time Robinson will have his phone back and can show us what he's got.'

'Or sell the pictures to the press.'

'I hope not. These sorts of shrines play out better in the public imagination than they do in a court room.' Henderson spread an arm in an expansive gesture: 'All this because Raymond Schofield dared to criticise him.'

'Tried to ruin him, more like. If you think of Khouri's humble beginnings in Syria, the death of his parents and being taken away from the place where he was born to live in a strange country with his uncle, I suppose he must have felt fiercely protective over what he had built: the business, the car, the house, his reputation.'

'For sure, and remember that Schofield himself isn't a nice man. Perhaps Khouri felt he would garner some sympathy by having a pop at him.'

'Well, it worked, didn't it?' Walters said. 'If you look at Twitter and Instagram – where everyone seems to have an opinion about their spat – even though people haven't a good word to say about cosmetic surgeons in general, Khouri was quite popular while Schofield's name was mud.'

'Disputes like this one never have a happy ending. It tends to eat up one or both of the protagonists.'

'Taking this place into account, it seems to have affected Khouri more than Schofield.'

'I suppose to someone like Schofield, it would feel like just another business rival he needed to crush, while Khouri would feel it was his livelihood, his legacy that was being threatened.'

'All this,' Walters said, spreading her arms wide, 'leaves me feeling a bit, I don't know, disappointed.'

'Why?'

'Robinson made it sound like he had solid evidence against Khouri. I'm sure what he meant was this place, but it doesn't do it for me. At most, it'll make good interviewing material, and if we engage a clinical psychologist, a terrific insight into his thought processes, but I still don't see his finger on the trigger.'

'I was thinking much the same. He could easily claim this isn't a contemporaneous account of events, but a glorified scrapbook compiled by someone with an unhealthy and overdeveloped interest in those events. A good brief will label him a twisted stalker, but not much else.'

'Nevertheless, I sure would like to see his reaction when we show him the pictures.'

'Angus, are you there?' a deep voice asked.

'Aye, I am.'

'Come over here and take a look at this.'

He walked out of the dressing room and towards Dave Cheshunt, another member of the SOCO team, raking through Khouri's wardrobe.

Cheshunt stood back and allowed Henderson to take his place. Wrapped in a t-shirt was a knife, beside it a Canterbury Clothing Company-inscribed woolly hat, and other items of dark clothing. The knife looked clean, but NIR, Near Infrared Spectroscopy, analysis would be able to detect any hidden blood spots. In fact, Henderson was sure he could see some flecks near the handle.

As usual, when faced with such a weapon, Henderson recalled the injuries inflicted on the murder victim: their width, depth, and the pathologist's assessment of the blade used. Yes, this was a good fit for the one used to inflict wounds on Martin Turner. He moved out of the way, letting Walters move into his place.

'You wanted firmer evidence,' he said. 'I think we've found it.'

FORTY-SIX

Early Saturday morning, Henderson went out for a long run. For a change, he headed east, past Brighton Marina and out towards the villages of Rottingdean and Saltdean. This was the most frustrating part of an investigation: waiting for something to happen. In this case, waiting for someone to locate Hassan Khouri. It made him feel helpless, unable to concentrate on anything else, and he used the run to dissipate some of his excess energy, otherwise he might be tempted to take some hasty action just to satisfy the urge to do something.

When he returned home, he showered, changed, ate a hearty breakfast, and then headed into the office. He had barely taken a seat and woken up his pc when Sally Graham arrived, breathless and obviously bearing some news.

A man fitting Khouri's description was seen entering a house in the village of Plumpton. This perhaps provided an explanation as to how Khouri knew about the abandoned cottage where Trevor Robinson had been held captive, as it was situated only a few miles from the village.

Within the hour, a car with Henderson and DS Walters, plus a van containing an armed response unit following behind them, were speeding towards

Plumpton. Since hearing the news, and while waiting for the raid party to assemble, he had dispatched two detectives to reconnoitre the property and they had spotted Khouri through a window.

They turned into Plumpton Lane, a long road running through the middle of the village. It was actually two villages. The smattering of houses they passed at the beginning of the lane were in Plumpton, while the railway station, the famous racecourse, and the house they were heading towards, were in Plumpton Green.

Before reaching the station, they pulled into the side of the road behind the Ford Mondeo containing Phil Bentley and Harry Wallop, the hastily-arranged surveillance team. Henderson got out of the car and walked over to talk to them.

Wallop opened the car door, got out, and stretched.

'Hi Harry.'

'Hi boss. Khouri's ex is called Kay Winter, and she lives in a barn conversion, the wooden building you can see over there,' he said, pointing over the hedgerow where Henderson could see the upper floors.

Looking over, Henderson saw what looked like a farmhouse and, about one hundred metres into the field on the right, the barn conversion.

'How did you see him from here?'

'We didn't. We used the track over there,' he said, indicating a gap in the hedge close to them. 'It leads into that small wood over there and brings you out facing the front of the property.'

'I think I would prefer to use that approach than to walk up the driveway. We'll advance on the property after a couple of officers are positioned at the back to stop him escaping again.'

'I agree. A full-blooded assault down the access road and he would be out of the house and across the fields at the back like a hare with a fox on its tail.'

Henderson nodded. He crossed the road and peered at the barn through the branches of the hedgerow. Even at this distance, he could see it had many large windows, and a glance up by any of the inhabitants inside and a full-blown assault would be exposed.

Henderson walked back across the road. 'When we're in position,' he said to Wallop, 'I'll radio you. Move your car up to the farm access road and block it.'

'Will do.'

Henderson turned to go.

'Boss?'

'Yeah?'

'Better luck catching the bastard this time.'

'Thanks Harry, we'll need it.'

Henderson walked back to his car where Walters was talking to the armed response officers. He briefed them with the information Wallop had supplied, and a few minutes later they set off into the field. The track they were on was shielded from the farm and barn conversion by hedgerow, but in early spring the fields contained nothing but grass, while the briary branches of the hedgerow windbreak were devoid of their usual lush covering of leaves.

They weren't exposed entirely as the barn was in a dip. Only someone in the upstairs rooms would have a decent view, but he suspected the small number of upstairs windows on this side was partly due to the amount of glass utilised on the ground floor, or perhaps there was a more agreeable outlook on the other side.

Standing inside what was no more than a small outcrop of trees, they had a decent view of the barn. He instructed two of the armed response officers to take positions at the rear of the building, and called Harry and instructed him to move his car and block the farm access road.

He allowed five minutes for the officers to reach their positions at the rear, before he ordered the team to move. There was no cover as the team sprinted across an open field.

Barn conversions to the DI looked flimsy, as if a big gust of wind would lift them up and drop them in a field fifty metres away, but there was nothing frail about the door. It was wide, made of solid oak and fitted with two deadlocks. It was a shame to damage such a fine and expensive fitment, but the door banger moved into position and two bangs later, they headed inside.

The heavily protected armed response officers checked the downstairs area, shouting 'Clear!' as they went. Seconds later, someone shouted, 'In here!'

In the kitchen at the rear of the house it was obvious the occupants had been eating breakfast. Two places had been set: avocado on toast. Despite the uneaten food, the diners were no longer at the table.

Khouri was standing at the back of the kitchen, a gun pointed at the head of his companion, Kay Winter.

'Put the gun down, Hassan,' Henderson said in a stern but calm voice. 'You are outnumbered, outgunned, and surrounded.'

'No way. I've done some bad things...I'm capable of doing more. It's you who should be worried, not me.'

'Take a look around. Look outside and you'll see more armed officers. Put the gun down, Hassan; you don't want to kill Ms Winter, do you?'

At the mention of her name, her previously stoic face crumpled.

'Please don't let him kill me? I haven't done anything wrong. I'm only thirty-three, I haven't done anything with my life yet.'

'Shut up, Kay!' Khouri hissed.

'Keep calm, Ms Winter. He's not going to kill you, are you, Hassan?'

'I will, unless you lot back off.'

'Let me make one thing clear. We're not going anywhere. You're the one who needs to give way, not us.'

It was a difficult situation. Khouri was in a corner with no means of escape. A desperate man was capable of doing desperate things.

His only way out was the back door leading into the garden. A man in such a hopeless position only had two options: he could either give up, or try to shoot his way out. If choosing the latter he would die in the process, as the moment he pointed his weapon at any of the officers, he would be shot.

'Hassan,' Henderson said, 'I'll ask you again, put the gun down.'

'No, no way.'

'Why did you kill Martin Turner?'

'How do you know it was me? I wasn't there. You've got nothing on me.'

'We've been to your house—'

'What? You bastards have been inside my beautiful house? Your dirty boots all over the carpet, your people rummaging through my things.'

All the time he spoke, the gun hand trembled as if he was going through some emotional turmoil. His poor hostage, whose legs had clearly turned to jelly, would be fearful he would pull the trigger, either accidentally or during this fit of rage.

'Let me go,' Winter said, struggling.

He was holding her by a handful of her long hair, the gun pointed at the side of her head. He yanked her hair with such force Henderson's fleeting thought about this perhaps being a set-up were dispelled.

'Argh!' she screeched. 'Khouri, you're an evil bastard!'

Khouri and Winter slowly stepped backwards.

'Where are you going?' Henderson asked.

'Move out of my fucking way.'

Henderson glanced at the senior ARU officer, Dave Fallon, indicating he should move back.

The strange dance made its way to the back door.

'Turn the key and open the door,' Khouri said to Winter. He eased her to one side so she could reach.

'No funny moves,' he said to Henderson, 'or she gets it, understand?'

'Okay.'

When the door was open fully behind them, Khouri and Winter edged towards Henderson and the ARU officers. Henderson was tempted to grab Winter when the gunman's attention was distracted by the door, but he feared Khouri would open fire in panic.

'Tell the guys you've positioned at the back of the house to show themselves.'

Henderson hesitated.

'Now!'

He nodded at Dave Fallon, who called them. Khouri then instructed them to stand away from the door. Khouri made his way outside and stepped away from the door. He turned and faced the two ARU officers, Winter in front of him, and instructed, 'Get in the house and close the door.'

They did as they were told. As soon as the door was shut, Khouri let go of Kay, stepped forward and locked it. Damn! Henderson hadn't noticed him removing the key, as the bodies of the surgeon and his hostage had blocked his view. Henderson watched from the window as Khouri, ignoring the shaking Kay Winter, set off at a pace down the back garden.

FORTY-SEVEN

When Khouri started running, Henderson barked orders to those in the kitchen before sprinting through the damaged and open front door, Walters behind him. A copper was assigned to deal with the traumatised hostage, and the rest of the team were scrambling back to their van.

He ran round the barn and entered the garden, running to the end as Khouri had done. He climbed the fence marking the border between Winter's property and the large field beyond. In the distance, nearing the end of the field, he saw Khouri. The surgeon looked comfortable running; he had an elegant, long-legged stride and appeared to be someone who often ran long distances over rough ground. Every now and again he glanced over his shoulder.

Henderson had already been out for a run this morning, so the additional distance didn't bother him too much, although he knew he would soon tire if it went on for any length of time. Without looking back, he knew Walters would be far behind. Even though Henderson wasn't shod in running shoes, he could still run at a reasonable pace in the ones he was wearing. Walters, on the other hand, was equipped for no more than a sprint along a Brighton pavement, not for a trek over a bumpy field.

To his surprise, Khouri seemed to dip down and disappear as if he had just jumped into a ditch. It was only when he got closer, and heard the sound of a train, that he realised Khouri had reached the culvert of the train tracks leading into Plumpton Station, now over to his left. A concern flagged in Henderson's mind: if the train tracks were sealed by a high fence, to stop local kids playing there, Khouri would have the choice of going either left or right. Henderson hoped when he got there, the fleeing man's direction of travel would be obvious.

When Henderson reached the dip, he realised there wasn't a fence, but due to a combination of a passing train and the general difficulty of crossing train tracks, Henderson was much closer to Khouri than he had been. He was close enough to shout, but decided to save his breath until he had closed the gap still further.

Away from the trains, they were now travelling along a country road and, surprise, surprise, it was Khouri who was starting to tire, not the DI. Clearly, what he'd eaten of his avo and toast breakfast was not good preparation for a long run. They approached what looked to Henderson like a disused industrial site and, without stopping, Khouri nipped through a gap in the fence.

It was clear to Henderson that Khouri knew what he was doing: how else would he know about the hole in the fence? The place looked like an abandoned brickworks, and had been closed for a decade or more, as many of the buildings were dilapidated and any remaining machinery was thick with rust.

Henderson moved to the cover of a hut, pulled out his radio and told the rest of the team where he was located. He put his radio away and set off after Khouri. His plan was to corner the surgeon and when the armed unit arrived they could overpower him. If the DI simply stayed behind the hut and waited for reinforcements to arrive, they would have no idea where Khouri would be and could spend the next few hours looking for him only to find he had already made his escape.

He knew he was right about this being a brickworks, as he could tell from the shape of the buildings, the red dust under his feet, and the debris lying around, but there wasn't a single brick to be found. He imagined local builders would have visited the site long ago and picked over the carcass as effectively as a vulture would do with a dead sheep.

The yard consisted of one very large building with a tall chimney, presumably the brickworks itself; a series of smaller buildings, many with their roofs caved in, looking like storage areas, and one low building in reasonable condition, considering its age, the offices.

He was unsure if Khouri had taken a left into the large building, or a right among the ruins of the storage buildings. He was about to investigate the large place when a shot rang out, emanating from the DI's right. It was dangerously close, suggesting Khouri had a better view of him than the other way round.

Henderson pulled out his gun and ducked down, keeping himself in the shade as he made his way past the storage buildings, taking special care when he came to openings, at what used to be windows or where a fissure had opened up due to movement of the structure. Through one of those he saw Khouri, but one moment he was there, and the next he was gone.

Approaching another fissure, Henderson was distracted by a movement: it was a bird, but when he looked back, a leg shot out and kicked the gun out of his hand. Not waiting for Khouri to appear and point his pistol at him, he launched himself at the surgeon. Henderson punched him in the face and they both fell into the dirt and detritus lying on the ground. Henderson wasn't sure, but he thought Khouri's gun skidded away.

Khouri punched Henderson on the side of the head but when Henderson went to smack him again, a hard blow struck his solar plexus and knocked the wind out of him. He doubled up, and due to the distraction and lessening his grip, Khouri squirmed away.

It took Henderson a few seconds to recover; when he did, he looked up: Khouri had a weapon trained on him.

'Think you can get the better of me, copper? Nobody does that.'

'Give it up, Khouri. How far are you going to get with no money and no car?'

'You don't think I've thought of that?'

'Have you?'

'You underestimate me, as many other people have done to their cost. Of course I have. Money, and any documents that I might need, are deposited in a safe place. I knew this day would come at some point.'

'Put the gun down!'

Henderson turned at the same time Khouri did. DS Walters was standing there, her gun trained on Khouri. Almost in slow motion, Khouri's gun moved from pointing at Henderson, and swung round to aim at the detective sergeant.

Henderson launched himself at the surgeon. From his low position, he executed a perfect rugby tackle, catching his opponent around the midriff and dropping him to the ground. The gun in his hand fired.

This time, Henderson wasn't letting go and punched Khouri repeatedly until he stopped struggling. Walters came running over and before Khouri could rally his resources and respond, Henderson grabbed the gun and held him still while Walters applied the cuffs.

'That shot, it didn't come near you?' Henderson asked.

'Nah, it hit a piece a wood above me, I had to jump out of the way as it came crashing down.'

'What happened to the ARU?'

'A train's broken down at Plumpton Station, the road's blocked.'

FORTY-EIGHT

'Following a major police operation today at Golding's Farm in Plumpton,' Henderson said, 'an armed suspect has been arrested and his hostage released unharmed. No police officers were injured in this operation. The arrested man has been charged with firearm offences, kidnap with intent to endanger the lives of two individuals, and the murder of two Brighton lawyers, Martin Turner and Alex Vincent.'

This provoked a tsunami of voices and questions from the journalists in the packed conference room, and Henderson suspected no one heard the next bit.

'Thank you, Detective Inspector Henderson,' DCI Houghton said beside him. 'If I can now open this press conference to some questions?'

Henderson and Houghton walked out twenty minutes later, the room still buzzing with excitement, some of the many questions asked by journalists remaining unanswered.

'I thought it went well,' Houghton said, turning off the television in his office, the pair of them like two actors viewing the first broadcast of their latest play.

'It did,' Henderson said. 'Although I would have preferred the camera to be on my right side, I think my profile looks better from there.'

'Ha,' Houghton said, walking over to a cabinet and retrieving a bottle of whisky. 'Is it too early for you, Angus?'

Henderson didn't need to look at his watch. 'It's never too early.'

Houghton handed him a glass and they both clinked. 'Here's to a successful operation and no further loss of life.'

'I'll second that. Cheers.'

'It could all have ended so differently,' Houghton said. 'If he'd made a move to shoot the hostage, or God forbid, actually shot her, you would have had no option but to shoot him.'

'Aye,' he said over the rim of his glass, 'at times like this we're operating on such slim margins.'

'Even though it doesn't seem like it, I do think the press know and appreciate it. I was talking to a journalist before the press conference who said as much. If he was in a room with a man holding a gun, he said, he wouldn't be able to speak or stand for his knees shaking.'

'Let's hope he puts something similar in his article so his readers can understand the dangers we face, all in the interests of public safety. Khouri seemed to be so unhinged, I didn't know if he would take a pop at us or shoot the woman.'

'At least the case against him is sound.'

Henderson nodded. 'Aside from the offences committed at Golding's Farm and at the abandoned brickworks, we've got the knife used to kill Martin Turner and the forensic data from the cottage where he held Trevor Robinson.'

'What about Alex Vincent? I'm a little unclear on his motive for that one.'

'From what's been appearing in newspapers so far, you would think all the things he did were in connection with the long-running vendetta between him and Raymond Schofield.'

'They weren't?'

'In part, but it's clear from the interviews we've conducted with him so far, behind it all was his desire to strike out at anyone who would do damage to his business and reputation. Schofield tried it, and we now see the results of their well-publicised feud. However, his main motivation for breaking into the offices of Jonas Baines was to remove a Medical Litigation case file raised by a lady called Lesley Fisk.'

Henderson took a sip of whisky before continuing.

'Lesley's a twenty-five-year-old lingerie model who claimed her career was ruined when Khouri botched up her lip enhancing and boob job. He made her lips pout, which she didn't want, and left visible scars under her boobs. Her grievances might have stopped there, if she didn't have an allergic reaction to the boob-filling material which left her in a coma.'

'Good lord.'

'She claimed she had told Khouri about her allergies, and in her file there were medical reports, expert statements, and photographs, most of which are irreplaceable. Jonas Baines say their removal from the file killed the case stone-dead. While Khouri was in the Jonas Baines offices, he decided to make a little mischief by going into Alex Vincent's office and removing several items from Rebecca Schofield's divorce file.'

'Where did he get the security badge?' Houghton asked.

'From Trevor Robinson, one night in a casino. Robinson rarely wore his work suit when gambling, but one time he did and Khouri removed it while he was in the toilet.'

'What did he take from Rebecca Schofield's divorce file?'

'His original plan was to plant some of the stolen documents in Schofield's house, thereby implicating him in the break-in. He jettisoned the idea when he realised a housekeeper also lived in Schofield's house. Instead, he resolved to use some of the more incriminating parts to shame Schofield on social media, and slow down the divorce process to make him suffer more.'

'Martin Turner's death was what, in the wrong place at the wrong time?'

'It seems so.'

'Khouri's a strange fish,' Houghton said. 'I wouldn't put him in the Broadmoor category, as he's intelligent and engaging, but it's like a part of his brain is given over to criminality.'

'In a way, you can understand his no-holds-barred approach when you understand his background. He'd arrived in the UK at the age of eleven to live with his uncle after his parents were killed in a terrorist bomb blast. He attended a state school; but he was bright and everything he achieved and owned was down to his own efforts.'

Henderson took a drink; it was nice whisky.

'We have enough to put him away for a very long time without it, but for the sake of Vincent's wife, we'll do our best to gain a conviction for his murder as well. The CCTV, as you know, isn't conclusive, but Khouri told us he was fearful of Vincent calling in the auditors, which is where he was headed the day he was waiting for the train. Khouri knew this as Trevor Robinson had inadvertently revealed what Vincent was planning during one of their casino chats. He feared it, as their work would have exposed the true purpose of his break-in.'

'Why bother? Medical Litigation would have discovered its absence in the end.'

He shook his head. 'Maybe not, as the trial wasn't scheduled to be held until the following year. By then, Khouri would have seen Schofield convicted of murder, although for the killing of Allan Blake and not Martin Turner as he tried to engineer, and the trail of his theft would have gone cold.'

'He would have been home and dry if it wasn't for his rashness at raiding the divorce file and trying to put one over on Schofield,' Houghton said.

'Aye, and if it wasn't for the irresponsible, although some would say, heroic actions of Trevor Robinson, he would have got away with murder.'

'On such small margins, right enough. Another?' Houghton asked, holding up his empty glass.

'I don't mind if I do.'

The End

About the Author

Iain Cameron was born in Glasgow and moved to Brighton in the early eighties. He has worked as a management accountant, business consultant and a nursery goods retailer. He is now a full-time writer and lives in a village outside Horsham in West Sussex with his wife, two daughters and a lively Collie dog.

Dying for Justice is the tenth book to feature DI Angus Henderson, the Scottish cop at Sussex Police.

For more information about books and the author:
Visit the website at: www.iain-cameron.com
Follow him on Twitter: @iainsbooks
Follow him on Facebook @iaincameronauthor

Acknowledgments

On the occasion of the publication of the tenth book in the DI Henderson series, I'd like to take the opportunity to thank all those people without whom I would never have made it.

Peter O'Connor at bespokebookcovers.com has been designing brilliant books covers for me since the beginning and has always been a pleasure to work with.

My editorial team of Zoe Markham, Vari Cameron, and the Advance Reader Team do a fantastic job reshaping my often rambling words into something coherent.

Last, but not least, I would like to thank my readers, many of whom have been here since Book 1, and others who have now got ten books to keep them occupied.

Also by Iain Cameron

DI Angus Henderson Crime Novels

One Last Lesson
Driving into Darkness
Fear the Silence
Hunting for Crows
Red Red Wine
Night of Fire
Girls on Film
Black Quarry Farm
Blood Marked Pages
Dying for Justice

Matt Flynn Thrillers

The Pulsar Files
Deadly Intent
No Time to Lose

All books are available from Amazon

A Small Request
If you have read any of my books, I would be grateful if you could please leave a review on Amazon. It helps other readers make an informed purchase decision.

Printed in Great Britain
by Amazon

74598607R00229